C000220616

'Burke mov̶e̶[...] of view, bringing [...] and a sympathetic feminine position . . . Burke's bubbly enthusiasm for London, where the novel is set, is infectious, as is his characters' passion for food, travel and romance' *Daily Telegraph*

'Clever romantic comedy' *Closer*

'I defy the most hard-hearted cynic not to find something seductive in his writing' *Sunday Express*

'Burke's characters and their unfolding story have depth and charm' *Hello Magazine*

'Refreshing' Adele Parks

'A very skilful practitioner of a genre hitherto dominated by Nick Hornby and Tony Parsons' *Time Out*

'Burke is very clever, a terrific find, a natural storyteller and definitely a talent to watch' *Bookseller*

Also by Paul Burke

Father Frank

Untorn Tickets

The Man Who Fell in Love with His Wife

About the author

Paul Burke's advertising work has won him almost every award in the industry and he has worked on campaigns for Barclaycard, VW, PG Tips, British Gas and Budweiser. At the same time he pursued a parallel career as a DJ on radio, in clubs and has worked for LBC, GLR and Heart 106.2. He has written for the *Guardian*, *Tatler* and *The Sunday Times* and he lives in North London with his wife and two children.

The Life of Reilly

PAUL BURKE

HODDER

First published in Great Britain in 2007 by Hodder & Stoughton
An Hachette Livre UK company

This paperback edition published in 2008

1

A CIP catalogue record for this title is
available from the British Library

ISBN 978 0 340 82819 9

Typeset by Palimpsest Book Production Limited,
Grangemouth, Stirlingshire

Printed and bound by Mackays of Chatham Ltd, Chatham, Kent

Hodder & Stoughton policy is to use papers that are natural,
renewable and recyclable products and made from wood grown in
sustainable forests. The logging and manufacturing processes are
expected to conform to the environmental regulations of the country
of origin.

Hodder & Stoughton Ltd
338 Euston Road
London NW1 3BH

www.hodder.co.uk

To my darling wife

ACKNOWLEDGEMENTS

Deep, deep gratitude to Alex Bonham and to Georgina Capel, my fabulous editor and agent respectively and to Hazel Orme and her HB pencil. Special thanks must also go to Toni D'urso, Italo D'urso, Kim Taylforth, Joe Fitzgerald and Alison Nowell for telling me all the stuff I needed to know in order to write what you are about to read.

1

Sean Reilly was fifteen when it happened.

He'd gone to bed as Little Jimmy Osmond and woken up as Barry White.

Unlike most teenage boys, whose voices crack and wobble their way down a gentle depth gradient, Sean's vocal drop had been rather more dramatic.

On that fateful morning, when he opened his mouth to speak, he heard not his own voice but the big bass tones of a total stranger. This, understandably, threw him into a terrible panic. He rushed to the mirror, not quite sure what he'd see looking back at him. Fortunately he saw what he always saw: a pale Irish complexion, piercing green eyes and hair as black as Guinness.

Touching his face and tugging that hair, he was relieved to find that everything seemed normal before a sudden thought turned that pale complexion even paler. It was 1979, *The Exorcist* was still doing the rounds and Sean, who had sneaked in to see it at the Screen on the Green, was now considering the very real possibility that he might be possessed. He turned, slowly and nervously, to face the crucifix above his bed and waited for his head to start spinning and vile blasphemies to spew forth.

Nothing. Phew. He still had a friend in Jesus. He cleared his throat and opened his mouth, but again heard a man with a very deep voice say, 'Mum.'

Another voice, shrill, Irish, with a slight note of alarm, replied from the kitchen: 'Who's that?'

My God! Even his own mother didn't recognise him! 'It's me. Sean.'

Maggie Reilly was kind and loving but from a hardy generation not terribly sympathetic to illness. However, even she had to concede that her mischievous, malingering son couldn't possibly put on a voice like that. 'What's the matter with your throat?'

'I don't know.'

'If you think you're bunking off school,' she began.

'I don't want to bunk off school.'

It was the first time Sean had ever uttered that sentence and the first time he'd uttered any sentence with such depth and majesty. 'In fact,' he continued, sounding like Shere Khan in *The Jungle Book*, 'I'm quite looking forward to it.'

The initial horror soon wore off, and by the time Sean got to school, he was desperate to test-drive his new acquisition. Having seen the reaction of others, he realised that the Voice Fairy had been exceptionally benevolent and that things would never be the same again.

Everyone around him began to treat him differently. Other boys decided that, with such a deep voice, Reilly must be hard enough to skate on. Even teachers, despite a wealth of evidence to the contrary, seemed to think the depth of Sean's voice reflected the depth of his intelligence. There was a new certainty to his tone that could almost convince Mr Smyth, the geography teacher, that the capital of Vietnam was Cornwall.

Outside of school, he was served in all the pubs around Islington where it was assumed that it was medically impossible for Bass Boy to be under eighteen.

The real bonus for Sean, though, was the number of girls who were suddenly attracted to him. Their subconscious assumption was that, since eunuchs were always depicted with high-pitched voices, Sean Reilly must be endowed with something that resembled a baby's arm holding a peach.

Like a lot of London children with Irish parents, Sean was bilingual. Or, bi-accental. At school, he spoke with a London accent, but the moment he crossed the threshold of the Reillys' council flat in Gaskin Street, he'd switch to broad Irish. His talent for mimicry, complemented by a voice that sounded twice as old as its owner, meant he could now effortlessly assume the timbre of teachers, parents and priests.

His impression of Father Carroll was so accurate that he was faced with two ways of using it. Either he could sneak into the confessional box and find out what his fellow parishioners had been up to. Or he could gather his mates round the phone while he rang Claire Carty, the most beautiful girl in London, N1.

'Ah, Cleere,' he leered, in Father Carroll's gentle Waterford lilt, 'tell me what you're weering? Do ye have on the shtockings and the shushpenders, Claire? And the black underweer, Claire. Jaysus, I love the black underweer . . .'

Claire was horrified, having only known Father Carroll as a kind, almost saintly cleric. She was just seconds away from a lifetime in therapy when Mick McKenna, puce with the pressure of unexploded mirth, collapsed into helpless hysterics.

Sean spent the next few days avoiding Claire or, more specifically, her two older brothers. When he finally bumped into her outside Steve Hatt's fishmonger's on the Essex Road, he expected her to grab the nearest wet haddock and slap him round the face with it. But her reaction surprised him.

'Sean Reilly,' she said, with a sultry smile, 'you're a very naughty boy.'

As every male knows, if a girl addresses him by both fore- and surname it's a coy sign of affection.

'Look, Claire,' he mumbled, crimson with shame, 'it was just a joke.'

'But tell me,' she teased, flashing her pale blue eyes and tossing back her ebony mane, 'do you really like stockings, suspenders and black underwear?'

'Look, I'm really sorry.'

'You haven't answered my question,' she purred, her voice dropping almost as low as his. 'Do you like black underwear?'

'Um . . . er . . . s'pose so, yeah,' he croaked.

'Good,' she said, slowly and deliberately. 'You know where I live, don't you?'

'Er . . . um . . . yeah.'

'Then come round about nine when my mum and dad have gone up the club. I've got a little surprise for you.'

Sean agonised about whether he should go, convinced that the 'little surprise' would be a good hiding from the two older brothers but, at eight forty-five, he finally yielded to the glorious thought of Claire Carty in black stockings and suspenders. At two minutes past nine, he was rewarded with the real thing.

From that moment, Sean Reilly knew that his life would be led by his larynx.

2

Under-achieving parents are a wonderful thing. Pity the poor child whose mother is a human-rights lawyer and whose father is an eminent neurosurgeon. Far better to be blessed, as Sean was, with a mother who was a cleaner and a father who collected the tickets at King's Cross station. Far better to have the bar of professional accomplishment set reassuringly low.

Sean had been subjected to the maroon blazer and scholastic rigour of St Vincent's Catholic Grammar School and, without his new voice, might well have stayed on for the sixth form, filled in his UCCA form and spent three years at a dull, provincial university. However, the new voice had brought with it an impatience to matriculate at the University of Life.

He'd worked out that St Vincent's was the worst of both worlds. It had the hard discipline, cold showers and tough academic grind of a public school without any of the social contacts. Boys left with excellent grades but with one vital lesson unlearnt: in the real world, it's not what you know but who you know, and unless they wanted poorly paid work on building sites, those boys knew nobody. What was more, they all carried the cross of Catholic humility, just to make doubly sure that their potential was never fulfilled.

Sean felt it was far better to get out as soon as he could and avoid a long, unexciting road that would lead, at best, to a job in IT and a small semi in Leighton Buzzard. He didn't care what he did for a living, as long as he could do it in Soho. For Sean, those mazy streets and twisted alleys encircled by Oxford Street, Regent Street, Shaftesbury Avenue and Charing Cross Road were the beating heart of the greatest city in the world.

Soho was what every other latterly fashionable and 'edgy' London neighbourhood, from Notting Hill to Hoxton, would try, and fail, to become. Nowhere else could ever be as central, as vibrant or as gloriously seamy as Soho.

This relatively minuscule area had always punched way above its weight in social and cultural significance. It was home to the British music, film and sex industries. Its borders boasted the country's biggest cinemas and theatres. Its magnetic pull had brought in generations of beatniks, bohos, writers, artists, poets and the sort of painters who weren't also decorators. Maltese pimps and Danish whores had journeyed thousands of miles to seek fulfilment in Soho so Sean, who lived just a short bus ride away, felt like he'd been born into shoes of solid gold.

He took the first job he was offered – as a runner for a sound studio in Wardour Street. He spent every day running errands – delivering parcels, letters and contracts. He collected spools of tape, cans of film, rounds of drinks and trays of sandwiches. As a Catholic boy schooled by the Christian Brothers, taking orders was second nature to him. He was happy to help, eager to please, and was known and liked by the eclectic inhabitants of what was still very much an urban village.

However, one Thursday afternoon his happy life as a runner was brought to a premature close. Patrick Brown, chief engineer, owner of the studios and Sean's boss, spoke with a half-lisp and a nasal twang. He also had a habit of closing his eyes when he was trying to make a point, and Sean had captured this comic combination perfectly.

He was holding court – or, as his mother would have put it, 'showing off' – in Reception for the benefit of Suzanne, the cute blonde punky girl who took the bookings. She could hardly breathe for laughing and was, therefore, making no sound at all. Sean, eyes closed for his pitch-perfect parody of Patrick, had no idea that the laughing had stopped, and that the subject of his hilarious routine was standing right behind him.

When Sean opened his eyes, he saw that Suzanne was flushed,

awkward and embarrassed. His own facial expression immediately followed suit.

Patrick nodded slowly. 'Very amusing, Sean,' he said, not looking remotely amused. 'Can I have a word?'

As he followed Patrick into his office, Sean felt as he had when he used to follow Father Gabriel into the headmaster's study to receive six strokes of the cane. At that moment, he would gladly have accepted a good thrashing rather than instant dismissal from the job he adored. Unfortunately, life and its punishments were no longer that simple.

'Sit down, Sean.'

Sean sat down and thought it best to say nothing.

'Quite a talent you've got there. Tell me, can you do any other impressions?'

'Um, a few. Not very well but . . .'

'Go on, then,' said Patrick. He seemed to enjoy watching Sean squirm. 'Let's hear them.'

Sean ran through the usual crop: 'Ooh, Betty . . . I wanna tell you a story . . . You dirty rat . . . Of all the bars in all the world . . .' and finished with Jimmy Savile's irritating yodel and a quick burst of 'Howzabout that then, guys and gals?'

Patrick still wasn't smiling. 'You're a gifted mimic and you have an uncanny ability to sound much older than you are,' he said, 'which suggests to me that you have a very good ear.' He paused. 'And that's the first requirement for a sound engineer.' He paused again. 'So how would you like to become one?'

3

'Are you lucky?'

This, apparently, was Napoleon's first question to his troops. In his view, strength and courage were nothing without luck. When he went into battle, he liked to be bolstered by the flanks of fortune.

'Are you lucky?'

Sean Reilly's truthful reply would have been 'Yes.' However, he would also have been lucky enough to possess the wit and savvy to say, 'No,' and avoid being blown to bits at the battle of Austerlitz.

Sean had always been lucky, even before the Voice Fairy had arrived. He'd been lucky enough to have two older sisters who practically forced him to watch *Top of the Pops* every Thursday night, so he was into Roxy and Rod when his classmates were still watching Sooty and Sweep. He was also lucky enough to have an older brother, who didn't mind him tagging along to football matches and gigs as long as they were within walking distance of home. Since home was Islington, they could walk to Highbury and see Arsenal beat Chelsea, Liverpool or Manchester United.

They could also walk across the road to the Screen on the Green to see an unknown band called the Clash play their very first gig supporting another unknown band called the Sex Pistols. That gig has since been elevated to almost mythical status. The number of people who claim to have been inside that little cinema on that occasion would have trouble squeezing into Wembley Stadium, but Sean Reilly really had been there, and was lucky enough to be able to tell people just how awful it was.

Far better were Dr Feelgood, supported by Ian Dury at the Lord Nelson, and The Beat, supported by UB40 at the Hope and Anchor, both venues, again, just a short walk from Gaskin Street.

Islington was also the home of Gary and Martin Kemp, so Sean was in the delivery room for Spandau Ballet and the nascent New Romantic movement. It was therefore only a matter of time before he was sitting in a jeweller's just off Chapel Market having his left ear pierced. Sean had always wanted an earring. He loved the romantic idea that sailors wore gold earrings so that if one were to lose his life either at sea or in a brawl over a quayside hooker he always had the price of a Christian burial.

His father, however, was less than impressed. 'Earrings,' he'd boomed, 'are for pirates and poofs. I tell ya, boy, there'd better be a feckin' boat outside.'

Sean was not discouraged. His new voice had given him the confidence to dress up, dye his hair and even borrow his sister's mascara for nights out at the Blitz and Club for Heroes. The fey, feminine appearance and deep masculine voice proved a bewitching combination for a succession of gorgeous girls.

In the spectrum of Sean's life, sex was at one end and his parents were right at the other. To keep them as far apart as possible, he had to leave home but he didn't want to leave Islington. Again, it was down to luck that he knew all about the Cash for Keys scam at Islington Council. To secure the tenancy of a nice little council flat in a low-rise block just off Liverpool Road, all he'd had to do was turn up at the Nag's Head on Upper Street to meet a shifty-looking employee from the Housing Department and pass him a thick brown envelope under the table. The only other way would have been to get himself pregnant.

Back at work, his luck and his larynx had brought him a new career as a 'sound designer', pushing the buttons and twiddling the knobs to create the sound for TV and radio commercials. Hard work, natural charm and that in-built Catholic desire to please had quickly made him one of Soho's busiest, with a reputation for being able to make ads jump out of the radio.

He soon picked up the tricks of the trade, and was continually devising new ones of his own. Cellophane, for instance, can be used to create the sound of fire, staple guns can be amplified to sound like real guns, motorbikes can sound exactly like light aircraft, and the sound of soldiers marching through long grass was actually Sean rustling an armful of quarter-inch tape. Although commercials featuring the famous line 'Have a break, have a KitKat' had been running for years, Sean wasn't satisfied with the sound of the KitKat breaking in the middle: he made it harder and crispier by snapping a pencil instead.

He felt lucky to work with some of the finest actors and most beautiful actresses in the world, who were only too willing, given the amount of money they were being paid, to endorse the products of whoever was writing the cheque.

He felt even luckier when his work began to include balancing and enhancing the sound of big movies in Dolby Surround sound and invitations to Leicester Square premières.

However, he'd never felt luckier than the day he felt the intangible thrill of a pair of beautiful eyes gazing at the back of his head. He turned round and fell in love with Nikki Turner, a honey-blonde PR consultant, who'd come in to record a radio commercial for the *Sex and the City* fashion event. 'The City', unfortunately, was Sheffield, so although the event lost its allure, Nikki lost none of hers. At the end of the recording session when she walked out of Sean's studio, he couldn't bear the thought of her walking out of his life.

It was two o'clock and his luck kicked in again. The next client had cancelled. He was free till three. Normally he would have grabbed those precious sixty minutes to stretch his legs around the streets of Soho. Not this time. Nikki had asked for a CD of the commercial to be biked over to her office in Knightsbridge. Sean delayed this until he'd put together a second CD to accompany it. At his disposal, he was lucky enough to have libraries of music and sound effects, which he plundered to great effect.

As with a lot of confident people, Sean's natural swagger deserted him when he was faced with someone for whom he harboured real feelings. Rather than ask Nikki out in an awkward, bashful mumble, he hid behind a stupendous production of sonic and musical wizardry. It began with a fanfare and Sean's voice, saying, 'Nikki, hi, this is Sean Reilly. I wondered if you could answer the following question. Do you like . . .' Then he cut together a succession of sound effects: the clinking glasses and cutlery of a restaurant, the moist creak of a cork being drawn from a bottle and the wine being poured into a glass, birds twittering, a brook babbling, an aeroplane taking off, seagulls, waves lapping a tropical shore, the thunk of a football hitting the back of a net, followed by the roar of a crowd, then some music: salsa, samba, soca, calypso, rock, reggae and soul, a snatch of big-band swing, some gentle sax and, finally, a crescendo by the Royal Philharmonic Orchestra over the tumultuous applause of the crowd. Then Sean's voice returned: 'If you do, then phone me at the studio.'

She phoned. That night they were together in Sean's flat. He'd lost count of the number of girls who'd seen his bedroom ceiling, but he wanted to make sure that Nikki was the last.

He loved everything about her: her natural, understated beauty, her intelligence, her sense of irony, her kindness and wit. After two blissful years and a wildly expensive trip to Hatton Garden, he arranged to meet her and a hundred guests at a beautiful country church in a picturesque village in Kent. He was happy to suffer the indignity of wearing a hired morning suit and a pink cravat to please his new in-laws. Without complaint, he'd allowed what remained of his credibility to disintegrate as he and his bride had their first dance together as man and wife to the nauseating warble of Chris de Burgh singing 'Lady in Red'. Even that couldn't spoil his happiness.

His luck followed him from the reception to the honeymoon where their first child was conceived amid the opulence of the Oriental Hotel in Bangkok. It went back with him to London, and was with him when he found a huge, dilapidated house in Chiswick and a smiling manageress at the Halifax, who was only too willing to give him a mortgage.

Again, he was lucky that so many of his ex-schoolmates had gone into the building trade: conscientious Catholics led by the ironically named Darren Crook ('With a name like mine, mate, I have to be honest'), who would never rip him off. They transformed the old house into a magnificent mix of original and luxurious features. With the paint barely dry, the final picture hooked into place and their daughter now almost two, Sean and Nikki felt ready to conceive again and, without difficulty, they did. With a gorgeous wife and two adorable daughters, Sean decided he wanted to spend more time with them.

He was Soho's most in-demand sound designer, and that was the problem: he'd become a victim of his own success. He was always booked out, sometimes weeks in advance. He'd had enough of sitting in a studio from nine until six, without a break, never seeing daylight from October till March. He began to dread the hours he had to waste with useless, indecisive people who didn't know what they wanted and made hapless actors do forty-three takes before deciding that they'd go with take two, after all.

Most of all he was fed up with talentless people on the other side of the glass. The household names were fine – the bigger the star, the nicer they were. It was the others on whom he wasn't so keen. The second-rate luvvies who took themselves so seri-ously. They thought they could expunge the guilt they felt at voicing a commercial by behaving as though they were on stage at the National. He detested the thespian theorists, who explained in great detail how they would approach the script, then fail to deliver what they'd promised.

Even these people were a joy compared with the E-list 'celebrities', who had found fleeting fame as models, boyfriends of models or contestants on reality TV shows. Seduced by the fast buck they thought they could make as voiceover artists, they then discovered it wasn't as easy as they'd thought. Entombed in soundproofed silence, they fluffed, they fumbled, they froze. They emphasised the wrong words, stressed the wrong syllables and breathed at the wrong times. Sean found himself cursing the fact that they were breathing at all, and it was this that pushed him into a life-changing decision.

After he had carefully spliced together the only usable bits of seventeen different takes, compressing and balancing each one so that the finished piece would sound like one seamless read, he decided that enough was enough.

He'd almost forgotten what a rich, mellifluous gift the Voice Fairy had left him all those years ago. Now he remembered.

Having spent most of his working life listening to the most exquisite and the most abysmal practitioners of this art, he knew exactly what to do with his voice and, more importantly, what not to do. He knew how to read quickly without sounding rushed. In less than four seconds he could tell you that your home was at risk if you failed to keep up repayments on a mortgage or another loan secured on it, that mortgages were subject to status and that terms and conditions applied. He could adjust his tone to a multitude of settings and could, thanks to the luck of the (second-generation) Irish, produce an accurate array of accents from the Emerald Isle.

It had taken years, but he had finally cast aside the crippling Catholic humility that had always prevented him using his sublime gift to make himself a fortune.

Feeling happy and liberated, he declared to himself, 'I can do better than these people. From now on, my place will be on the other side of that glass. I can work a lot less and earn a lot more. I can spend more time with my family. I am the luckiest man in the world.'

And that, of course, was when his luck ran out.

4

'Eggs fighting.'

Lucy Ross had no idea what the beaming woman with the glasses, short lank hair and prominent overbite was talking about.

'Eggs fighting,' the woman repeated, augmenting her buck-toothed smile with some enthusiastic nodding.

Lucy was about to ask where the eggs were fighting when, with a sudden clunk, the penny dropped. 'Oh, yes,' she agreed. 'Very exciting.'

This was a lie.

'Would you like a vol-au-vent?' was the next enquiry.

'Oh, yes, please,' said Lucy. Another lie, but the truth, 'I'd rather eat my own gall bladder,' seemed a little harsh.

The woman and her tray of unappealing comestibles bustled back through the crowded church hall and Lucy realised that this was now, officially, the most tedious experience of her whole life.

It was no mean feat since Lucy's life had so far included sitting through *The Unbearable Lightness of Being* on DVD and studying *Jude the Obscure* for A level. It was a life in which her boyfriend, Adam, had played a significant part. He had once fancied himself as a latter day Renoir and Lucy had sat by riverbanks with him and his easel in loyal and encouraging silence: she knew what it was like to watch paint dry and that it was a hell of a lot more interesting than this.

'This' was general-election night in a musty church hall in a small village in Essex. As features editor for *Cachet* magazine, Lucy was there in the line of duty. Her editor had decided that *Cachet* readers, bright and sassy, would appreciate some political acuity alongside the usual 'Is your man a love rat? Ten tell-tale signs.'

So there she was, purgatorially bored, wishing she was somewhere – anywhere – else. Tonight would have offered the ideal opportunity to get a table at The Ivy or a ticket for *The Producers* because a significant proportion of potential patrons would be sitting at home watching Peter Snow and his giant swingometer. However, like everyone else in the hall, she was waiting for the Count. Oh, how she wished that the Count was a mysterious Balkan aristocrat with twinkly eyes and a twirly moustache. But, no, this Count, like innumerable others up and down the country, would involve some puffed-up self-important volunteers heaving metal ballot boxes on to creaking trestle tables.

Lucy's knowledge of politics was practically non-existent, ranking somewhere between her knowledge of late Etruscan pottery and the mating habits of slugs. To her glazed, tired eyes, the most interesting things in the hall were the radiators. Old, cast iron, painted Corporation Beige, they were just like the ones she remembered from school. She caught herself thinking how chic they'd look in her minimalist sitting room in Clapham, before attempting once more to concentrate on the parliamentary candidates.

They all looked fairly relaxed. The man with the yellow rosette and the girl with the red one weren't particularly nervous because they had nothing to lose. The result was a foregone conclusion. Brian Marsden, MP, deputy leader of the Conservative Party, blue rosette adorning his elegant hand-tailored suit, would be returned to the seat he'd occupied so comfortably for the past twenty-two years.

He was working the room like an old pro. Smiling, pumping hands, turning his hearty chuckle on and off and occasionally raising his eyebrows at Lucy, like a louche old uncle. This wasn't her first encounter with Marsden. She'd profiled him for *Cachet* a few months earlier after he'd allegedly made some ill-judged comments to a journalist from the *Observer*. Apparently he'd opined that all mothers with small children should abandon their careers and stay at home. As he had pointed out, with an exasperated grimace, he had been misquoted. All he'd said was that women who'd been brave enough to sacrifice their careers to look after their children should be supported and encouraged for doing so. Instead of an unreconstructed right-wing chauvinist, Lucy found a decent, compassionate man. A little vain, perhaps, and more than a little pompous, but it would be hard to imagine anyone standing for Parliament who wasn't. She'd come away from the House of Commons with a grudging fondness for the Right Honourable Member for Chelmsford South.

She found herself interviewing him again. 'Nervous, Brian?'

'Well, not really,' came the reply – practised, avuncular, just the right side of smug. 'Anyway,' he said, 'nothing we can do now. Polls have closed, boxes should be here any minute.'

He paused for a puff on one of his tiny, trademark Café Crème cigars. 'I mean, one must never take anything for granted,' he said, exhaling a slender plume of creamy smoke, 'but I've always done my best for the people here and I think they know that.' Then smugness got the better of him. 'They knew it last time,' he chuckled, 'and five times before that.'

As yet another fawning constituent came up to wish him the best of luck, Lucy turned to consider his opponents.

The Lib Dem's yellow rosette was now wilting. It knew that the mousy-haired creep wearing it was on a hiding to nothing. He was standing around awkwardly, looking like the child he used to be: the weedy kid at school who was always last to be picked for the football team. As he drank warm Lambrusco from a plastic cup, his little piggy eyes darted round the room. He just wanted the boxes to arrive, Lucy thought, and their contents to be counted. He wanted the TV news crew to hurry up and film his electoral humiliation so he could go home, put it all behind him and try again next time for a seat that he might have some chance of winning.

The Labour candidate seemed a bit more interesting. She, at

least, in her smart black Joseph two-piece, was giving Brian Marsden a sartorial run for his money. What was more, she was making an effort to talk to people. She'd wandered on to Marsden's patch and was now chatting to the local vicar. As she watched the Reverend Jennings chatting amiably back, Lucy thought how irritated he must be with this five-yearly procession of heathens through his hall. Oh, they all wanted to talk to him now, only too keen at election time to make hefty donations to repair the church roof. As he smiled politely, and accepted their alms, she wondered whether this benign clergyman was ever seized by an overwhelming urge to tell them all to fuck off.

She gazed up at the old-fashioned wall clock, which, like the radiators, reminded her of school. The hands on this one, like those of its classroom counterparts, seemed to move painfully slowly in a time zone that bore no relation to the real world. She'd always thought time had moved more slowly in Miss Chapman's history lessons than anywhere else on earth. That record had just been broken.

The fixed smile on Lucy's face was now causing her actual pain, and she was starting to worry that if the wind changed she'd be stuck like that: a cross between Tony Blair and Jake from *The Tweenies*. Fortunately, just moments before Bell's palsy set in, she could relax into a brief expression of solemnity as the ballot boxes were carried in and the quaint old process of British democracy creaked into action. Despite the advent of the Internet and text-messaging, the system of voting hadn't changed since 1832. Every single vote had to be counted individually by hand, and as this lengthy ritual began, so did Lucy's own with the return of the fixed smile.

She was just mastering the art of sleeping while smiling when the woman with the overbite presented herself once more. 'Can I get you anything, dear? Tea? Coffee?'

This time, Lucy told the truth: 'No, thank you. I'm fine.'

'I'm Sheila, by the way, Mr Marsden's assistant.'

Lucy warmed to the old-fashioned description, 'assistant' rather than 'PA', and found herself warming to Sheila, too, with her cold food, warm smile and indefatigable enthusiasm.

'Of course,' said Sheila, whose genuine smile made Lucy feel guilty about her fixed one, 'you're the girl from the magazine. Mr Marsden told me all about you. He said how . . . oh . . . Excuse me, dear, won't be a moment.'

Sheila's acute antenna had picked up a slight change in the atmosphere, imperceptible to anyone else. Lucy wouldn't have noticed it but now her journalistic eye was following Sheila across the room.

Marsden still looked confident and relaxed, silver hair and navy suit still immaculate, Café Crème still being casually puffed, but Sheila must have registered a slight flicker in his expression. Lucy couldn't work out what it was but now, for the first time, she found herself more interested in the people than the radiators.

Ten minutes later, the first signs of Tory tension were rippling through the hall. A little of the confidence seemed to have drained from Marsden's face. The Café Crèmes were being smoked a little more quickly. Something wasn't right. Clearly things weren't going as swimmingly as they had at the last election. Or at the five elections before that.

Suddenly Lucy wanted to hang around. There was now a possibility that Chelmsford South was about to witness a major electoral upset. For the first time ever, the readers of *Cachet* might get an eye-witness account of a momentous political event.

The Lib Dem's wilting rosette seemed to be reblooming, as though it had been doused by an invisible elf with a tiny watering-can. Lucy tried to read his thoughts. No doubt he was imagining his triumphant picture in the following day's papers, to be seen by all those bastards who wouldn't pick him for the football team.

Then she realised that the Labour girl was attracting more attention. Like a dumbstruck lottery winner, she appeared unable to compute the fact that her numbers were coming up. Literally. It was becoming more and more apparent that an awful lot of voters had put an X next to her name rather than Brian Marsden's.

Lucy's eyes swivelled over to Marsden. His tie was loosened and he looked rattled and unkempt. He was now chain-smoking the Café Crèmes and gulping down his warm white wine from his plastic cup almost as fast as Sheila could fill it. It was like watching a particularly tragic episode of *ER*, Lucy mused. Brian Marsden's political career lay prone and helpless on the operating table and time was running out. Not even George Clooney could save him now.

The doors at the back of the church hall suddenly swung open and the place was besieged by reporters, not just from the local Chelmsford free-sheet but from the BBC, ITV and most of the national newspapers. They were all there to record the Right Honourable Brian Marsden's spectacular fall from grace. They weren't there for the victor. Most of them couldn't even remember her name. They were spitefully thrusting their cameras and microphones towards the man she had beaten, gloating over his trauma and disbelief.

Looking at Marsden now, politically dead and physically exhausted, it would have taken a hard heart not to feel a twinge of pity as he faced his tormentors. Lucy was impressed by how gracious he was in defeat, even though he seemed to have forgotten that the victor was meant to speak first.

'May I take this opportunity,' he said to the millions of people who had stayed up late to watch this, 'to thank the people of Chelmsford South whom it has been my privilege to represent for the last twenty-two years and to wish my successor the very best of luck. She fought an excellent campaign and thoroughly deserves her victory. I hope she enjoys the job and its many responsibilities as much as I did.'

Lucy, so cynical only hours before, now understood just how electrifying real-life political drama could be. To her surprise, a lump formed in her throat and real tears trickled down her cheeks.

Poor old Marsden. It wasn't that Chelmsford South had turned against him personally, more that they'd turned against his party.

The grudging fondness she'd felt for him had increased over his election campaign and she only wished there could have been a happy ending. However, almost all political lives end in failure because almost all politicians outstay their welcome. Brian Marsden was no exception. Nonetheless, Lucy really wished he'd won.

No, she really, really, *really* wished he'd won.

As she snuffled back the tears, only one thought was running through her mind. Oh, fuck! she thought. What am I going to do? I know nothing about politics. And I'm the new MP for Chelmsford South.

5

Clichés are clichés because they're true, and none more so than 'This must be a bad dream, any minute now I'll wake up.' However, having given herself three hard pinches and a slap, Lucy realised that her happy, apolitical life really was about to end so, almost on cue, its latter stages began to flash before her.

She saw herself at her desk a few weeks earlier, subbing a piece about another miracle cure for cellulite when Simon Burridge, her editor, had flounced past. He had always reminded her of Elton John, in that his looks and personality were horribly mismatched. Both men were colourful, outrageous queens trapped in the bodies of tubby, balding accountants and, unfortunately, no amount of flamboyant behaviour or Versace attire would ever make either of them look anything other than wrong. 'Darling,' he'd trilled breezily, 'how do you fancy standing for Parliament?'

'About as much as I fancy you,' was Lucy's response, 'and even less than you fancy me.'

'Ooh, saucer of milk for our features editor.' He'd laughed, with his Cruella de Vil cackle. 'Come on, I'm talking about a serious – all right, semi-serious – political piece. It's just what we need to get our noses ahead of *Marie Claire* and *Cosmo*.'

'What are you on about?'

'A first-hand account from our intrepid reporter on what it's like to try to become an MP.'

Lucy wasn't impressed. 'Oh, please,' she said, rolling her eyes, 'what am I, Simon? Some sort of plucky Bridget Jones character? Am I going to have to wear big knickers and have 'hilarious madcap adventures?'

'If you insist, dear. But seriously, why not? It'll be a bit of fun, won't it, standing against your old pal Brian Marsden?'

Lucy was only attracted by the lack of effort involved. In Britain, she could 'stand' for election; in America, she'd have to 'run'. 'Brian Marsden?' she said. 'He's got one of the safest seats in the country. I've got no chance.'

'Exactly. Well, you don't want to win, do you, and give up your fabulous life working for me? Don't worry, politics isn't for you. It's for people without the personality to become account-ants or the principles to become estate agents. Oh, come on, it'll be a scream.'

Simon had flicked the fatal 'Why not?' switch in Lucy's head. It had been getting her into trouble since she was at school. It had made her throw that snowball at Sister Mary, the head-mistress, sing 'Saving All My Love For You' at a karaoke party and order the magic-mushroom omelette at a beach café on Koh Samui. The 'Why not?' switch made her ask Simon for more details. 'I suppose you've got me lined up to stand for some loony fringe party?'

'Well, sort of,' said Simon. 'You'll be standing for Labour. Which, in Chelmsford, amounts to much the same thing.'

A couple of weeks later, Lucy was being vetted by the selec-tion committee of the Chelmsford South Labour Party. Her chances of being picked were doubled because there was a 'women only' shortlist, and since she had no real desire to be picked, she was relaxed, charming and articulate. Far more so than her drear-ily ambitious rivals, with their sturdy calves and undistinguished careers in local government. One spectacularly ugly hopeful was an equal-opportunities adviser. Lucy was appalled by how anyone who promoted 'equal opportunities' could take advantage of a selection process that excluded half of the human race. When she told Simon, he smiled wearily. 'Welcome to the world of poli-tics, dear.'

So, Lucy Ross, who was exactly the sort of person required to boost the Party's flagging image, was duly selected as Labour candidate for Chelmsford South. The selectors knew they were bound to lose, so why not lose with a degree of panache and sex appeal?

Brian Marsden's backside was practically superglued to the seat, so there was very little interest in Lucy. Even the local paper had only given her a brief, perfunctory interview. She'd told the reporter something she vaguely remembered from school: that the term House of *Commons* was derived from House of *Communes*. The original purpose had been for each commune to send a representative to Westminster to make sure its views and wishes were expressed. Lucy had expressed her own view that the House of Communes should be just that. Her intention would be to listen to the wishes of the people in her commune and to ensure that they had a voice in Parliament. She said, quite truthfully, that she had no parliamentary ambitions and that her only interests were those of her constituents.

She'd struck a chord with the voters. Contrary to what she'd thought, they really had turned against Brian Marsden personally. He may have been a decent chap and an eminent politician, but he was a lousy constituency MP. His preoccupation with the business of government and the advancement of his own career had left him with little time for the people who'd voted for him.

Lucy's campaign slogan 'Change for Chelmsford' may have been trite and meaningless but what she did with it was inspired. She'd placed red collection boxes in local shops, pubs and restaurants with the words 'Change for Chelmsford' written on the side and a brief message from Lucy Ross, Labour candidate for Chelmsford South, asking local people to help one another. The loose change that plinked into the boxes would be distributed among local charities so that change for Chelmsford would lead to 'Change for Chelmsford'.

Coins in collection boxes were swiftly followed by votes in ballot boxes – enough to propel Lucy into Parliament.

She rippled back into the present and felt the full force of microphones and cameras being turned towards her. It was like facing a firing squad. Through those lenses, millions of people could see tears in her eyes but no one knew that they were tears of horror, rather than joy. Oh, God! She had to make a victory speech for which she was wholly unprepared. 'Pull yourself together,' she muttered to herself. 'Come on – eyes and teeth.'

She took Brian Marsden's place on the stage. Her voice, high and breathless, made her sound like a nervous child reading in assembly. 'Um, er, well, as you can imagine, I didn't expect this, so the few words I had prepared were to congratulate Brian Marsden on another victory. Um . . . I'd still like to congratulate Brian on his long and distinguished . . . er . . . parliamentary career and on his many political achievements—'

'Such as?' shouted a wag from the *Daily Mirror*.

'Er – I don't know . . . Um . . . I'm sure he must have done something.'

There was uproarious laughter from all around the hall.

Lucy tried to protest: 'No, no – I didn't mean it like that. I – I just want to thank the people of Chelmsford South for voting for me and . . . um . . . giving me this wonderful opportunity to represent them. I will do everything I can to be a really good MP.'

Cheers and applause echoed round the hall as the media circus packed up and headed for Romford.

Lucy found herself being fêted and congratulated by people she'd never seen before, all from Party HQ in Millbank. People who, until a couple of hours ago, didn't even know who she was. Now suddenly they all wanted to be filmed and photographed next to her as though they'd been in some way responsible for her success. In truth, Chelmsford South had been considered such a hopeless, unwinnable seat that Lucy had just been left to get on with it. Now she wanted to be put out of her misery. Please, someone, she thought, just draw a sharp knife slowly over my throat. It would surely be preferable to having her hand shaken and her cheeks kissed by these slimy people and to being told what an asset she was to the Party. She felt like screaming, 'You didn't want to know me before and I was quite happy with that! Now, please, just go away, all of you, and leave me alone!'

Eventually they did. Word had come through from Millbank that another victorious candidate was waiting to be smothered in fake sincerity.

Brian Marsden, naturally, had been first to flee – keen, perhaps, to swap his parliamentary seat for some rather more lucrative ones on boards and committees. The media hadn't been far behind, and now the party apparatchiks had gone. Lucy's friends hadn't gone because they hadn't come. It was just work, she'd told them, just another silly assignment. It would be very boring and she'd rather they didn't witness the most excruciating moment of her life.

Adam would probably have been there but he was away filming in South Africa. The musty church hall, which had been rammed only half an hour before, was now almost deserted. Lucy had never felt so alone in her life. She'd had a feeling that she might drink a little too much cheap white wine and had therefore taken the precaution of booking into the Travel Motel, just off the Chelmsford bypass. The prospect of a night there was almost as grisly as that of five years in Parliament.

She was about to burst into floods of desperate uncontrollable tears when something stopped her. Amid the helpers folding up the trestle tables, sweeping the floor and tipping plastic cups into bin bags, she saw one of the saddest sights she'd ever seen. Alone in a corner, unnoticed by anyone else, a woman of about sixty was sobbing silently. Lucy went over and placed a comforting arm round her shoulders. With her short white hair and buck teeth, the poor woman looked like a small, defenceless rabbit, whose mother had just been shot. 'Oh, I'm so sorry, dear,' she wept. 'It's your night and I shouldn't be spoiling it like this but, well, I don't know what I'm going to do. I've worked for Mr Marsden for twenty-two years. It's been my life. And now it's all over.'

Lucy had always found something particularly tragic in tears shed by the bespectacled. The sight of a handkerchief dabbed between crying eyes and glasses always had Lucy's own tear ducts welling up in sympathy. It was this that prompted her to make her first political decision. 'No, Sheila, it isn't all over,' she said, suddenly strong, kind and resolute. 'I'm the MP for Chelmsford South, and for as long as I am I want you to be my assistant.'

6

Lucy had always blamed her addiction to shopping on the fact that she'd been born above a shop. It was in the blood. Sorry. Nothing she could do about it. The Amalfi delicatessen on Clerkenwell Road was owned and run by her Italian-born parents. Her father's name had originally been Rossi, but anti-Italian feelings during the Second World War had led her grandfather to anglicise it by dropping the last letter. In later life, Lucy was grateful for this – not that she wanted to deny her Italian provenance: she just didn't want anyone to think she was related to the lead singer of Status Quo.

Ever since her grandmother, her *nonna*, had walked her, as a small child, up to Chapel Market, Lucy had been in thrall to the 'So if I give you these coins, that lovely thing becomes mine' rush of pure, unmitigated joy. If she could have seen a list of every item she had ever bought, she would have been very happy with just about everything on it.

Everything, that is, apart from holidays, particularly those of the packaged variety. From the crammed and delayed charter flights, which dumped people in Málaga at two in the morning, to the horrible realisation that the travel agent's brochure could have won the Pulitzer Prize for fiction, holidays had been a constant disappointment. Yet, each year, the boredom, misery and impotent anger of the previous summer would be somehow forgotten as she leafed through another brochure, hoping, with the glorious folly of the eternal optimist, that this time things would be different.

They never were.

Small wonder that, like thousands of other ex-victims, she'd jumped for joy when the Internet arrived to give greedy airlines and lying tour operators the kicking they so richly deserved. Travellers were finally unshackled and able to take spontaneous trips to exotic places on cheap, flexible flights. At last holidays could join perfume from Les Senteurs and chocolates from Pierre Marcolini on Lucy's long list of pleasurable purchases. Smart hotels were a particular delight. She adored their gloss and polish, their lifts and lobbies, their amplified sense of serenity. To her, they were temples of beauty, luxury or Zen-like simplicity: havens of calm in breathtaking locations. She loved the fact that, on arrival, she could forget all aspects of domestic drudgery. When the receptionist took the initial imprint of her Visa card, she had no past, only a present and a future. Her whole life was starting again.

That was how she felt when she checked in at the Travel Motel, but this time it was a truly gruesome feeling.

The Travel Motel was clean and functional but it was also the most soulless and depressing place Lucy had ever stayed. She knew that half of the rooms would be temporary homes for lonely sales reps called Alan with Ford Mondeos and Matalan suits. The other half would be cubicles of timid infidelity where married men also called Alan, could have clammy, clumsy relations with girls called Zoë who worked in Accounts.

She was welcomed by a receptionist in a woundingly foul polyester uniform and handed a complimentary leaflet that promised her a 'comfy bed' and everything she needed 'for a good night's sleep'. The word 'comfy' on a piece of official literature made her want to twitch, as did the knowledge that, after the life-changing shock she'd just sustained, no bed in the world would be 'comfy' enough to deliver a good night's sleep. Tonight nothing short of an anaesthetist would send her to the Land of Nod.

The functional, featureless room was a monument to blandness and, as she lay on the bed, gazing blankly at the muted fawn walls, Lucy wondered if this was how it felt to be dead. Painless, not unpleasant but utterly devoid of anything resembling life.

All hideous accoutrements were present and correct: the tiny bathroom with its horrible nylon shower curtain that would seem wet even when it was dry, the thin disposable shower cap, the mean ungracious little slivers of soap and, of course, in the bedroom, the tea and coffee-making facilities, replete with artificial sweeteners and non-dairy creamers.

Lucy knew she'd had precisely the wrong amount to drink: not enough to help her sleep but just enough to keep her awake: not enough to drown her sorrows but just enough to keep them afloat. She'd briefly considered drinking a bit more, then driving recklessly home in the hope that the Essex Police would catch her. She'd be breathalysed and forced to resign, having served approximately three and a half hours as an MP. Tempting as it was, she knew that this would instantly make her the most famous politician in the country, her shamefully short tenure enshrined for ever in *The Guinness Book of Records*. She thought about offering a straightforward 'Look, this has all been a terrible mistake' resignation, but that, too, would bring the unwelcome glare of media attention. She reflected bitterly on her ironic, post-modern reason for booking the room, and how spectacularly it had backfired.

Oh, it was meant to have been such a hoot: the dreadful but wittily reported climax to the whole Chelmsford experience; the fitting end to her disastrous but amusing flirtation with politics. Her plan had been to fly off the following morning to a sumptuous hotel on the other side of the world. She was supposed to be fulfilling a lifetime's ambition by checking in at the Mount Nelson in Cape Town where Adam would be waiting for her in a luxury double. This majestic colonial palace had topped Lucy's accommodation wish list for years, and the idea had been to compare it, hilariously, with the Chelmsford Travel Motel.

The thought of opening her laptop on the terrace of the Mount Nelson and heaping superlatives on its old-fashioned grandeur and opulence had sustained her. She'd been longing to luxuriate in the sheer acreage of a four-poster bed for which 'comfy' would be insultingly inadequate.

Apparently the Mount Nelson combined the best of both hemispheres: an old English country house complemented by the perfect South African climate. 'Apparently', however, was as close as she would get. The trip would have to be cancelled. Alone in her cheap little cubby-hole, Lucy couldn't even bring herself to look at the SAA club-class ticket that would have made her long-cherished dream a reality.

She imagined the scene eight thousand miles away: Adam's mouth agape as he saw the result flash through from Chelmsford via Sky News. She knew exactly how he'd be feeling. He'd encouraged her, supported her and egged her on. In their relationship, he had always been the more politically aware. He was the *Guardian*-reading metropolitan liberal, so surely he'd be bursting with joy and pride to discover that he'd helped the woman he loved become a Labour MP.

Not exactly.

Lucy knew that he'd only been so supportive and encouraging because he'd never imagined she'd win. She knew that now he'd be consumed with confusion, guilt and envy.

He hadn't phoned, he hadn't texted. He'd leave it to her. He always did. Adam was an Olympic sulker, and when they argued it was always Lucy who had to give in first and make everything all right.

She thought of a random number in her head – forty-three – and decided to count to it. He had forty-three seconds to call. If he didn't, she'd call him. And unless he had a cast-iron excuse for not calling, involving serious injury and a herd of wild elephants, she vowed it would be the last time she would ever call him.

The forty-three seconds expired. She called. He answered.

The conversation and its outcome were much as she had predicted. And although she would have expected it to cause her hours of sobbing insomnia, it didn't. In fact, within another forty-three seconds she was fast asleep in a surprisingly 'comfy bed'.

7

'Caught single'. Ironically, it was Lucy who had coined this phrase for a piece she'd penned for the previous month's *Cachet*. She'd written sympathetically, if a little condescendingly, about women who'd invested the 'settling-down years' between twenty-five and thirty-five in a relationship that they'd assumed would find its way to the altar. Instead they'd discovered that the Romance & Relationship Building Society had suddenly gone bust, leaving them emotionally penniless. Overnight they'd found themselves 'caught single' in their mid-thirties and having to start dating all over again, ten years older, desperately out of practice and becoming gradually deafened by the relentless ticking of their biological clock.

Those poor wretched creatures, she'd thought, never imagining that, within weeks, she'd be one of them.

Having had precisely the wrong amount to drink, Lucy had worked out that by around six a.m., she would have limbo-danced back under the limit and be legally able to escape. She couldn't bear to contemplate having breakfast alone in the hideous Country Fayre dining area at the back of the Travel Motel, sitting alone with a stale greasy croissant and the little jar she'd chosen from the 'selection of homemade preserves'. The very thought of receiving a cup of instant coffee from a fat, sullen teenager dressed as a medieval serving wench had her heading back to London long before the sun had got its hat on.

By seven fifteen, she was in Smith's of Smithfield, her favourite breakfast haunt, right in the heart of London's famous meat market. The handsome old Grade-II listed building had once been a wholesale butcher's store-house; the sort of place where

Sylvester Stallone had used carcasses as punch-bags in the first *Rocky* film. Reborn as a four-floor stack of restaurants and bars, the place had the gritty, urban feel of a New York warehouse. Huge windows, heavy industrial ironwork and grimy exposed bricks made it the antithesis of the cheap, flimsy prefab from which she'd just fled. Now she needed its metropolitan vibe to seep into her, with a wake-me-up concoction of fresh apple, carrot and beetroot juice.

Even an environment as familiar as this looked different now. Lucy felt like a child in an oxygen tent, there but not there. Everything was the same but not. She could see her old life but was no longer able to participate in it. Lolling on a battered leather sofa, head back, she emitted the slow moan of simultaneous relief and despair. Her loyal friend Karen took this as her cue to start the questions.

Karen Fisher was Lucy's closest confidante and a long-standing *Cachet* colleague. Her contributions to the magazine were seldom made under her own name. She was Helen Style, fashion and beauty editor, she was Tracy Garden, horticultural expert, but this morning she was Anna Wise, everybody's favourite life adviser. 'Anna' could always take an impartial view of other people's problems and offer inspired, perceptive solutions. However, like a Michelin-starred chef who comes home pissed to a microwave meal, she could never be as intelligent and objective about her own life. Like a pinball, she'd pinged from one disastrous entanglement to another, each time picking up the bittersweet experiences that informed her wisdom.

'Promise me you didn't drink and dial,' she began.

'I didn't drink and dial.'

'But you had drunk.'

'Not enough to *be* drunk.'

'Then you dialled?'

'Only to tell him that I wouldn't be joining him in Cape Town.'

'What did he say?'

'Well, he just fumbled and mumbled a bit, and said he's been offered more work out there so he'd be staying for another month. I was welcome to join him but – and you'll hate this – *the ball was in my court.*'

'Well, any sort of balls would never be in his,' said Karen. 'And now, I suppose, it's all your fault. If you hadn't gone and won that seat, everything would still be fine.'

'That was the implication, yeah.'

'So you dumped him?'

'I took the honourable course of action,' said Lucy, trying out politico-speak for the first time, 'and resigned from my relationship. I felt my position had become untenable.'

'Well, I suppose it had. Can't have your career being as important as his, now, can we? Even though you're a Member of Parliament and he's a . . . What is it he likes to call himself?'

Adam was a lighting cameraman, or what Americans call a director of photography. When asked what he did for a living, he always said, 'I'm a DOP.' The fact that nobody knew what this meant gave him immediate licence to explain, by boasting about all the commercials and movies he'd worked on.

'So how do you feel?' said Karen.

'Well, surprisingly calm about the whole thing,' Lucy said. 'Maybe I'm still numbed by the shock of the election, but even this morning I'm waiting for the hurt to kick in and I'm beginning to wonder if it ever will. I think our relationship was well past its sell-by date. We were never that compatible. Maybe we were together out of habit rather than anything else. And if so, it was a habit I should have kicked a long time ago. You were never that keen on him, were you?'

Karen knew that she was about to step on to very thin ice and lightened her tread accordingly. There's a fine line between taking your friend's side and deriding her judgement. 'Oh, he was okay,' she said cautiously, 'but there was always this sort of vanity about him. He took himself a bit too seriously.

Everything had to be just so, all a bit measured, all a bit too thought-out.'

She was right and Lucy remembered the litany of prissy affectations that she had found so irritating. Adam was pathologically neat and tidy. His wardrobe was immaculate, shirts beautifully ironed and perfectly hung, jumpers folded properly, as though they were still on the shelf in Prada. The way he said he enjoyed 'film', rather than films, and took his snaps with a vintage Pentax when a digital Canon from Argos would have done the job so much more easily. Then there was the original Fender Stratocaster on which he could only play the opening bars of 'Smoke On The Water' and 'Stairway to Heaven'. And the ridiculous vintage Citroën DS that spent most of its time being either towed or repaired. The way he drove it! she thought, in shades and a black cashmere polo-neck, as though he were an extra in a Claud Lelouch film . . .

Lucy felt like Julie Andrews in reverse. Instead of consoling herself by thinking about her favourite things, she simply remembered the least favourite and then she didn't feel so bad. 'He was a bit of a cock, really, wasn't he?' she said.

Again, Karen hesitated. Couples who split up have a tendency to get back together, but she decided to be honest. 'Yes.'

And for the first time Lucy laughed. If Karen had been entirely honest, she'd have told Lucy that Adam was also a notorious 'lingerer' – a man who lets a friendly kiss on the cheek linger just long enough for the recipient to feel slightly uncomfortable.

'Well,' said Lucy, 'I really needed him last night and he wasn't there for me. I don't mean physically, I mean emotionally. I needed his love and support last night more than ever. I'm actually quite scared about being an MP.'

'I bet you are,' said Karen. 'Anyone would be. Trouble is, he was even more scared. He'd never be able to cope with you having a high-profile parliamentary career. A man like that would be no help at all.'

Lucy took a sip of her drink. 'You're absolutely right,' she said.

'Anyway,' said Karen, with a smile, 'how did your mum and dad react?'

Lucy's response to her friend's innocuous question was to splutter fresh apple, carrot and beetroot juice through her nose in true comedy style. But this was no joke. 'Oh, my God!'

'You haven't you told them, have you?'

Lucy didn't reply: she was wiping juice off her chin and heading for the door.

8

Not only had Lucy failed to tell her parents that she had won the seat: she'd also omitted to mention that she was even standing for it. She had no excuse. Bruno and Ella Ross were not dead, estranged or living in Italy: they were alive, adored and living in East Finchley. They still ran the Amalfi delicatessen, having relocated it from Clerkenwell some twenty years previously.

She hadn't told them because it had been just work and, like everyone else, she'd never thought for a moment that she'd win. And, anyway, Bruno and Ella weren't particularly interested in their youngest daughter's career. Lucy was thirty-three and their primary concern was when she was going to get married and weigh in with a couple of *bambini*.

The more she thought about it, the worse it got. In Italy, politicians are viewed with even more loathing and distrust than they are in Britain. Bruno, in particular, regarded them all as vile, corrupt, scheming narcissists. His heart would break when he found out that his beautiful daughter had become one.

Lucy's upbringing had been typically Italian, filled with laughter, music, food and wine. Pleasure was only tempered by the strictures of the Catholic Church. Her bright, industrious parents had no interest in politics. At their happy, bustling mealtimes, extra seats at the huge dining-room table were filled with noisy Neapolitan friends and relatives, and the bonhomie was never besmirched by dreary political discourse.

For something as significant as this, Lucy knew that a mere

phone call would not suffice. She'd have to battle her way through Islington and Holloway to explain herself in person. Oh, God, becoming an MP was bad enough, but to have split up from a possible source of grandchildren was a tragedy of operatic proportions.

To most people, her frantic journey would have seemed a waste of time. Surely her parents would already have heard about Brian Marsden's political demise, and who had replaced him, on that morning's eight o'clock news. But Lucy knew Bruno and Ella's early-morning routine. They made the fresh pasta, took delivery of the warm, dusty ciabatta and the sweet honeyed pastries, packed the freshly ground coffee beans into the giant Gaggia 6000 to create the most potent espressos in London, arranged the Italian hams and cheeses, and replenished the shelves with balsamic vinegar and extra-virgin olive oil. She knew it so well because, as a child, it had been her morning routine too. She was also aware that in the authentic Italian atmosphere of the Amalfi delicatessen, there was no room for Terry Wogan, Chris Moyles or mendacious politicians on the *Today* programme. Bruno never listened to the radio. He'd tried Classic FM in the hope of hearing a stirring piece of opera – *Turandot*, perhaps, or *La Traviata*. Instead, he had heard constant ads for hernia clinics, and matey presenters, saying, 'We're just going to take a little break but, hey, stay tuned for a really cool bit of Bach.' After a few days of that, he had tuned out for ever and returned to the CD player that sat on a shelf in the corner, half-hidden by tins of San Marzano plum tomatoes, and played Verdi, Puccini, Tony Bennett and Dean Martin, or the pre-war tunes of Carlo Buti and Luciano Tajoli. The customers, however, did listen to the radio so Lucy knew she had to get to the deli before the shutters were pulled up, the awning hooked down, and the cat let out of the bag.

She screeched to a halt outside at eight fifty-six and saw her father cheerfully lugging a couple of tables out on to the pavement, while he treated East Finchley to a bellowing version of 'Primo Amore'. Bruno had always suffered from a musical strain of Tourette's syndrome: as soon as a tune entered his head, he had no vocal control – he had to burst into song. Lucy winced at a childhood memory of when the song he'd felt compelled to sing was Joe Dolce's 'Shaddap You Face'.

His voice and spirits seemed equally good and, although she hated to spoil things for him, Lucy was consoled to see that no one else had beaten her to it.

'Loo-cheer,' he boomed and beamed. His smile extended his white moustache to the width of a draught-excluder.

Lucy had been christened Lucia, pronounced 'Loo-cheer', but most people didn't know that: they'd called her 'Loosia', as though she were a Caribbean holiday destination. At the age of twelve, she'd decided it might be easier to call herself Lucy.

'What a lovely surprise,' said Bruno, kissing her on both cheeks, 'Ella! Ella! Look who's here.'

Lucy's mother appeared from the back of the shop. Contrary to popular myth, this Italian woman had not grown dumpy and hirsute: Ella Ross, at sixty-eight, was still slender, elegant and striking. She embraced her daughter but, unlike Bruno, sensed immediately that something was wrong.

Maybe it was the heavenly smell of the coffee and the freshly baked ciabatta, or the sound of Pepino di Capri crooning 'Nessuno Al Mondo' from among the tins of tomatoes, maybe it was just the comforting warmth of undemanding love. Whatever it was, it pulled the plug and the long-postponed deluge of tears that Lucy hadn't realised were so close to the surface finally arrived. She slumped down at the one table that Bruno had yet to pull out on to the pavement.

Ella, though she couldn't say why, was not surprised. She had no idea what was wrong but she had thought for some time that something wasn't quite right. She gently stroked her daughter's thick dark curls and waited patiently for the sobbing to abate.

Bruno's brow, rarely furrowed, was now displaying deep lines of bewilderment and concern.

He turned to close the shop before it opened but was about three seconds too late. In the middle of this real-life Italian opera, the first customer had arrived.

9

All priests have an in-built crisis detector. It's a bit fuzzy when they're first ordained, but the longer they spend comforting the sick and the sinful, the more acute it becomes. After forty-six years, Father Salvatore de Luca's was tuned to perfection.

At seventy-two, he should have returned to the little village of Minori in the south of Italy to enjoy his retirement, but since the Archdiocese of Westminster wasn't exactly overwhelmed with young men queuing up to take holy orders, they were keen to retain the services of old men who already had. Father Sal was one of them and his morning routine, like Bruno and Ella's, seldom varied. He said the eight o'clock mass at St Anthony's in East Finchley. By Holy Communion, he was gagging for the Gaggia and often shoved the little round wafers into parishioners' mouths with unseemly haste and irreverence. Within ten minutes, he'd be out of his vestments and heading across the road to the Amalfi delicatessen for his high-octane caffeine fix.

Father Sal was also unaware that his best friend's daughter, whose tiny head he had held over the font some thirty-three years earlier, was the new MP for Chelmsford South. He'd heard that Labour had been re-elected but wasn't particularly interested in the details.

As he approached the Amalfi, the sensor lights on his crisis detector started to flash and hum. He entered, saw Lucy sobbing in her mother's arms and quietly turned the sign on the door from *Open* to *Closed*.

As small boys playing hide and seek in the lemon groves around Minori, Sal and Bruno had been able to communicate without

saying a word. They still could. Bruno's helpless shrug said, 'I've
no idea what's wrong with my daughter.'

Sal's arched eyebrow said, 'We'll wait till she's ready to speak.
And a double espresso, please.'

When Lucy lifted her head she saw Father Sal's kindly smile.
She'd been confessing her sins – most of them – to him since
she was seven so his unexpected presence made her feel a little
easier. 'Bless me, Father, for I have sinned.' She sniffed, with a
watery smile.

'What is it Lucia?' said the old priest. 'What have you done?'

'Well', she said, 'I haven't exactly sinned.'

Father Sal left the warm, open, non-judgemental pause that
always elicited further details. 'So what is it?' he asked gently.
'What has made you so unhappy?'

'You haven't heard?'

Three ageing Italians shook their heads.

'I stood for Parliament,' she said, 'and I won. I'm the new MP
for Chelmsford South.'

Bruno jolted, spattering his starched white apron with dark
brown espresso. He and Ella stared at each other in silent horror.

Father Sal nodded.

'It's not something I ever wanted to do,' Lucy went on. 'It was
just a little stunt for the magazine. I stood against Brian Marsden.'

A little more espresso hit Bruno's apron. He and Ella had no
interest in politics but even they'd heard of Brian Marsden.

Lucy looked at her father. His shiny bald head remained bowed
in silence. He'd either been struck dumb or he was deferentially
allowing Father Sal to do the talking. Probably both.

'How did this happen?' said Father Sal, genuinely curious. 'I
didn't realise you had political ambitions.'

'I haven't.' She sighed. 'It's the last thing in the world I wanted
to do. It was just a stunt for the magazine. They gave me a really
safe Tory seat to contest, one that I had no chance of winning.
I don't know what happened but I won. Not by much – only

two hundred and thirty votes – but now I'm the Member of Parliament for Chelmsford South, and as far as a certain person is concerned . . .' She nodded at her father. '. . . may as well have sold my soul to the devil.'

Bruno still hadn't looked up. It was as though he and Ella were in silent, contemplative prayer.

Father Sal took this as his cue to give Lucy the benefit of his wisdom. 'Well, Lucia,' he said, 'God moves in mysterious ways. This was clearly His will. He must have wanted you to do it.'

Oh, please, thought Lucy, spare me the Catholic platitudes. God's will, my arse. Catholics had done this for centuries: anything you can't explain, from the creation of the universe to an electoral upset in Chelmsford, just say, 'God did it.'

Lucy's views on religion were quite strident. Like a lot of lapsed Catholics, she lapsed into laughter whenever she thought of the ridiculous things she was supposed to believe. As a child, she'd believed in Father Christmas, the Tooth Fairy and God. As she grew up, she'd let each belief go. She couldn't comprehend how anyone, having let go of numbers one and two, somehow failed to let go of number three. How was God any different from the others? Was there any more evidence for His existence than for theirs? Not a shred – and, in her view, anyone who believed otherwise was condemned to live in a state of permanent infancy.

She had never wanted to upset the people she adored, three of whom were with her now, so those views had remained unspoken, and never more so than now. But just as she was about to dismiss Father Sal's theory as textbook Catholic nonsense, she realised how convenient an explanation it might prove. 'I'd never thought of it like that,' she said. An invocation of Our Lord at this juncture would make her shocking career change more palatable to her parents.

She looked expectantly at Father Sal, waiting for him to do the dirty work for her. He didn't disappoint.

'Lucia,' he said, 'I may live in a fairly cloistered environment but I'm not a fool. I know that things have changed. I know we live in a far more secular world now. People are no longer so willing to become priests or nuns, but they are willing to become politicians. You have a wonderful opportunity, to treat your constituents as your flock. You also have a responsibility towards them. All those people voted for you. They want you to represent them. God wants you to represent them. You can't let them down.'

Lucy nodded. This was great. She could never have dreamed up such a plausible justification.

Father Sal took the first sip of his double espresso. 'My parishioners didn't vote for me,' he continued, 'they just got what they were given, but it is my moral duty to look after the flock.'

'And you think,' said Lucy, 'that it's my moral duty to look after mine?'

Father Sal nodded.

Oh, Christ, thought Lucy. Not only am I the MP for Chelmsford South, I'm the parish priest as well.

Still, now indemnified by God and his representative in East Finchley, she turned to her parents. To her astonishment, Bruno was smiling. This was a miracle on a par with Saul's conversion on the road to Damascus.

'Loo-cheer,' he said, his first word in twelve minutes, 'why the tears? You have done a wonderful thing. We are very proud of you, aren't we, Ella? I bet Adam is too.'

Oh, shit. Lucy had forgotten about him. Her parents adored Adam. Their pride and joy would be short-lived. Lucy knew she might be pushing her luck if she claimed that God had also told her to dump her boyfriend. 'Um . . . that's the other thing I've got to tell you,' she said. 'I'm no longer with Adam. We've split up.'

She watched the smiles vanish. Bruno and Ella gazed at each other with rather strange expressions, as though they'd been sharing a guilty secret for the past ten years. They glanced at Lucy, then at each other. Her mother was first to speak: perhaps because Father Sal was among them she too felt the need to confess. 'Don't worry,' said Ella. 'He was nice enough, Loo-cheer.'

'Yes,' said Bruno, faltering slightly, 'but maybe he wasn't right for you.'

'To be honest,' said Ella, finally able to admit this, 'your father and I were never that keen.'

10

It was a problem to which Sean Reilly had grown wearily accustomed: the dumb creatives. Only in the advertising industry could certain people be known, without irony, as 'creatives': the writers and art directors who created the commercials, though the word 'creative' was highly inappropriate for most of them. In Sean's experience, the better they were, the less seriously they took themselves and the more open they were to the suggestions of others. Unfortunately they were the minority. Sean had a code for the rest, the precious, po-faced pillocks so lacking in either talent or charm. In his mind, they were all called Matt and Jez, because their names were usually something similar.

The Matts and Jezes were the 'creative teams' recruited from art college in pairs because it was believed that, when it comes to creativity, two heads are better than one. It's a theory with which most artists and authors might beg to differ, especially since neither Matt's nor Jez's heads contained much in the way of original thought. Often when Matt or Jez were asked who did the pictures and who did the words, they would reply, quite shiftily, that they both did a bit of each. In which case, one might reasonably ask, why do we need two of you? The most preposterous, self-regarding explanation came from one particular Jez who had declared that when he and Matt worked together they became a 'third person', and it was that third person who created the ads.

Although Sean knew that the ad industry employed a great many smart, talented people, he could see why it was so easily ridiculed. In fairness to Matt and Jez, they had been visually trained and when, as an engineer, Sean had dubbed the sound on to their TV commercials, he'd had to concede that many of those commercials were visually stunning. Then again, that was usually down to the artistic talent of the director or the technical wizardry employed in post-production. For Matt and Jez, it was invariably radio commercials, with no visual content, that exposed their shortcomings and that was what was happening now.

Gazing at them from his silent glass booth, Sean awaited the next absurd instruction. Would they ask him to read it 'faster but slower'? Or would they want it 'more innocent but sort of, like, knowing'? Or perhaps it would be the one he always remembered, 'Could you sound a bit more fat?' He was looking at idiots who didn't know what they wanted and didn't know what they were doing.

He watched them conferring before attempting to articulate their requirements.

'Um,' mumbled Matt, 'we . . . er . . . we want it to sound sort of like Bob Hoskins.'

Sean nodded.

'Or maybe,' added Jez, helpfully, 'You know, a bit Stephen Fry.'

Curiously enough, Sean was able to give them exactly that. Both Hoskins and Fry spoke with London accents, so Sean reproduced Fry's clarity of diction while lengthening the vowels and adding some of the gruff North London growl common to both his own and Hoskins's youth.

Almost unique among his peers, Sean had never been an actor, comedian or presenter, yet his vocal talents were far greater than theirs who had. This made him ideal for clueless nitwits like Matt and Jez. He could sound cool, cold or cruel but had cornered the market in sounding reasonable. Clients queued up to put him behind the microphone because he could make anything, whether it was taking out a mortgage or taking out your own spleen, sound like a really good idea. His was a reassuring, deep London accent on which he could push the posh fader up or down. It wasn't one of those unnaturally heavy, rich and over-intrusive voices that left listeners feeling aurally violated.

Sean sounded real and he sounded trustworthy. Although he was quite capable of affecting accents from outside the M25, he always steered clear of doing so.

His years as a sound engineer had left him with a loathing for southerners adopting northern accents, posh people pretending to be common and white people pretending to be black. In every case, with the genuine article so easily available, he could never understand why people used ham actors from the Dick Van Dyke school of impressionists.

Having satisfied Matt and Jez, he was released back into the community to walk unrecognised by any other member of it. That was the beauty of being a five-star general in the invisible army of voiceover artists. Although his voice was instantly familiar, having graced countless commercials, talking books and documentaries, his face was not. He could still wander anonymously through the West End of London. Instead of fame and fortune, his voice had brought him the best of both worlds: the fortune without the fame.

Sean Reilly, however, belonged to another invisible army, one so secret that even its own members were unaware of its existence. Since it didn't exist, it didn't have a name, but if it had, it would have been known as SODS – the Society of Disaffected Spouses: men and women from all walks of life whose marriages hadn't turned out quite as they'd hoped. They loved their spouses, adored their children and had no intention of divorcing, yet their souls ached with disappointment.

The women were more easily identified, their grievances more readily expressed. They talked to one another; they sought advice from friends and from magazines like *Cachet*. In any newsagent at any time, they could find a dozen articles devoted to 'getting the most from your man'.

Their male equivalents were harder to pin down. They suffered silently, having no such forums for complaint. What was more, many would have had to be tortured in Guantánamo Bay before they'd own up to their unhappiness. They knew that whingeing of this nature would be viewed, even by other men in identical situations, as an unseemly sign of weakness, so their disappointments remained unspoken, unacknowledged and unresolved. Yet they all harboured poignant, even pathetic dreams and wishes about their own wives: the solicitor from Malmesbury, who listened every week to Steve Wright's *Sunday Love Songs* hoping that one of those schmaltzy requests would be for him; the dentist from Solihull, who secretly longed to receive one of the huge pink satin-hearted Valentine cards that he saw every year in the window of WH Smith; the plumber from Hounslow, who kept himself trim and smart in the vain hope that his wife might give him a saucy wink, pinch his bum and tell him how nice he looked – the sort of thing he did so frequently for her. How little effort would that take? It would have made him feel wonderful all day. What had happened? Why couldn't she be bothered any more?

Sean was similarly bewildered. Why, before they married, had Nikki deluged yet ultimately deluded him with physical and emotional generosity then withdrawn it, for no apparent reason, a few years afterwards? He didn't expect to be fed and fellated on demand: he just wanted his wife to be his girlfriend. For Sean, it wasn't about sex but affection: something he was always happy to give but seldom seemed to receive.

Even though, or perhaps because, his wife was forty and had produced two children, Sean found her just as gorgeous as he had on the day he met her. She hadn't let herself go physically – but, boy, had she let herself go emotionally! She seemed to have settled into a rather cruel complacency where the man who'd devoted his life to providing for her and the children no longer seemed to matter. When he exploded periodically with the fury of unrequited affection, she accused him of being 'stupid' and 'over-reacting'. She wasn't hateful towards him – but the opposite of love isn't hate, it's indifference.

Like other disaffected spouses, Sean felt he'd been duped. The woman he'd married had been wearing a mask, and when it was removed, he'd found himself sharing a matrimonial cell with someone totally different. 'Who are you?' he wanted to say. 'And what have you done with my lovely wife?'

Nikki's attitude towards him had changed with the arrival of the children. She regarded herself as a mother now, rather than a lover, and Sean had failed to figure out why she couldn't be both. The children had made him love her even more. He thought that they could, and should, make life even more romantic for the couple who'd created them. Instead he'd watched in horror as his wife turned into a cross between Martha Stewart and Bree from *Desperate Housewives*.

He still bought her flowers, booked tables at romantic restaurants and wasn't afraid to venture into Jo Malone for honeysuckle and jasmine body lotion, which he offered to apply himself, but it made no difference. He felt as though he was trying to force the fizz back into a once sparkling glass of champagne that had long gone flat.

His marriage, no longer buoyed up by the deep blue sea of reciprocal affection, had run aground and all because of that age-old problem: once married, women want their husbands to change and hate it when they don't; men, conversely, never want their wives to change and hate it when they do.

Sean racked his brains but couldn't remember a bit in the marriage service where he'd said, 'And one day I promise to become interested in barbecues, DIY and garden centres.'

He was a loving husband and doting father. He didn't have a drink, drug or infidelity habit. He was kind, thoughtful, funny and unselfish. He didn't spend all week at the office and all weekend on the golf course. He wanted to stoke the flames of marital romance by treating his marriage like a courtship. He wanted to hold his wife's hand in the park and snuggle up with her in the back row of the cinema.

He didn't want an extramarital affair, he wanted an intramarital one. Was that really too much to ask? If the kids were at school, the sun was shining and he didn't have a booking that afternoon, he wanted to take his wife for a lovely, languorous picnic by the river. Is this it? he thought. Do we remain locked in this loveless liaison for the rest of our lives? Till death do us bicker?

He'd worked hard, he'd earned a hell of a lot of money, he'd got up in the night hundreds of times to feed the children when they were babies. He'd understood that love, fun and romance would have to be put on hold for a while. But now that the children were growing up, he wanted it back – and he thought that Nikki would too.

He thought wrong.

11

Darren Crook was evidently excited about the new residential development that he was currently carving out from an old porn warehouse in Soho. It was round the corner from the Dog and Duck, where he and Sean were enjoying a lunchtime pint. Darren was covered with grime and brick dust, while Sean was basking in the incredulous satisfaction of a man who'd just earned five thousand pounds for ten minutes' work.

'Nah,' said Sean. 'I've just got a thing about being a landlord.'

'Oh, for fuck's sake, Reilly, you've got to lose that council-house mentality. You're earning a fucking fortune! You've got to start investing it properly.'

Sean had no interest in investing his money. Only recently his bank had called to tell him that having sixty-seven thousand pounds in his current account wasn't particularly clever, and that perhaps he might like to transfer sixty of it to a high-interest savings account. Sean had never owned a stock, a share, a TESSA or an ISA. Although his voice was often heard on TV commercials, advising people on the smartest ways to invest their money, he had never taken his own advice.

He had a healthy disregard for matters financial and viewed those who fell for get-rich-quick schemes as either greedy, stupid or both. Houses and flats, he believed, were homes. They were not 'investments', and although the 'yield' from a 'property portfolio' could easily have trebled his income, he'd always felt that there was something slightly horrible about making huge profits from people's basic need for shelter.

'No', he said, 'I'm not interested.'

Darren was not deterred. 'Listen,' he said, 'I'm only telling you this because you're a mate and I know you've got a lot of cash sloshing around. Believe me, if I was making the sort of dough you are, and I'd tied a knot in it after two kids instead of having four, I'd buy one like a shot.'

Sean could see that his friend was only trying to help him. He also knew that if Darren was involved, the build quality, finish and attention to detail would be superb. And, although he hated himself for even thinking these words, so would the 'investment potential'.

'They're not going on the market just yet but if you wanted to buy one off the plans, I'm sure I could sort it for you,' said Darren, looking at his watch. 'Come on, finish your drink and we'll pop round and have a look.'

Sean hadn't seen Darren so excited since he'd invited him along to a recording of a radio commercial without telling him that the two voice-overs would be Ian Wright and Dennis Bergkamp. Darren was a fanatical Arsenal fan whom Sean had first met on the terraces at Highbury. He'd admired his friend's red and white Arsenal T-shirt, which bore the defiant motto, 'These colours never run.'

To Sean the streets of Soho were more familiar than the back of his own hand, but Darren led him towards a little alley down which he'd never ventured. At the end, it broadened out into a cul-de-sac. What had once been an old NCP car park was now the chic Soho Hotel and next to it was the old warehouse that Darren and his crew were fashioning into loft apartments.

'What's this?' said Sean, as Darren handed him a hard hat.

'What does it look like?' said Darren. 'Just stick it on and shut up. Suits you, mate. Very Village People.'

Sean climbed the half-built bare timber staircase, amid a cacophony of hammers, drills, saws and sanders, and couldn't help noticing how this building site differed from the ones he remembered from his youth. The raucous banter of Irish voices was no longer in evidence. In fact, there was no banter at all. One man's conversation would have been incomprehensible to another. Poles didn't understand Estonians and Turks didn't understand Serbs, so they worked largely in silence, leaving Darren, as project manager, to interpret. He didn't understand any of them but, in the time-honoured way of speaking English slowly and loudly, and with the occasional 'o' on the end of each word, 'Me-o needs you-o to knock-o down that wall-o,' he managed to make himself understood.

'So, you're not actually doing any of the work?' said Sean.

'Nah,' said Darren. 'I'm not twenty-one any more. It's just so fucking hard, carrying bricks, underpinning, putting steels in. Builders are like footballers, mate, there comes a time when you're too old to play and you have to manage instead. I'm the project manager. The developer's employing me because, after twenty-odd years, I know every trick in the book. I have to make sure he doesn't get tucked up. Not that this lot would do anything wrong. They're as good as gold and grateful for the work.' An expression of pity passed over Darren's face as he gestured towards a big bearded Ukrainian on his hands and knees laying a timber floor. 'See him over there?' Sean nodded. 'That's Victor. Concert pianist back home in Kiev and he's laying fucking floors. It doesn't seem right. You've never seen anyone work like this lot.'

Sean, however, was more interested in the timber floor than in the man who was laying it. Solid oak, resin bonded, it was the Ferrari of floors. As he looked around what would soon be a stunning apartment, it was now very clear why Darren had been so excited. Sean loved the abundance of natural light from the huge double-height windows. He loved the massive expanse of living space, the exposed brick, the galleried bedroom, and the clean, white, heavy-duty bathroom where the showerhead was the size of a satellite dish. The sleek stainless-steel kitchen bristled with Teutonic efficiency. Most of all, he loved the commanding views of the city he adored: the London Eye, Big Ben, Regent's Park and Canary Wharf were all clearly visible, depending on which of those double-height windows he chose to face.

He was enthralled by the peculiar feeling of being right in the heart of Soho yet quietly secluded from it. He'd fallen in love with this half-finished apartment as quickly and deeply as he'd fallen in love with Nikki.

He knew he couldn't live in it, yet he also knew he had to buy it. He was going to have to 'buy to rent'. He was going to have to become somebody's landlord, even though the idea made him feel dirty, horrible and usurious. He was now smitten with the idea of owning something as beautiful as this. Suddenly he understood why people paid obscene sums of money for paintings, sculptures and jewellery. They, too, had been overawed by sheer beauty.

Darren's pragmatism interrupted Sean's reverie: 'You could make a fucking mint out of this place. Wealthy American bankers, Japanese tycoons. And I'll tell you something else, mate, you could hire it out for films and photo shoots. What a location.' Unaware that he was pushing a door that was already open, Darren went on, 'You've just got to ask yourself one question. How are you going to feel if someone else buys it? And the first person who sees it will do just that.'

It was Sean's cavalier attitude to money that had ensured he had so much of it languishing in the bank. Not a penny was 'tied up' so it could all be released instantly from its virtual vault and turned into bricks, mortar and double-height windows. With about as much thought as he'd have given to buying a pint of milk, Sean decided to buy the fiendishly expensive apartment. 'That drink,' he said to Darren, heart racing, with the unique thrill of a wild and ridiculous purchase, 'that innocent pint round the Dog and Duck, is now going to be the most expensive drink I've ever had.'

'And the most lucrative,' said Darren. 'Come on, back to the pub. I think you owe me another one.'

'We'll have it tomorrow,' said Sean. 'I want to go home and tell Nikki.'

'Can't you ring her?'

'Nah. This calls for celebration. Bottle of Krug and a bunch of flowers. She'll be delighted. Her old man's a stockbroker, always telling me to invest my money. She'll see this as a sign of me finally growing up. Cheers, mate.' With that, Sean turned and ran, almost tripping over Victor, the giant Ukrainian, in his haste.

He rushed through Berwick Street market still wearing his hard hat, only pausing to buy Nikki a huge bouquet from the flower stall, that would require an extra seat on the tube to accommodate it.

Twenty-five minutes later, head and shoulders concealed by petals and foliage, he was home. 'Hello?' he called to Nikki as he put his key in the door. 'Anybody in?'

She didn't reply. It was half past two. Sean had said he'd be back at half past three. Unwittingly, he'd caught her out. He heard her voice and that of an unfamiliar male coming from the bedroom. He burst in and was alarmed to see his wife with a handsome blond man at least ten years her junior.

Sean's expression tautened from confusion to anger. 'What the fuck,' he said, 'is going on here?'

12

Nikki, at least, had the grace to look thoroughly embarrassed.
'Um . . . Sean,' she said, 'this is Greg. He's from Prickett & Doyle,
you know, the – er – the estate agents.'

Sean nodded curtly at Greg but didn't want to make the
poor bloke feel any more awkward. He'd reserve his fury for
Nikki.

'Well, um, thank you, Mrs Reilly,' said Greg, hastily gathering
his notes, clipboard and electronic tape measure. 'I'll, er, e-mail
you the valuation – um, tomorrow morning.'

Sean allowed Greg approximately five seconds to vacate the
premises, then turned to his wife, almost too angry to be angry.
'What's the matter?' he said, his voice quietly quivering with
rage. 'I thought you loved this house.'

'I do,' said Nikki.

It was then that Chas and Dave started singing in his head,
as they always did on occasions like this. Chas Hodges was no
Sinatra but the blustering lyrical poignancy of 'Ain't No Pleasing
You' encapsulated Sean's feelings about his marriage. 'Then why,'
he growled, 'are you putting it on the market?'

'Well,' she said, 'my mum phoned this morning, and you know
that gorgeous old oast house right on the village green down in
Offham?'

Sean knew the one. It was about half a mile from his in-laws
and Nikki had frequently told him that it was the house of her
dreams. She'd wanted to live in it since she was a little girl. He
nodded.

'Well, it's for sale,' she went on.

'So?'

'Oh, do I have to spell it out?' said Nikki, unleashing her biggest, most charming smile. 'It's beautiful.'

'On a lovely summer's day, I grant you,' said Sean, 'but it's fucking miles away.'

'It's fifty minutes from here.'

'At three o'clock in the morning,' he said. 'No, no, no. We're not moving.'

Sean knew exactly how this conversation was going to go. First, Nikki would show him a glimpse of the affection he craved but was habitually denied.

Almost on cue, she slipped her arms round his neck. 'Kent's gorgeous,' she said. 'I grew up there. It's the Garden of England.'

'It would be like living in a fucking salad,' said Sean.

Right, the *faux*-affection hadn't worked. Now for the challenge.

'Come on,' she said, in a gung-ho, show-jumping sort of tone, 'it'll be an adventure.'

'An adventure?' said Sean, incredulously. 'Trekking in the hills of Burma would be an adventure. Smuggling Kalashnikovs out of the former Soviet Union would be an adventure. Moving to a boring village in Kent is *not* an adventure.'

The challenge hasn't worked, thought Sean. Brace yourself for the insults. He gazed into the middle distance and tried to keep a rein on his explosive Irish temper as he was told how un-adventurous he was and how unwilling to try new things, how wedded he was to London and, finally, how little he cared for the welfare of his children.

He had to take issue with that. 'What?'

Out came the old chestnut about London being a bad place to bring up kids and the countryside a good one. Never mind that they ran the risk of growing up dull and parochial. Never mind that they'd be bored rigid by the age of thirteen with nothing to do but drink cider at bus stops. Never mind that, if they had even a few active brain cells and the merest spark of curiosity, they would head straight for London, as Nikki had, at the earliest opportunity.

What really bothered Sean was that his wife, knowing he adored London and earned his living there, was prepared to force him to move into rural seclusion with no concern for how unhappy it would make him. He had come to realise that if Nikki was happy, everyone else had to be. The same applied when she was unhappy. And she'd now decided that she was unhappy in London.

He knew that if he moved to this *Darling Buds of May*-style village, his next move would be to an asylum. Although the inhabitants would be perfectly nice, they would work in finance, tee off at the local golf club and play cricket on the village green. Most enjoyed a pint of real ale on a Sunday lunchtime, took pride in their patios and knew how to assemble flat-pack furniture. Sean would have more in common with the Bobo people of Wagadodo.

As Nikki dug her heels in, Sean longed for the days when she had dug them into the small of his back. She wanted that oast house and she was going to have it. If he loved her, he'd move. If she loved him, she wouldn't. Who's right? Who's wrong? Who cares? Watching his wife's face harden into that look of selfish determination that he'd seen so many times before, he knew two things. One was that nothing would deter her from fulfilling this bucolic idyll. The other was that he wouldn't be feeling uncomfortable about becoming someone's landlord. He now knew he'd never have to be.

13

Like most people, Lucy had her first day at school saved indelibly on her emotional hard drive. She remembered her fear and apprehension at having to let go of her beloved *nonna*'s hand and the wobble in her throat as she did so. She remembered some of the other children crying, which, like yawning and throwing up, can be contagious. But just as she was about to add her own snuffles to the poignant choir of tears, she'd heard the most heartwrenching sobs from the other side of the classroom. They were coming from a lumpen, ungainly child who was clinging to her mother's skirt. As Miss Higgins, the teacher, gently tried to unclench the podgy little fists, the decibel level soared off the scale. Lucy remembered thinking, Either there's something seriously wrong with this child, or she knows something we don't.

The first assumption was nearer the mark. Her name was Mary Mannion and, unfortunately, her education predated the phrase 'special needs'. In a class full of children whose needs weren't special, Mary would always be rooted to the bottom. She was useless at everything, by far the worst at reading, writing, speaking and sport. She'd also been at the back of the queue when good looks were handed out. By the time she reached the front, all that was left were some thick, unprepossessing features and a perennially gormless expression. With the cruelty found only in Paraguayan torture chambers or primary-school playgrounds, the boys in Mary's class decided that she had fleas. No one could go near her without their fingers crossed for immunity. By the age of ten, her lack of intellect and elephantine appearance had earned her the nickname Dumbo. When Paul O'Mara discovered a broken chair that would have buckled whoever had sat on it, he knew he'd get the biggest laugh if he placed it under the biggest backside.

For years afterwards, Lucy hoped that she might one day see a BBC2 documentary entitled *The Hidden Talents of Mary Mannion* that would reveal her unfortunate classmate as a sylph-like supermodel, a poet, painter or pianist. She knew such hopes were in vain, though, so she'd packed Mary into cerebral storage. However, as she entered the House of Commons for the first time, she felt a burning empathy with that unfortunate child. Her throat was dry, but no one was holding her hand and there was no skirt to cling to.

The sheer majesty of the Palace of Westminster can be hugely intimidating to anyone who has never been inside it. Lucy had only ever viewed it at a distance, either whizzing past in a taxi or from a riverboat party on the Thames. As she went through the doors, the weight of history bore down on her shoulders. With its high, vaulted ceilings, leaded windows, pew-like benches and images of British patron saints in the Central Lobby, it had an imposing, ecclesiastical feel.

Other new MPs seemed similarly awestruck, but only Lucy felt like Mary Mannion: she was the only one who genuinely didn't want to be there. Others may also have been surprised at their victories, but theirs were pleasant surprises. They'd wanted to win and had worked hard to secure their triumph. Their delight was written all over their obedient, on-message faces during the short induction programme. A little map was then issued to help them negotiate the labyrinthine corridors and to locate the fourteen restaurants and seven bars. They were congratulated, welcomed and reminded of the burden of responsibility and privilege. Lucy now felt like a bewildered prisoner, convicted of a crime she hadn't committed. As she walked back along the ancient corridors, she imagined her clothes as prison fatigues, and that she was carrying an itchy blanket, toothbrush and tin mug back to her cell. But for Lucy Ross there would be no gallant attorney battling for her release. There would be no Shawshank Redemption.

Her nightmare, or 'daymare', was interrupted by an amiable woman with short hair, small eyes and a face as plain as a slab of Madeira cake. 'Hi,' she said, in a prim Scottish accent. 'You must be Lucy Ross. I'm Hilary Knowles. Labour, Bedford North. Third time lucky.'

'First time unlucky,' said Lucy, with a dry smile, the irony of which was lost on Hilary. It was then that Lucy noticed something unusual about her parliamentary colleague. She'd either been overdoing it on the deep-fried Mars Bars or she was pregnant.

'Six months.' Hilary had noticed Lucy's quizzical look at her convexity.

'Congratulations,' said Lucy, 'but what about—'

'Oh, it'll be fine,' said Hilary with a smug smile. 'The important thing was getting in. Had to keep this under wraps – literally – when I was campaigning. Might not have played too well with the voters.'

'I'm not surprised,' said Lucy, before she could stop herself.

'What do you mean?' said Hilary, who had clearly been expecting a little more sisterly support.

Quick, thought Lucy. You're a politician now. Think of another angle to deflect the blame from yourself. 'W-well,' she stuttered, 'you know what the punters are like. They expect you to be there for them twenty-four/seven. They won't want you to have any sort of life, will they?'

'No, no, you're quite right,' smiled Hilary, seemingly satisfied that Lucy was on her side. But Lucy wasn't. She found it hard to comprehend how Hilary could stand for Parliament knowing she was pregnant and deliberately deceiving the people who'd voted for her. She knew she'd have to go off on maternity leave almost as soon she'd started, leaving them unrepresented. And how would she feel once the baby was born? Would she want to return to the Commons? And even if she did, how effective would she be? None of that seemed to matter: as Hilary had just said, 'The important thing was getting in.'

The balance between looking after constituents and looking after children reminded Lucy of how Simon had fulminated at the revelation that Tony Blair allegedly got up in the night to feed baby Leo. 'He's the fucking prime minister,' he'd said. 'We're paying him a shitload of money to run the fucking country. We don't want him getting up in the middle of the night to feed a baby, then falling asleep in a G8 summit meeting.' He was consoled by the thought that the prime minister almost certainly did not get up in the night: it had been an example of ill-considered spin, designed to earn the nation's approval but, as usual, having the opposite effect.

Out of the corner of her eye, Hilary had spotted someone potentially useful. 'Anyway, Lucy,' she concluded, 'great to meet you.' She waved to a man with glasses and an ill-fitting suit. 'Gavin . . .'

He turned. 'Hilary.' He smiled, and they were gone. The networking had begun and, not for the first time in the last twenty-four hours, Lucy felt horribly alone. As she looked around, it became clear that the majority of the new intake of MPs were career politicians. Had they entered the Commons in the eighties, they would have been Tories because as Conservatives they would have had the best chance of getting in. Now the political pendulum had swung a little to the left and Labour had swung more than a little to the right, that was the party they'd joined.

She was hoping to find a few left-wing firebrands or right-wing libertarians. However much she disagreed with their views, at least their passion and conviction might make them interesting human beings. Where were they? The truth was, they were practically extinct. However, as she was soon to discover not quite.

14

'Are you sure you want to do this?'

'Of course I'm sure,' said Lucy. 'The question is, are you?'

'Well, yes,' said Sheila. 'I just can't believe you want me as your assistant, you being Labour and me having spent the last twenty-two years working for the Tory Party.'

Lucy was having coffee in the immaculate front room of Sheila's three-bedroomed thirties semi just outside Chelmsford. There was something very reassuring about the big blue three-piece suite, bought on interest-free credit with free delivery from DFS, the volumes of Dick Francis and Danielle Steele on the shelves, the photos on the sideboard of the children and the baby grandchildren, the homely smell of furniture polish.

'Oh, that doesn't bother me,' she said. 'All I want is to do my best for the people who voted for me. It's got nothing to do with party politics.'

'So you're not actually Labour, then?' asked Sheila, warily.

'I'm not actually anything,' admitted Lucy, 'but don't tell anyone.'

Sheila seemed relieved by this, but Lucy sensed there was a little more to it. 'What does your husband think?' she asked.

'Well, to be honest,' said Sheila, 'he's not too happy about it.'

'Ah. Well, like I say, are you sure you want to do it?'

'Oh, I am, yeah. I said to him, "It doesn't matter nowadays whether the MP is Labour or Tory. There's not much difference between them. It's all about trying to help people. Very often their MP is the only hope they've got."'

There was a pause.

'But he still needs a bit of convincing,' said Lucy.

Sheila nodded. 'I mean, don't get me wrong, he wouldn't stop me doing this.' She chuckled. 'I'd like to see him try. But he liked Mr Marsden, had a lot of respect for him. The thing is, though, I know he'll like you even more.'

Lucy knew what Sheila was about to say, so courtesy dictated that she made a pre-emptive offer. 'Shall we pop round and see him, then?'

'Oh, that'd be nice,' said Sheila, reintroducing her trademark buck-toothed smile. 'He'd like that. He rants on a bit – don't they all? – but he's a good man. If he wasn't, I couldn't have put up with him for the last thirty-seven years.'

'I'm sorry – how rude of me,' said Lucy. 'I've been so pre-occupied with what you and I are going to be doing for a living that I've never asked you what George does.'

'He's a greengrocer. The shop's on King's Parade. It's only five minutes' walk.'

When Lucy saw King's Parade it was instant love. Built in 1929 when the king in question was George V, it was built to serve the local community, which, against all the odds, it still did.

King's Parade was known as 'the shops'. *The* shops were not to be confused with shops. *The* shops were always a local parade and people tended to 'pop out' to them. All over the country, supermarkets had destroyed 'the shops' but King's Parade, quirky and English, was alive and kicking. Over the last few years, a tradition had developed that involved shopkeepers naming their establishments with excruciating puns. The motor-accessories shop was called Carnoisseur, the optician's Eye Society and the hairdresser's, almost inevitably, British Hairways. Even the estate agent's was dubbed Sherlock Homes. Newcomers were happy to play too: the Chinese takeaway had changed its name from the Happy Garden to Kung Food, although the proprietor was never quite sure why. Lucy immediately promised herself a visit to her favourite; a tanning salon called Tanz In 'Ere. Right in the middle, steadfastly refusing to join in, was George Webb & Son, Quality Fruiterers & Greengrocers.

'Mauve tissue paper,' said Lucy, enthralled as she walked through the door. 'Oh, wow, it's years since I've seen it.'

The proprietor was surprised but pleased with her reaction to his traditional display of Granny Smith apples in mauve tissue paper.

'Sorry.' She smiled. 'I'm Lucy Ross . . . um . . . MP.'

'George Webb,' said the greengrocer, formally shaking her hand. 'How do you do?'

George was sixty-three but not in a Mick Jagger/Paul McCartney way. He looked like sixty-three-year-olds are supposed to look: stocky, craggy-faced, short grey hair neatly combed and brilliantined. For work he was wearing a blue nylon overjacket, not unlike a barber's, beneath which there was a clean white shirt and dark tie. He was the sort of greengrocer who doesn't exist any more. Lucy was tempted to prod him to see if he was real. Looking around, she noticed that the Granny Smiths were not the exception but the rule: every piece of fruit and vegetable was perfect. 'Oh,' she gushed, 'what a wonderful shop.'

'That's very kind of you,' George replied, with a tight, modest smile. 'Trouble is, this business was full of shysters. They'd put all their best fruit on display, then give you all the old rubbish from underneath. So when the supermarkets started letting people choose their own, well, it was all over.'

'Oh,' said Lucy. 'Still, you're doing okay, aren't you?'

'Absolutely,' he replied, as if only a heretic would suggest otherwise. 'Most of my stuff is home-grown, either on my allotment or from places I know and trust. Places I've been dealing with for years. I only sell what's in season.'

Lucy nodded approvingly. 'So it's mostly organic?'

'I suppose it is,' he replied, 'but what does that mean anyway? Years ago, people started using pesticides, saying it was essential to keep the produce fresh. Naturally they charged you more for it. Then they said it was "organic", free from pesticides, and charged you even more for what you had in the first place. I've just sold good-quality fruit and veg for years and everyone round here knows that, so, yeah, this shop's doing fine.'

'Even better now,' said Sheila, 'thanks to Mark.'

'Mark?' said Lucy.

'Our youngest,' said Sheila, proudly, as a group of youths nodded politely to George and carried on through to the back of the shop.

'Where are they going?' asked Lucy.

'Well, a couple of years ago,' George explained, 'Mark turned the back into a second-hand record shop.'

'Not just second hand,' said Sheila, quick to correct him. 'He does all the latest stuff too. Mail order and on the Internet.'

'Oh, fantastic,' said Lucy. 'Can we go round and have a look?'

Mark was an amiable creature in his late twenties with a long dark ponytail and a black Babyshambles T-shirt. He struck Lucy as having been the sort of boy who had listened to John Peel when he was supposed to be doing his homework but, unlike most sixth-formers up and down the country, Mark had probably liked most of the offal that the great man had played. His merchandise wasn't arranged with quite the same care and precision as his father's, but he was friendly, enthusiastic, and his part of the shop was clearly thriving.

Fruit and veg at the front and music at the back; it was just the sort of shop that Lucy adored. 'I notice,' she said to George, 'that you haven't joined in and given your shop a comedy name.'

'No fear,' came the swift reply. 'It was George Webb and Son when my dad was the George and I was the son and it was just a barrow on Bethnal Green Road. That name remains.'

'See what I have to put up with?' said Mark, with a sigh.

'What were those daft names you suggested?' said George to his son. 'Fruitopia? Melon Cauli?'

'Rhythm and Greens, Dad,' said Mark. 'Brilliant name. And I still think you ought to change it.'

'Over my dead body.'

'Don't tempt me,' laughed Mark. 'Anyway, um . . . Lucy . . . good to meet you.'

As they walked back to the mauve tissue paper, Lucy decided to cut to the chase. 'George, I know I'm technically Labour but I'm sure Sheila's told you how I ended up winning this seat.'

'Yes, she did,' said George. 'And, to be honest, though I always liked Brian Marsden, he had it coming. He didn't look after the shop, didn't look after his customers. Do that in any business and those customers will go elsewhere.'

George was no fan of the Labour Party. In his mind, they were still in cahoots with the unions and he retained bitter memories of what he had regarded as the militants' selfishness, greed and dishonesty back in the seventies and eighties. He'd never done anything to harm the miners, yet they'd deliberately plunged his home into darkness. He'd done nothing to hurt the dockers, yet they'd driven him to the brink of bankruptcy by letting his oranges rot on the quayside. As he'd said more times than he could count, 'Hurting innocent people in pursuit of your own pay claims: how socialist is that?'

Still, he could see why Sheila would want to work with Lucy. He liked the way Lucy had stipulated that his wife would be working *with* her, not *for* her. He liked the way she'd been honest enough to admit from the outset that she'd be unable to do her job unless Sheila did it with her. How often do you find that level of candour in a politician? 'They're good people round here,' he explained. 'Salt of the earth. Yeah, we've got more than our share of rascals but they're solid. They'll always help you. They're a bit like the Palestinians.'

Sheila rolled her eyes to the ceiling. 'Here we go,' she muttered.

'But they are,' he insisted. 'Driven out of their homeland, whether they liked it or not. Most of them were quite happy in London, but they were uprooted and relocated miles from every-thing they ever knew. Luckily, that sense of community is very strong and it's been re-established out here.'

Lucy's journalistic training and eye for angle was deployed

perfectly with her next comment. 'Well,' she said, 'you say they're always happy to help anyone but sometimes, I suspect, they need a bit of help themselves.'

'Got it in one,' he said.

'Well, hopefully,' said Lucy, 'that's where I come in.'

George's craggy face broke into a broad and surprisingly handsome smile.

'Anyway, lovely to meet you, George,' said Lucy. 'I promise to do my best.' She saluted him. 'Scout's honour. Anyway, off to the local Labour Party HQ. It's along this road, isn't it?'

George's smile was replaced by a frown. 'Yeah, about a hundred yards up, next to Bloomin' Chic, the florist.'

Lucy also frowned. 'You mean it's a shop?' She remembered her own father's fury when Glynn's, the baker's next door to the Amalfi deli, had closed down. Old Mr Glynn had retired and the shop had been taken over by a firm of chartered accountants. 'Shops should be shops,' Bruno had fumed, his hands windmilling. 'Accountants belong in offices. They bring no benefit to the community.'

Even though she was only twelve, Lucy had understood what he meant and agreed with him.

She now found herself repeating what he'd said: 'Shops should be shops. You don't want a political party occupying a perfectly good shop.'

George's smile was now broader than Broadway. A girl after his own heart. 'I'm always saying that, aren't I, love?'

'Yes, dear, you are,' said Sheila, then turned to Lucy. 'But where will you have your surgeries? Where will you hold meetings?'

'I don't know. The local library? The town hall?'

George, had turned in five minutes from staunch Labour hater to Lucy's biggest fan, said, 'You know what? I might have just the place.'

15

There are two sides to every matrimonial breakdown and Mrs Nicola Reilly wasn't entirely to blame for hers. She was guilty, if that's the right word, of trying to change the very things that had attracted her to Sean in the first place. Yet she would argue, and frequently did, that to expect some sort of change wasn't unreasonable. She'd expected him to evolve as a human being but, to her increasing frustration, he hadn't. He was exactly the same as the day she'd met him. Sean believed that the qualities that had made him such a great boyfriend were all that were required to make him a great husband, but Nikki didn't agree.

As he matured, she had thought he might start taking pride in his house and garden, but no: her home-making skills and the way she'd toiled to create a lush and well-stocked garden were wasted on him. As he'd often rather tactlessly remarked, he'd rather live in a luxury hotel or a council flat, freed from all domestic responsibilities.

She'd have loved Sean to help her choose carpets or curtain fabrics but he wasn't interested. It would have meant so much to her if, just once, he'd brought home something made by Black & Decker and had attempted to use it. Instead he sneered at DIY, which, in his opinion, was almost always borne out of meanness. He told her that at least half of Darren's work involved unbodging some tight-fisted amateur's attempt to do his own wiring or plumbing. Nikki accepted this but had foolishly thought that Sean might *want* to do something practical, even if it was just painting a wall in the spare bedroom. She reminded him of something else Darren liked to say: 'If you can piss, you can paint.' Sean would just smile, kiss her and tell her he was having terrible trouble with his bladder.

He didn't seem to understand that no amount of red roses bought from a florist would ever mean as much to her as a small bunch from the garden they had tended together. He didn't realise that he may have got the warmth and affection he craved if he'd spent a little time with a spirit level or a pair of secateurs.

She wanted him to have a bit more in common with her friends' husbands. When the conversation turned to loft conversions, she'd have loved him to join in, instead of gazing gormlessly into the middle distance, as if he'd had a stroke – she frequently had to kick him under the table – but when he regained the power of speech, he could be enchanting. He was a wonderful storyteller and Nikki would watch her doe-eyed friends and their wide-eyed partners as he regaled them in his gorgeous deep voice, with scurrilous off-the-record tales about the famous people he knew.

Trouble was, Nikki had heard all these tales before and longed for Sean to take the same delight in talking about things they had done, or were planning to do, together. Other people may have been impressed by his compendious knowledge of music, film, literature and sport, but that knowledge was useless and she'd much rather he'd known how to put up a shelf.

In her frustration she had cruelly accused him of being 'common in all the wrong ways'. He still spoke, when he was not being paid to speak otherwise, in an accent very similar to those of the builders and bouncers who had also grown up around Gaskin Street. He drove like a maniac, usually with the windows open and the sort of heavy-duty seventies funk on the CD player that made James Brown sound like James Blunt disturbing the leafy affluent calm of their neighbourhood. All he needed was a pair of furry dice. He still loved football and frequently yelled obscenities at the TV if he felt that the ref might benefit from a visit to the optician. However, she said, when it came to things that common people might be good at, like fixing a boiler or plastering a wall, he was useless.

Over the years, they had developed the irreconcilable differences that, in any British court, would constitute reasonable grounds for divorce, so their parting became inevitable.

Inevitable, but surprisingly amicable. Like so many couples, they found agreeing to disagree much easier than agreeing to agree.

Nikki wasn't a bad person and knew that Sean adored his children. Without question, he could have unlimited access to them. There would be no need for him to join Fathers4Justice and hang, dressed as Batman, from the roof of Buckingham Palace.

Sean, for his part, had no great interest in material possessions. Apart from his books, CDs and clothes, he was happy to let Nikki take everything she wanted from Chiswick to Kent. He would buy her dream house for her without a mortgage, but would now need a huge one to pay for his own. There would be no wealthy American bankers or Japanese tycoons renting it from him: he would have to pay that mortgage himself. And how the hell was he going to do that?

16

It would have been easy to dismiss Jonathan Wilson-Love as typical of the smooth new breed of Chelsea fan. He was wealthy, confident and came to matches in a sports jacket, chinos and Gucci loafers, his little finger adorned by a signet ring bearing the family crest. It would be understandable to assume that he had been at least thirty before he began to prefer round balls to oval ones. He looked exactly like all the other public-school Johnny-come-latelys who'd only bought their season tickets to Stamford Bridge once all threat of violence had been removed.

Nothing, however, could have been further from the truth. Jonathan had been known as Chelsea Jon since prep school, when his little section of the dormitory had been festooned with pictures torn from *Shoot*! magazine of old Chelsea legends like Peter Osgood and Charlie Cooke. What was more, Jon was born and bred in Chelsea and had never lived anywhere else. The one thing he'd hated about boarding-school was missing all the home games. His own family had regarded 'soccer' as perfectly ghastly, but Joan, their cleaner, her husband Bill and their three sons were all season-ticket holders from the World's End estate and were happy to let little Jonny, with his wooden rattle and blue and white scarf, tag along with them.

Thanks to a billionaire's benevolence, Chelsea had become the most glamorous and successful club in the country but when opposing fans taunted them by singing 'Where were you when . . . Where were you when . . . Where you when you were shit?', they weren't talking to Jon. He remembered exactly where he had been in 1983 when his beloved Blues were languishing near the foot of Division Two. He was standing on the terraces at the Shed

End. When he'd stood there with Bill and Joan, fifty thousand other fans had stood with him. Watching Chelsea struggle against Cambridge United, there had been fewer than eight thousand but Jon had been among them. He remembered manager John Neal's promise to lead Chelsea out of Division Two, which he very nearly did – straight into Division Three. From then on, things could only get better, and they did. But not for Joan and Bill: season tickets had become prohibitively expensive and, like thousands of other loyal fans, they were priced out of Stamford Bridge.

As proprietor of Take One Voices, the biggest voiceover agency in the country, Jon could now afford one of the corporate boxes in the West Stand and, no doubt, have got himself on first-name terms with Frank Lampard and John Terry, but this was something he would never do. Those people were his heroes. Even though they were much younger than him, they would always be men and he would always be the little boy with the wooden rattle and the blue and white scarf. He didn't want to meet them: they belonged on the pedestals once occupied by Osgood and Cooke. Instead, when Joan told him that she and Bill would no longer be going, he paid for their season tickets and vowed to do so forever: it was his way of thanking them 'for providing the only thing about my horrible, loveless childhood that I ever really enjoyed'.

Joan and Bill were now in their seventies, but Chelsea Jon still took them to every home game, along with his two eldest children. Football still had the mesmeric power to transfix him. While the ball was in play he could think of nothing else. When the referee blew the whistle for half-time, it was as though a hypnotist had clicked his fingers and snapped Jon out of a trance. It was only then that he remembered the call he'd meant to make before kick-off to his number-one client. 'Sean? Hello, it's me. Listen, when are you moving into this amazing bachelor pad of yours?'

'About three weeks' time. Why?'

'I've got the most brilliant idea.'

17

Sean was acutely aware of the terrible irony in being a voiceover artist: his career could collapse at any time, not because he was bad but because he was good. His brilliance had made him extremely popular so he ran the risk of becoming overused. Suddenly, through no fault of his own, he might find himself dumped by advertisers who, understandably, didn't want their ads to sound like everyone else's.

So far, Sean had avoided becoming a dumpee by developing a random list of things he refused to advertise. It had nothing to do with morals or principles, just the things he didn't like. Teabags, for instance, the congestion charge, multiplex cinemas, the RSPCA, British Airways or any ad that included the words 'retail park' or 'just off the M25'. Still, that gnawing uncertainty remained, so Jon's 'brilliant idea' was very timely. He'd suggested that Sean install a microphone and an ISDN line in his flat to link himself up, in digital clarity, to sound studios anywhere in the world.

Sean took the idea several stages further. The first piece of furniture he unpacked was a brand-new matt-black Fairlight mixing desk for the spare room. Around it, he created a compact, state-of-the-art recording studio. Often, around midnight, he'd put on his headphones, open his mic and the words 'Hello, this is Sean Reilly in London' would arrive by satellite in New York or Hong Kong, where English voices on commercials and movie trailers were always in demand. He could work long after other Soho studios had closed or, if he got an urgent wake-up call from Sydney or Auckland, long before they opened. He was available as a voiceover artist, and occasionally as a sound engineer, practically twenty-four hours a day, happy to operate in alien time zones. Word got round, Sean got busy and cheques flew in from all over the world.

Sitting up late into the night, pouring those deep, honeyed tones down the line with the lights of London twinkling behind him, Sean felt like Dr Frasier Crane, his voice providing the answer to somebody's problem.

His new flat had been the answer to his. It was very cool. Not just for its look and location but because it was, quite literally, cool. Nikki, who felt the cold, had forced Sean to feel the heat. With the radiators boiling, he'd spent years enduring the stuffy discomfort of a prickly fever, never quite sure whether he was about to be struck down with cholera. The joy of no longer living in a house where the sitting room was hot enough to grow tropical fruit was far greater than he could ever have imagined.

Greater still was the joy of opening the front door and not being ordered to take off his shoes. He remembered reading *An Evil Cradling*, Brian Keenan's harrowing account of his four and a half years as a hostage in Beirut. Although far worse was to come, Keenan recalled the helplessness he had felt when his captors took away his shoes. 'Without your shoes,' he wrote, 'you have no dignity,' and Sean, looking down happily at his chunky-soled footwear, felt that his own dignity had finally been restored. He danced a heavily shod shuffle on his resin-bonded floors to celebrate this wonderful new sense of liberty. It gave him the same puerile frisson that he derived from driving diagonally across empty spaces in supermarket car parks.

At last he could relax in his own home. He did a lot of relaxing on the Most Comfortable Sofa in the World: huge, dark and infused with the almost pornographic scent of new leather. It was positioned opposite the sixty-inch plasma TV while its identical twin luxuriated on the other side of the room beneath a giant Anglepoise reading lamp. A discreet but immensely powerful pair of Bose 901 speakers were connected by underfloor wiring to the studio in the spare room where the ten thousand tracks he'd downloaded were now stored on a hard drive, which he could operate from a laptop on the sofa. Home entertainment didn't get much more spectacular. At last he had the means to live like an eighteenth century peasant. Like the average artisan before the industrial revolution, Sean worked when he needed to. Yes, he did jobs for people but the idea of being permanently yoked to one employer was now as alien to him as it would have been to that artisan. He had time now to become a twenty-first-century *flâneur*, wandering the streets of London, proud of his place as a small cog in a huge metropolitan machine. From Soho, he would amble west to Notting Hill, south to Battersea Park, east to Brick Lane or north to Hampstead. For Sean, who'd spent twenty years as a sound engineer, sitting on his arse, walking was its own reward. Not for him the hills and dales so beloved of the rural rambler. To his urban eye, one tree looked pretty much like another, but every street in London was unique. His was the most cosmopolitan city on the planet, which was why he could never have been exiled to a village in Kent. London's cultural diversity was hugely attractive but it was only the icing on a cake that had taken hundreds of years to bake. Now Sean wanted to immerse himself in its history, heritage and tradition. Like many a native Londoner, he'd never been inside Westminster Abbey, St Paul's Cathedral or the Tower of London. He had no idea what treasures lay within the National Gallery or the British Museum, but he would make it his business to find out. He'd been too absorbed working, ironically, in the centre of London to appreciate its cornucopia of cultural delights.

He walked for miles every day and soon discovered that it was the only exercise he needed. For years, he'd hauled himself on to the treadmill and various other instruments of torture at the Hogarth Health Club in Chiswick and now there was no need to do so. He'd never derived an atom of pleasure from going to the gym. He'd hated the continuous assault of MTV: all gyms expected their members to have the disposable income of affluent forty-somethings but the musical tastes of teenagers.

Worse, in a gym, he could never ignore the fact that he was

exercising. His urban meanderings, however, kept him trim without making it painfully and sweatily obvious. He was never tempted to quicken his walk to a run and do twenty-six miles for charity. Why was it, he wondered, that the London Marathon featured very few fit young men of twenty but every year was crawling with desperate-to-prove-they were-still-fit men of twice that age? Their training schedules often left them with twisted ankles and knackered knees and, however worthy their aims, Sean thought it might be better for all concerned if they'd simply got themselves sponsored to sit naked in a tub of baked beans.

The pleasure of ambling was all very well, he thought, as he wandered through an elegant, secluded little mews in Mayfair, that he'd never noticed before, but there was still one empty room in his flat and it was high time he filled it.

18

The 'empty room' wasn't strictly a room: it was Sean's designated space in the underground car park, and his was the only one not occupied by a chic set of wheels. He'd always been rather embarrassed by his car. Nikki had chosen it and Sean, as he had with the cream sofas and elaborate curtains, had gone along with it, despite an internal entreaty of taste and discretion, imploring him not to. The car was a BMW X5, which he detested for two reasons. First, it was a BMW. Although he loved the cars, he couldn't say the same for the people who drove them. A disproportionately large number of selfish motorists who refused to let others emerge from side turnings and didn't bother to thank those who extended this courtesy to them could be found at the wheel of a BMW. What was worse was that the X5 was a big, hefty 4X4, which seemed vulgar and unnecessary for the streets of West London. Nikki was unrepentant. In her view, speed humps were vulgar and unnecessary for the streets of West London and a 4x4 offered the only way of going over them without dislodging a couple of vertebrae.

Sean had conceded the point, but was still embarrassed because the X5 was the vehicle of choice for either footballers or drug-dealers. Whenever he sat parked in it for more than thirty seconds, he expected an anxious tap on the window from an emaciated youth in a hooded top, asking if he could score. Either that or he felt that, with an X5, he should be in a car park at two a.m., spit-roasting a pole-dancer.

The X5 had now moved to Kent, its spiritual home, where at least some use might be found for its off-road capabilities, and Sean, for the first time since he was seventeen, was without any form of transport. One Thursday morning, he received a size-able windfall from a film studio in LA and decided to spend it. Given his aversion to BMWs, it was odd that he was planning to visit a BMW showroom. He wanted to buy a Mini Cooper made, of course, by BMW – though this was something that the Bavarian Motor Works wisely chose not to advertise.

'Hi, I'm Chris Perrett,' said a tall, handsome salesman, with an easy charm and informality untypical of his profession. 'Anything I can do to help, just let me know.'

This was a double bluff. Chris, in his casual shirt and G-Star cargo pants may not have been smartly dressed but he was smart enough to know that he had a far greater chance of parting customers from their cash if he stood back and didn't hassle them. It was up to Sean to do the hassling.

'Well, you can sell me a Mini Cooper, if you like,' he said.

This wasn't what Chris had been expecting. 'Right. Any particular colour?'

'Yep. The hot orange metallic.'

Now this really wasn't what Chris had been expecting. Even he, a Mini evangelist, thought that the hot orange metallic was a particularly vile colour. It was a bit like buying a car with ginger hair. 'Okay,' he said, raising an eyebrow. 'Any accessories?'

In for a penny, thought Sean. 'Yeah, I'd like the Union Jack roof with spoiler, extra headlights and the full aerodynamic body pack.'

The salesman's opinion was clear from his expression. A thought bubble might as well have been floating up from his head: 'Sad fucker in mid-life crisis.' All he said was 'Will you be requiring one of our finance packages?'

'No, no,' said Sean. 'I'll pay cash. Well, when I say cash I can write you a cheque now.'

Make that '*Rich* sad fucker in mid-life crisis'.

'Okay,' said Chris, pulling up a chair at his desk to close the easiest deal he'd ever make. 'If I could just take a few details.'

Sean sat down. 'So how long before I can take delivery?'

'Well,' said Chris, 'obviously it's going to be a factory order. At the moment we're looking at ten to twelve weeks.'

'Twelve weeks?' said Sean, standing up and putting away his cheque book. 'I need it before then. I haven't got a car. In twelve weeks I'll have spent the price of this motor on taxis.'

'Well, if you'd consider another colour . . .'

'No,' said Sean. 'It's such a funky little car. It looks amazing in that metallic orange. Is there nothing you can do?'

Chris shook his head.

'Thing is,' said Sean, 'I've just split up from my wife. Freedom at last.'

'Oh, don't say that.' Chris grinned. 'I'm just about to get married.'

'I wouldn't bother, mate,' said Sean. 'Just find someone you don't like and buy her a house.'

Chris laughed and Sean deepened his tone to an almost professional level. 'So, twelve weeks, then?'

'I'm afraid so. Unless, as I say, you'd consider another colour. How about that one over there?' He pointed to a dark silver metallic model on the other side of the showroom.

'No,' said Sean. 'It's . . . so boring, colourless – so grey.'

'Not when you drive it,' said Chris, defaulting for the first time to sales patter.

'No, thanks,' said Sean, getting up. 'It's the orange or nothing. I'm sure I can get one somewhere else.'

'Wait a minute,' said Chris, dropping the long-practised routine at the thought of Sean and his chequebook walking out of the showroom. 'Are you sure you don't want that dark silver one?'

'Quite sure, thank you. It's supposed to be a fun car. Not having it in a bright colour is sort of missing the point.'

'I wouldn't say that,' said Chris. 'Especially that one. It's got all the toys, black leather seats, chrome trim, sixteen-inch alloys.'

'Yeah, but it's been in the showroom.'

'Only since Thursday.'

'It's like an ex-display model.'

'No one's actually driven it.'

'But I bet quite a few people have sat in it.'

Chris changed tack. 'Do you like music?'

'Yeah.'

'Okay, I'll up-rate the stereo. If you can wait till tomorrow, I'll change it for a Harmon Kardon system that would rival any club in Aya Napa. Have you got an iPod?'

'Yeah. Why?'

'Well, I'll throw in an iPod interface that you can plug straight into the system.'

Sean was wavering.

'And since it's been on display and you're paying cash, I'm sure we can do something on the price.'

Sean looked again at the dark silver metallic Mini Cooper and thought for a moment. He nodded, shook hands with Chris, sat down again and took out his cheque book. It was too good a deal to turn down.

Especially as he'd seen that car in the showroom the day before. It was exactly what he wanted and he wouldn't have been seen dead in a hideous orange metallic one.

19

Sean buzzed Jon into his flat at ten thirty one Tuesday night, and found himself simultaneously appalled and impressed by the way Jon treated his wife. He wasn't unkind or unfaithful but he did as he pleased. If that meant, as it frequently did, drinking and carousing in Soho until the early hours, then so be it: the long-suffering Alex Wilson-Love had to accept it. She stayed at home in Chelsea or, during school holidays, at their cottage in Wiltshire and took care of the three children.

Jon, having fallen into a cab at three a.m., would be deeply asleep (and often still deeply drunk) when the children left for school. Most weeks, even though his house was only fifteen minutes from his office and he came home every night, he didn't see the children between Sunday night and Saturday morning.

But who was Sean to criticise? Jon and Alex were still together, which was more than could be said for him and Nikki.

'To what do I owe the pleasure of seeing my agent?' he asked.

'Oh, I haven't come to see you,' said Jon. 'I've come to see this flat. Wow!' He plonked himself down on one of the huge sofas. 'I'm obviously getting you too much work. This place is amazing. All you need now is a snooker table just here and table football over there, which would still leave you room for a pinball machine by the door.

'Aren't you forgetting the Hawaiian-style bar in the corner, you tasteless twat?'

'Oh, but, seriously, it's fabulous. Makes me want to get a divorce.'

'Christ, if Alex hasn't divorced you yet,' said Sean, 'she never will.' He lobbed a cold bottle of Budvar and an opener to Jon, who uncapped it and took his first glug in one seamless movement.

'Cheers. Right, pleasantries over, I need a favour from you. Tomorrow morning I want you to do a job for no money.'

Before Sean could say anything, Jon continued, gesticulating expansively around the huge loft apartment, 'And don't even pretend you can't afford to.'

'Of course I can. What is it? A charity job?'

'Not exactly.'

'And what exactly does "not exactly" mean?'

'It's for a friend of Alex. Her name's Emma Tate and she's just set up this little thing called Top Table. It's basically a dating agency but that's not how she's marketing it.'

'Don't tell me,' said Sean, 'one of those supper clubs for "busy professionals". In other words, ex-geeks who got their confidence late in life. Too late to find themselves a partner.'

'Maybe,' said Jon, 'but I think it's more for people on round two. They fucked up the first time and now they're in their late thirties or early forties and don't want to hang around waiting for it to happen.'

'Or not happen, as the case may be.'

'Exactly,' said Jon, taking another long swig of Budvar. 'As the old saying goes, "Try to marry your second wife first." Anyway, Emma's bought a few radio spots and the station offered to produce the ad for her. Well, can you imagine how fucking cheesy they'd make it? So, I've managed to blag her an hour at the Sound Suite tomorrow morning.'

'Let me guess – nine o'clock?'

'Yep. I told her she needed a bloke with a lovely voice, bit of an edge so he won't sound like a total saddo. A bloke who'll make going to Top Table sound like a really good idea. I told her she needed you.'

'Well, thanks for that,' said Sean. 'Please call again when you've got less time.'

'So can I tell her you'll be there?'

'Yes,' said Sean, with a weary sigh.

'Good, because I already have.'

Sean had to smile. He'd do anything for Chelsea Jon, and Jon knew it. He'd never forgotten that it was Jon who had persuaded him to have a crack at being a voiceover artist. It was Jon, a former actor himself, who had worked so hard with him to put his showreel together, teaching him how to make the most of his exceptional raw material. Finally it was Jon who had suggested he install the ISDN link in the spare room, enabling him to afford the flat in Soho, the house in Kent and the brand-new Mini Cooper.

'Right,' said Sean, looking at his watch. 'I've got an ISDN to San Francisco at eleven, so off you fuck.'

'Nine o'clock tomorrow, then,' said Jon, as he left. 'You'll like Emma. You'll like her a lot.'

'I hope so,' said Sean. 'Then I won't mind doing this for free. Good night. Love to Alex.'

Jon looked at his watch. 'Blimey,' he said. 'It's only ten to eleven. I might actually see her tonight.'

Sean closed the huge warehouse-style door, opened the big bright red Smeg fridge and gargled with some freshly squeezed pineapple juice to make sure his voice was clean and clear for California, then poured himself a refill. He went into the little studio and booted up the Fairlight. 'Hello?' he said, deeply and clearly. 'This is Sean in London. Anybody there?'

'Hey, Sean,' said a Californian voice that was audibly tanned. 'This is Brad in San Francisco. How are you?'

'Fine, thank you,' said Sean. 'You?'

'I'm good,' said Brad, tanly. 'Do you have the script?'

Sean had the script. He'd read it, worked out various approaches to it and the glass of fresh pineapple juice was ready to assist him. This was an important job, a big coast-to-coast US TV campaign, so although Brad and his tanned associates in the City by the Bay would marvel at the ease and perfection with which Sean would deliver his lines, his preparation had been meticulous.

For his quick nine a.m. freebie, there would be no preparation at all. Yet that little job would turn out to be the most significant he'd ever done.

20

Unusually for Sean, he hadn't shaved. Especially as he was one of the few men in the world who adored the whole process. He loved the luxuriant lather on his face, the satisfying scrape of the razor debristling his chin. He loved splashing on freezing cold water when he'd finished and, best of all, the astringent sting of the aftershave fragrantly closing each pore.

Like many people Sean had often imagined himself on *Desert Island Discs*. The eight records he'd choose would change from one day to the next, but his luxury items never altered: an unlimited supply of Mach 3 razors and Kiehl's shaving cream. Whenever a man is stranded on a desert island, whether it's Robinson Crusoe or Tom Hanks in *Cast Away*, he's invariably depicted with a big, bushy beard. As long as Sean had his razors and his shaving cream, he would never feel like a castaway, nor lose hope of being rescued.

All well and good, but when he woke up ten minutes before his nine o'clock booking, the splashing of the freezing cold water was the only part of the routine for which he had time.

Not sure whether the light stubble made him look like Mickey Rourke or an old lady who needed her chin plucked, he rushed into Sound Suite's reception.

'Hi, Sean,' said Chloë, the stunning, flirtatious but-she's-young-enough-to-be-your-daughter-so-don't-even-think-about-it receptionist. 'That's Emma over there. You're with her.'

'Okay, thanks.'

Maybe because he'd only been awake for twelve minutes, maybe because he hadn't shaved, but Sean's voice was deeper than ever.

'Emma?' said an almost subterranean rumble. 'Hello, I'm Sean Reilly.'

'Wow, you are, aren't you?' smiled a woman in her mid-thirties, whose playful attractiveness was enhanced by the subtle scent of Michael Kors. 'What a magnificent set of lungs.'

Sean knew he had a great voice, of course, but he was unaccustomed to such direct, fulsome praise and found himself blushing.

'Studio's ready when you are, Sean,' said Chloë.

'Right,' he said, turning to Emma. 'Shall we go through?'

'With a voice like that, baby,' she laughed, 'I'll go anywhere you want to take me.'

Sean, caught off guard again, smiled bashfully, knowing the bristles couldn't hide the blushes.

Emma Tate was known as the Jane Austen of Notting Hill for her legendary matchmaking prowess. She would put together a dinner party for eight people at her flat in Bassett Road, and if she'd invited an unattached man and an unattached woman, you could guarantee they'd be attached to each other by the time dawn broke the next morning. Her strike rate was so impressive that it was suggested by each half of every lovestruck 'item' that she strike out professionally.

So, here she was at the Sound Suite, making her first radio commercial. Ben, the young engineer, was delighted but nervous to be sharing his studio with The Great Sean Reilly. 'Can I have a bit for level, please?' he asked, once Sean was seated in the booth with his headphones on. Sean, who had an almost pathological aversion to saying 'One-two, one-two', recited a little poem:

> 'I went to the market
> With my brother Jim,
> And somebody threw a tomato at him.
> Tomatoes are soft, they don't break the skin
> But this fucker did, it was still in the tin.'

'That's great, Sean,' said Ben. 'Okay, let's go for one. This is Top Table Thirty, second radio commercial, take one.'

Sean took a deep breath and began: 'This commercial isn't aimed at you. You're happily ensconced in a relationship but maybe you have a "friend" who isn't. Maybe your "friend" is a busy professional man or woman who never seems to have time to meet that special person. We may be able to help. At Top Table, we organise private dinners at chic and discreet London venues where people can meet and relax. There are only twelve places each time, six men, six women, so if your "friend" would like to come along, the number is 0800 12 12 12. Top Table, because . . . well, you never know . . .'

Emma squealed with delight. 'Fabulous! No wonder Jonny calls his agency Take One.'

'How was it for time?' Sean asked Ben.

'Thirty-one seconds, but it's fine. I'll just take out a couple of pauses.'

'No, no,' said Sean. 'I'll have another go. Might as well.'

Take two was even better, Sean's voice slightly more matter-of-fact, which suggested that joining a dating agency was nothing to be ashamed of. In fact, it was positively cool.

'How was that for time?'

'Oddly enough,' said Ben, 'even though it sounded more relaxed it was shorter. Twenty-eight point seven.'

'Good,' said Sean. 'Is that okay, Emma?'

'*Okay?*' she squawked. 'Darling, that's like asking whether Michelangelo did an okay job on the Sistine chapel. It was perfect. Thank you so much.'

Sean found himself blushing again. There was something about Emma that made his face and neck redden without warning. Fortunately, he was in the glass booth and nobody could see what he could feel.

'Well, I've left a tiny bit of room,' he said, 'to establish maybe a second of lounge piano up the front that you can run under me. Perhaps some cutlery, gentle hubbub, you know the sort of thing.'

He took off his headphones and came out of the booth, while Ben began to mix in the gentle piano music and sound effects. 'Thanks, Ben. See you soon.'

'Yeah, cheers, Sean.'

As he left the studio, Sean was made to blush once more.

'Thank you so much,' said Emma, kissing each unshaven cheek and simultaneously pressing a card into his hand. 'Look, why don't you pop along to our first one? On the house. It's the least I can do. Two weeks on Thursday at the Soho Hotel.'

'Um, er, that's very kind,' said Sean, 'but it's not really my . . . um—'

'Of course not,' said Emma, looking right into his eyes with Austenesque perspicacity. 'But I'm sure you've got a "friend" who might be interested.'

21

Brown Windsor Soup. Lucy had never known what it was but she was sure she'd find it, along with soggy roast beef, over-cooked vegetables and jam roly-poly, on the menu at the House of Commons canteen. Instead she discovered that the fare on offer was rather more appealing. There was lobster and tarragon risotto, steamed fillet of John Dory, breast of duck with peanut and noodle salad. The chicken was corn-fed, and even the sausages were free-range and organic. There were vegetarian options, low-carb options, fine wines and fruit smoothies.

There had clearly been a dramatic improvement in the stan-dards of parliamentary cuisine: politicians had been spectacu-larly kind to themselves. As Lucy ordered the grilled swordfish with rocket salad, she wondered why they hadn't been quite so kind to the nation's schoolchildren.

Feeling again like a schoolkid herself, she gazed round the crowded dining hall, tray in hand, looking for a spare table. She didn't know anyone, she didn't particularly want to know anyone, but in a corner she saw two people she recognised. Both were high-profile household names, and both had been in the House of Commons for as long as she could remember, so it was no surprise to find them there. What was surprising was that these sworn political adversaries were fraternising quite openly over a bottle of claret.

The political heyday of 'Mad Jack' Dodds and Sir Michael Huntley had been in the mid-eighties when Dodds, a bolshy ex-miner from South Yorkshire, had led the vehement and often violent opposition to Huntley's plans to close the pits. Each man had believed sincerely that what he was doing was right. With the benefit of 20/20 hindsight, both had been right – and wrong. The truth, as always, lay somewhere in between.

The middle ground, for better or worse, was where British politics had now settled. It was a bland, beige sofa of ideology on which neither man sat comfortably. Consigned to the backest of back benches, affectionately tolerated and patronisingly called 'characters' by both sides of the House, Huntley and Dodds had unexpectedly found themselves friends rather than foes, united by their loathing of the current regime. Huntley, though nearly seventy, was still charismatic, with thick silver hair, smooth skin and an exquisite navy suit, hand-made like all his others by Douglas Hayward in Mount Street. He was like Brian Marsden only more so: taller, more elegant, more urbane, more distinguished. Lucy could see at once that Marsden had based his sartorial and political persona on Huntley.

Jack Dodds couldn't afford to grace the Commons in a hand-tailored suit. Actually, after the recent success of his memoirs, he almost certainly could. His loyal Yorkshire constituents, however, would never forgive him if he did, so he stuck with his Marks & Spencer's tweed sports jacket and slacks. Like Huntley, he also had a generous head of thick grey hair, but while Huntley's was expensively silver, Dodds's had that working-class grey which, in a certain light, looks green.

Lucy was a journalist. She'd never been shy about getting herself on the right side of the red velvet rope to gatecrash a celebrity party. Gatecrashing a celebrity lunch like this was too good an opportunity to miss. 'Mind if I join you?' she said, eyeing the empty seat next to Huntley. They could hardly say no. Huntley gave a short gentlemanly smile and Dodds's grunt seemed to signify some sort of assent so she sat down. 'Hello,' she said, with her special-edition gatecrasher's smile. 'I'm Lucy Ross.'

'Oh, I know exactly who you are,' said Huntley, raising a silver eyebrow. 'You ended the political career of one of my closest friends and greatest allies.'

Maybe this hadn't been such a good idea.

'Bollocks,' was the first word Lucy heard Jack Dodds utter in person. She was delighted to find him exactly as she'd expected him to be, as bluff and blunt as one of the Four Yorkshireman in the Monty Python sketch. 'Brian Marsden lost that seat all by himself and you bloody know it.'

The point-scoring that kept them constantly amused had begun.

'I think you're being a little unfair to Lucy here,' said Huntley, 'by suggesting that she had nothing to do with her own electoral victory.'

Lucy suspected that both men loathed everything they thought she stood for. Dodds abhorred New Labour for abandoning its socialist principles while Huntley despised them for mugging his party in the mid-nineties and making off with most of its ideas. They had assumed that Lucy had no real political convictions and therefore no business being in Parliament. They were absolutely right. However, their joint assumption that she was yet another biddable bureaucrat who would never think of not toeing the party line was spectacularly wide of the mark.

Lucy had come to regard her new career as an elaborate version of jury service: something she knew she had to do but didn't care much about. And, as Jack Dodds in particular was fond of saying, 'You can't beat a man who doesn't care.'

'I'm sorry about Brian,' said Lucy. 'I don't expect you to believe me but I never wanted to win. I was quite happy working as a journalist. That whole election thing was just a stunt. If I could turn back the clock and lose, I would.' She looked at their stony, sceptical faces. 'You don't believe me, do you?'

Huntley's clear blue eyes gazed incisively into Lucy's chocolate brown ones. 'Oddly enough,' he said calmly, 'I do.'

'Do you?' said Lucy.

'Certainly,' said Huntley, with a sad smile. 'I remember Brian phoning me when he heard that Labour were putting you up as their candidate. He couldn't believe his luck. Laughed out

loud and made no effort at all with his campaign. I don't think
he knocked on a single door. He took their loyalty and their
votes for granted.' He nodded at Dodds. 'Even he doesn't do
that.'

'Served him bloody right,' said Dodds. 'Talked a lot of crap,
did Marsden, and you know what they say – "MPs are like
nappies and they have to be changed for exactly the same reason."'

'Well,' said Huntley, with a wicked smile, 'I suppose he does
have a point about our dear departed friend. Cheers.'

'Cheers,' said Lucy, raising her glass.

'What's that?' asked Dodds, looking at the orangey contents
of Lucy's glass.

'An Innocent smoothie,' said Lucy.

'Ooh,' said Dodds, disdainfully, 'a *smooo*othie, is it?' Perhaps
you should have one of those, Mickey.'

'Maybe,' replied Huntley. 'And I believe they do one with
yoghurt called a Thickie. Now, I wonder who should have one
of those?'

Fifteen–love to Huntley.

Lucy wasn't sure which would be more impolite: laughing at
Dodds or not laughing at Huntley's lightning riposte. 'I'm the
Innocent Thickie,' she said. 'I've got myself a job I never wanted
and don't know how to do. Will you help me?'

Huntley and Dodds looked at each other. They'd each known
countless MPs about whom this appraisal was true but they'd
never heard one admit it. It was hard not to find such honesty
disarming.

'Come on,' said Huntley, 'it's early days. It's a great honour
to be an MP.'

'It used to be,' Dodds grunted, 'but not any more. I know I'm
getting old but people go into it younger and younger. Most of
them have bugger all experience of the real world. Absolutely
nowt in common with ordinary folk.'

'He's got a point,' said Huntley. 'I was forty before I even
considered standing for Parliament. Until then I felt I hadn't done

enough with my own life to tell others what to do with theirs. Most New Labour MPs have only ever worked as policy advisers or college lecturers or in local government. Every penny they've ever earned has come directly from the taxpayer.'

'Got yourself an office yet?' asked Dodds, in a tone that suggested he already knew the answer.

'No.'

'You can bet *they* all have,' said Huntley, gesturing round the room. 'There'll have been a lot of jockeying for the best offices, biggest desks and what-have-you. You see, for these people it's a career.'

'Like it wasn't for you?' said Dodds, perennially unwilling to let Huntley get away with anything.

'Well, of course it was,' said Huntley, 'but my ambitions were based on serving my country and trying to make things better for people.'

'Like the ninety-seven per cent of miners who lost their jobs after your lot had finished with them.' Dodds snorted.

Fifteen–all.

'Most of these new MPs are just malleable lobby fodder,' said Huntley, 'with less power than the average traffic warden. They're happy just to have the letters MP after their names. That's all they want. They're not particularly well paid.'

'Tell me about it,' said Lucy, who'd just remembered the salary cut she'd have to take to do a job she didn't want.

'But it's the most money they've ever earned, and are ever likely to earn, so they're hardly going to risk losing it by stepping out of line.'

'It's also a class thing,' said Dodds, unsurprisingly. 'When I started I'd say about seventy per cent of Labour MPs were from what you might call working-class backgrounds. Now I reckon it's nearer ten.'

'You've got to decide,' said Huntley, 'how you want to play it. You're here now and, whatever you think, it's an opportunity you really shouldn't waste. Also, you put yourself up for election and thousands of people voted for you. You have a duty not to let them down.'

Huntley's reality check sent guilt seeping into Lucy's mind, evident in the slight reddening of her cheeks. 'I know,' she said, 'and you're quite right. But I really have no desire to make a career out of this.'

'Well,' said Huntley, 'that's up to you. Though, I have to say, becoming a minister is very satisfying. It's like having a brand-new Jaguar and spending years stuck behind a caravan on a narrow country lane, then suddenly coming to a dual carriageway and getting the chance to put your foot down.'

Lucy spent three seconds thinking of herself as a barren, unmarried cabinet minister with grey hair and a navy twin set before saying 'No!' a little too loudly.

'So you've no desire,' said Dodds, sensing, at long last, the possibility of a kindred spirit, 'to progress within the Party?'

'None whatsoever.'

'Right, love.' He smiled. 'Then you can become what some folk like to call "a maverick". I've been doing it for thirty-odd years and enjoyed every minute of it. If you don't want anything from the Party and you don't break any parliamentary rules, there's nowt they can do to you. Drives 'em mad.'

Lucy wasn't convinced. 'I can't just be a maverick,' she said. 'There's got to be more to it than that.'

'Of course there is,' said Huntley, always the more rational and pragmatic of the two. 'But there's nothing wrong with having the courage of your convictions and speaking out against your own party if you think they're wrong. Goodness knows, the House could do with a few more people like that.'

'Okay,' said Dodds, seemingly unfurling an invisible guide to being an MP. 'First things first. Always do your casework. Hold your surgeries, look after the people who voted for you. At the end of the day, that's why you're here.'

'To a point,' said Huntley. 'Even if you worked twenty-four hours a day, you could never sort out every problem brought to you by your constituents. A lot of them are insane anyway, expecting you to solve problems that are nothing to do with you. You have to work out where you can and should use your position to help someone, and where you either can't or shouldn't.'

'Also,' said Dodds, taking his turn in what Lucy was beginning to think was a well-rehearsed double-act, 'people like their MP to be on telly, on the radio or taking part in debates. They like to know that you're doing something important in Westminster. If they don't see you doing that, you might as well work for the Citizens Advice Bureau.'

'Like everything else, it's a balancing act,' said Huntley, 'but you'll soon get the hang of it. Anyway, I hear you've taken on Sheila Webb as your assistant. Very shrewd move.'

'How did you know that?' said Lucy.

Huntley gave a suave chuckle. 'Oh, my dear! You think magazines are a gossipy business? Wait till you see what politics is like. Sheila's wonderful. She used to do most of Brian's constituency work. Wrote all his letters for him. He'd have been sunk without her.'

'You mean,' said Dodds, 'you've nicked an ex-Tory minister's assistant to come and work for Labour?'

'Um . . . well, it wasn't quite like that,' said Lucy.

'I don't care what it was like,' said Dodds, and gave a gravelly, almost emphysemic laugh. 'Ee, I like you already.'

'Well,' said Huntley, 'if you're going to take what I would prefer to term the "principled, independent-minded" route, then you have to select something about which you care passionately and feature it in your maiden speech.'

'Mine, for instance,' said Dodds, 'was keeping the pits open, and his was closing them down.'

Another weary sigh from Huntley. 'Mine, Lucy, was liberating our country from the terrible effects of bullying and self-serving trade unions.'

'In other words,' said Dodds, 'closing down the pits.'

'We introduced sensible legislation to prevent our nation being continually held to ransom and, interestingly, not one piece of that legislation has been repealed by your party.'

'My party?' sneered Dodds. 'They're not my party.'

'Anyway, Lucy,' said Huntley, 'as I was saying, find something you feel passionate about.'

'And don't bother talking about improving education or the health service,' said Dodds. 'Everyone wants to see them improved and they never will be. Try and be a bit more original.'

'It doesn't matter how trivial it seems,' added Huntley. 'It will strike a chord with someone.'

'Well,' said Lucy, before she could stop herself, 'I really care about shopping.'

As the two seasoned parliamentarians looked at each other, she could see that neither had been expecting anything quite as trivial as that.

22

Sean didn't so much drive his new Mini Cooper as wear it. When he buckled it on, it felt like a high-speed bomber jacket.

Missing the children one sunny Tuesday afternoon, he swung it out of its underground parking space, pointed the bonnet towards Kent and took off. As he whizzed over Tower Bridge, then through the back-streets of Rotherhithe and Deptford, he was thrilled by the sort of responsive handling he'd only ever experienced in a go-kart. But then, as Chris the salesman had told him when he took delivery, the car did have 'class-leading road feedback'.

Driving had always excited and relaxed him. Social mobility had been one of man's greatest achievements in the twentieth century and, sitting in a long queue of traffic next to an empty bus lane, he felt hatred for local councils' spiteful attempts to restrict it in the twenty-first.

Driving gave him time to collect his thoughts and today, snaking slowly round Blackheath, he thought about the term 'mid-life crisis'. Was he having one? Absolutely not. Far from being symptomatic of a mid-life crisis, the new living arrangements and concomitant Cooper were steps he'd taken to avoid one. If he'd moved to Kent, he would have been mired in mid-life crisis now and it would have been only a matter of time before he'd pitched up, in full leathers, at the nearest Harley Davidson dealership. As it was, he'd never felt so out of crisis in his life.

Fiddling with his iPod to locate his 'fast-driving' selection, which he would activate once released on to the open road of the A20, he thought of that other symptom of mid-life crisis:

the sudden obsession with new music. As a sound engineer, he'd had a purely professional interest. If Matt or Jez had wanted something a bit 'like, you know, Razorlight or the Paddingtons', Sean had to know what they meant. This was different from dads in their forties raving about the latest Bloc Party or Snow Patrol albums. They'd had their turn as teenagers but, more often than not, had been too busy swotting for their O levels and were now treating music and football as subjects that could be studied in the same way. 'Too late, mate,' was what Sean wanted to say. 'You should have been doing all this when you were sixteen. It's no good trying to catch up now.'

That said, Sean's choice of music for the A20 veered embarrassingly towards Dad Rock. Generally he didn't like rock music but allowed himself a shameful blast of ZZ Top's 'Sharp Dressed Man', Robert Palmer's 'Bad Case Of Loving You' and Led Zeppelin's 'Rock and Roll'. All he needed were some tight jeans and a curly perm, and he'd be Jeremy Clarkson.

Robert Plant gave way to Edward Elgar as he slowed down for a spot of country driving. The fun he could have had round the twisty lanes was invariably ruined either by someone driving a tractor or by someone who might as well have been.

Arriving at the house, he resisted the urge to perform a spectacular handbrake turn into the gravel drive, but only just. Nikki was happily trowelling compost into a huge terracotta pot containing a plant that must have escaped from *Day of the Triffids*. She greeted him with a healthy wholesome smile. 'Oh, I'm so glad you're here,' she said.

Sean was pleasantly surprised. My God, this was perilously close to affection. 'Really?'

'Yeah. I need you to move this pot.'

Sean's heart, having momentarily lifted, immediately sank again. The first half of so many of her sentences began with 'I need you to . . .' The second half was never '. . . be my boyfriend; be my soulmate; satisfy my carnal desires'. Instead it would involve carrying out some sort of domestic chore. With Nikki's horticultural, if not carnal, desires satisfied, Sean wiped his hands and sped off to collect the children from school.

Kent is not noted for artists, writers or any other males who aren't chained to either a desk or a combine harvester at three thirty in the afternoon. Its menfolk tended to toil either in small businesses in Maidstone or large ones in London, EC3. The sight of Sean in the school playground therefore produced the sort of gawping curiosity normally reserved for a dwarf with three heads.

A confluence of Catholic humility and his wife's long-term indifference had made Sean forget that he was far more hand-some and youthful than most men of his age. He hadn't yet succumbed to a life of back pain and UK Gold, and his pres-ence elicited a lot of nudge-nudging and admiring glances from young mothers. Sean, though, only had eyes for two females: Katie and Rosie Reilly, his five- and seven-year-old daughters. Shrieking with surprise and delight, they raced into his arms to be swung round in a carousel of love, affection and fun. Those admiring glances became almost dewy-eyed as a dozen wives wished their husbands were more like Sean. He carried his little girls off to meet his 'naughty car', which, he told them, had a mind of its own.

'Now, naughty car,' he told it, 'I want you to go very, very slowly. I have two very nervous children in the back who don't like going fast, okay?' To squeals of excitement, the naughty car took off through the country lanes and delivered them home in five minutes rather than ten. Sean made their dinner, helped them with their homework and tucked them into bed, then told them one more naughty-car story before they went to sleep.

He came downstairs, hoping for a little light chat with Nikki before he headed back to do an ISDN link to Toronto. He should have known that she'd already be slumped motionless in front of *Holby City* and, until it was over, would have no interest in anything he had to say.

Heading back up the A20 he was relieved, but at the same time vaguely insulted, by how quickly and easily Nikki had settled into her new life in Kent and by how little she seemed to miss him.

The iPod was now shuffling some randomly poignant songs like Millie Jackson's 'Hurt So Good', Dusty Springfield's 'If You Go Away' and the Paris Sisters' 'I Love How You Love Me'. Suddenly, when Toni Tennille started singing 'Do That To Me One More Time', Sean found himself wanting someone to feel that way about him. The wonderful life he'd created for himself counted for nothing unless he could share it with someone: someone with whom he could make love and laughter before it was too late.

He'd thrown away Emma Tate's card with Top Table's number on it, but not before he'd saved the number into his phone. Even though he was doing 100 m.p.h., he scrolled down and dialled it because over the last few months he'd come to realise one important thing. Forget oysters and rhino horns: the greatest aphrodisiac in the world is boredom.

23

Joe Callanan had sat next to Sean at school. Or, rather, he hadn't. When the teacher called, 'Callanan,' in the register, Joe was invariably absent. His curly red head would usually burst through the door just as the teacher reached 'Reilly'. Although Joe lived opposite the school and his bedroom was approximately two minutes walk from his desk, he never managed to get there on time.

Sean's flat was a similar distance from the Soho Hotel, yet he was displaying an attitude to timekeeping that was worthy of the master himself. Sean was in no hurry because he still had huge doubts about whether he wanted to go. What for? Did he really want to meet someone else? And even if he did, was this the way to do it? No matter how attractive he found the women around the table, there would always be the smack of desperation about anyone who joined Top Table. Never mind the sassy way it was presented, it was still just a glorified dating agency.

Like most people in moments of bored curiosity, Sean had scanned the Lonely Hearts columns of *Time Out*. He'd noticed a disproportionate number of 'mental-health professionals' and wondered whether they were 'professionals' who worked in mental health or 'health professionals' who were mental. He was also struck by the prevalence of 'tall, slim, attractive' people. There was a distinct paucity of 'short, fat ugly' ones, though the words 'well-built' were usually a bit of a giveaway.

Top Table didn't work like that. Emma vetted all applicants, picked twelve and told them nothing about the other eleven. It was no good describing yourself as Cameron Diaz if you had a face like a bulldog licking piss off a nettle: Emma would reject you. Liars were not welcome at Top Table.

The invitation said drinks at eight, dinner at eight thirty. Sean looked at his watch. It was already a quarter past and he was still dancing alone with a towel round his waist. Frank Sinatra and Dean Martin had long provided his favourite getting-ready music: their old standards made him feel as though it was 1961 and he was heading for a night out in Vegas with some of the guys and a couple of broads. He got the feeling that the broads tonight might be very broad indeed.

Appropriately enough, on came Sinatra singing 'Love And Marriage'. Sean had to chuckle: in his experience love and marriage went together like a horse and water-skis. This was followed by his favourite rat-pack number: Dino crooning 'You're Nobody Till Somebody Loves You'. Unfortunately, given the nature of Sean's night out, it suddenly sounded like a co-dependants' theme tune. He quickly scrolled down to find some other getting-ready tunes. Slave's 'Just A Touch Of Love', Barrington Levy's 'Here I Come' and, obviously, the Temptations' 'Get Ready'.

Over the years, he'd become accustomed to the word 'dinner' being followed by 'party', though before the age of twenty he would have considered them two incompatible forms of pleasure. The term with which he still had trouble was 'drinks'. Serious imbibers had always gone for 'a drink', while prissier people preferred 'drinks'. The irony was that 'drinks' usually meant a single glass of wine or champagne and 'a drink', in the Islington of Sean's youth, usually involved at least eight pints of Guinness and a punch-up.

He'd decided to skip the drinks and arrive just in time to sit down and be asked whether he'd like a white or wholemeal roll delivered by a pair of tongs to his side-plate. Unfortunately, the Temptations had been followed by Syl Johnson's 'Ms Fine Brown Frame', which demanded several minutes of nostalgic musing and eighties dancing. By the time Sean had snapped back into the twenty-first century and rushed next door to the Soho Hotel it was nearly ten to nine. Joe Callanan would have been proud of him.

The place was achingly chic and living proof that London really had caught up with Manhattan in the hip-hotel stakes. Emma was waiting in the wood, metal, glass and stone lobby, standing next to a ten-foot-high bronze sculpture of a cat. 'Ah, Sean, you made it,' she said, with a welcoming smile.

'Nothing gets past you, does it?' he winked.

'They've only just sat down,' she continued. 'Come and meet everyone.'

Sean was ushered through to the Swirl Room, a dark riot of bold colours round a central chandelier, where eleven people looked up from a beautifully laid round table. The looks he received from the men and women were very different: the women viewed him as a potential partner, the men as a potential impediment to finding one.

As Emma ran through the names, as though they were all contestants on *University Challenge*, Sean recalled an old maxim he often quoted when making radio commercials. In an effort to prevent greedy advertisers trying to cram too much information into thirty seconds, he told them they'd be wasting their money. Listeners wouldn't remember a single word, and certainly not the thrice-repeated phone number. 'If you throw one ball at your listeners,' he explained, usually in vain, 'they'll catch it. If you throw half a dozen, they'll drop the lot.' Emma had to introduce each person by name but that was eleven balls in quick succession and Sean dropped the lot.

As soon as he sat down, he wanted to get up and go home. What on earth was he doing? The last time he'd gone out with the sole purpose of pulling was more than twenty years ago, and all that was required back then was a slow dance. It was simply a matter of waiting for the opening bars of 'Three Times A Lady' and asking a girl to join him in a vertical demonstration of horizontal intent. After three minutes, he knew whether or not you'd pulled. Suddenly he thought of Nikki, and could sum up what he felt she'd removed from their marriage: the metaphorical slow dance.

It seemed so much more complicated now. This ritual was going to take much longer than three minutes but, unfortunately, it was too late to back out now. Just treat it, he said to himself, as an ordinary dinner party. The food will be great, you're hungry, you've got nothing in the fridge and it saves going to Waitrose.

Naturally it was boy-girl, boy-girl, so Sean was seated between two women who, to his surprise, hadn't fallen straight out of the ugly tree. The one to his right had had only one ball to catch. 'Hi, Sean,' she announced, in a rich, confident voice. 'I'm Sophie.'

Sophie Benson was thirty-six, but with the thick, flaxen hair and peachy complexion found only in the well bred and well-fed, she looked no more than thirty. Her clothes were made to last, in both quality and style. The light cashmere jumper, Thomas Pink shirt and almost obligatory string of creamy pearls were neither high fashion nor out of date. Sean found her rather alluring in a jolly sensible, very English sort of way.

Everyone round the table had a secret. Nothing particularly dark or sinister but they all had their reasons for resorting to this method of finding a partner. Sophie's was just thoughtless conceit: she had been the prettiest, wittiest girl in her class at Francis Holland School. Amid the throng of braying Sloanes in the White Horse pub on Parsons Green, she had been the one for whom any chap in a blue stripey shirt and red spotted tie would make a beeline. The last twenty years had been a gregarious merry-go-round of drinks parties, charity balls, skiing, sailing and sex. Sophie had been in no hurry to settle down: there had always been 'plenty of time for all that' – until she discovered that there wasn't. Having attended the smart country nuptials of both her sisters, all her friends and most of her ex-boyfriends, she had driven back to Fulham one Sunday morning and realised that the only wedding she hadn't been invited to was her own.

Not given to self-pity or introspection, she'd 'jolly well pulled herself together' and called Top Table first thing on Monday morning. Ten days later, she was interviewing Sean Reilly for the position of serious boyfriend.

'Sorry, darlin',' he said, inexplicably defaulting to Cockney, as he always did when talking to posh people. 'I didn't catch your name. I must be goin' senile. Won't be long before I'm hidin' me own Easter eggs.'

'Sophie.' She smiled, displaying perfect teeth. 'Sophie Benson.'

'Sean Reilly.'

'Gosh! I do like your voice,' said Sophie, characteristically direct. 'You sound just like Ian Dury.'

'Well,' said Sean, 'as long as I don't look like him.'

'What do you do?'

'I'm a voiceover artist,' he said, shifting his tone from Ian Dury towards Ian McKellen. 'And you?'

'Oh, I've done all sorts of things. Publishing, a few ski seasons in Verbier, crewing on yachts, and then I ran an equestrian centre down in Somerset. Do you ride?'

'No,' said Sean, who had seldom seen a horse without a policeman on it. 'You're not doing that now, I take it.'

'No. I work for a charity.'

Oh, I bet you do, thought Sean. Having waived his fee and voiced countless charity commercials, he'd met more women like Sophie than he cared to remember. Some were very nice, but too many thought the moral high ground implicit in working for a charity gave them *carte blanche* to be bossy and hectoring, and to take shameless advantage of other people's good nature. He counted to three in his head and, almost on cue, Sophie said, 'Look, we're shooting a little DVD to raise funds. I don't suppose you'd consider doing the voiceover for it. No money, of course.'

Sean sighed silently but nodded, thanking God he hadn't

mentioned that he was also a sound engineer with his own studio. It would almost certainly have meant spending the next few weeks being bossed around and putting the whole thing together for nothing.

Mission accomplished, Sophie turned her attention to the slender, blond, fey little chap to her left. Jason Foley was the boy at school who had always played with the girls. While the other boys in his class had entered the 1983 fancy-dress party as soldiers or footballers, Jason had donned a wig, lipstick, his sister's swimming costume, augmented by a pair of oranges, and gone as Miss World, to waltz home with first prize. Naturally, it was no surprise to find him on Friends Reunited, unmarried, working as an interior designer, with hobbies including singing in an otherwise all-female chorus. However, as he explained, in his camp, theatrical manner, he harboured a terrible secret: 'I wasn't really gay', he said, 'I was just going through the motions.'

Sean thought this an unfortunate choice of phrase but listened, quite rapt, as Jason continued: 'It was never really me. Don't let anyone tell you otherwise, it's far easier to meet someone if you're gay than straight. You poor loves, it's an absolute nightmare. I mean, whoever heard of heterosexual cruising bars? Gay men are far more direct about their intentions. It was so much easier. I assumed I must be gay because I love receiving bouquets, I know every word from *Oklahoma!* and I shriek with delight every Christmas at Selfridge's window display. I thought it was just a matter of time before I met the right man. Then it occurred to me that the right man might actually be a woman, so I've finally come out of the closet. Say it loud, I'm straight and proud.'

The whole table gave him a round of applause and Jason did indeed shriek with delight. It was impossible not to like him. Sean thought he was great, certainly not the sort of bloke he'd expected to find at Top Table.

He'd thought they'd be more like Clive, who was sitting

opposite him. Clive was quietly spoken and cripplingly shy. After more than hour, he'd barely uttered a word. Clive's secret, though it was hardly a secret, was that he was bald. He'd had a full head of jet black hair until just before his twenty-first birthday when, with distressing alacrity, it began to fall out. Within a couple of years, it was practically all gone, apart from the thick dark tufts at the back and sides.

The sudden and dramatic loss of his hair had been a spiteful whack from the cruel hand of Fate. If his hair had been fair or sandy, its loss would have been far less noticeable. Clive's fragile self-esteem had never recovered. Even now, twelve years on, the most striking thing about him was his smooth, shiny cue-ball baldness, accentuated by an unusually high forehead. Of course, it would have been better for him to shave off the whole lot but that would have taken a level of confidence that he simply didn't possess. Something irrational inside him believed that if he clung to its last vestiges his thick black hair might one day return.

Sean tried to bring him into the conversation a couple of times, and noticed both Jason and Sophie trying too, but Clive's shyness was so intense that his face, neck and bald head blushed horribly whenever anyone spoke to him. Rather than cause him such obvious discomfort, people stopped speaking to him.

Sean's ears pricked up when he heard a man two seats to his left talking about poetry. 'I'm rather like a poetry jukebox,' the man boasted, in a sonorous tone. 'Just give me a subject and I'll oblige.'

'How about love?' said the woman next to him, whose name was one of the many balls Sean had dropped.

The man gazed pensively at no one in particular and began:

> 'All the love the whole world knows
> Is said to be in a single rose.
> Yet all the love you'd find in two,
> Could never match how I feel for you.'

The table didn't quite know how to respond, though Clive's head had turned blood-pumpingly crimson.

'That's beautiful,' said the woman, whose name, Sean suddenly remembered, was Katy.

'One tries,' said the would-be poet laureate, with nauseating mock-modesty. 'I'm Laurence, by the way – Laurence Mills.'

Clearly he was expecting someone to reply, 'What – *the* Laurence Mills?' When no one did he continued, pompously, 'Anyone else care to throw a subject at me?'

Sean was tempted, so tempted, to piss on this idiot's parade with some random suggestions. 'Roast turbot,' he wanted to shout. 'Michael Aspel, prolapsed haemorrhoids . . .'

'Life?' called someone else.

Again, the great man furrowed his brow to bring to mind another piece of doggerel he'd either written himself or memorised from the *Reader's Digest*.

> 'Forty years, where have they gone?
> Tell me, I don't know.
> But the biggest question of them all,
> Is death a door or just a wall?'

His attempt at an enigmatic expression was met with a rather awkward silence, which he was not embarrassed to fill. 'The thing with poetry,' he explained, 'is just to express your feelings. Open your heart, open your mind and let it flow.'

Sean had discovered poetry only recently when reading an anthology of verse for the BBC. He knew that Laurence was talking out of his arse. Writing poetry requires an understanding, however basic, of form, metre and rhyme. No one tells a first-time pianist to 'Open the lid, express your feelings, just let it flow.'

Laurence was overweight and profoundly unattractive, but he believed that the most important part of any man was his mind and that women would be seduced by his towering intellect. Lacking in natural flair, he'd worked extremely hard to amass the knowledge that he was now so keen to display. Knowledge is power, and he wanted power over women. He believed that cerebral prowess would lead to sexual prowess and couldn't comprehend why such success had always eluded him. He was a 'consultant psychologist' with his own practice in Wimbledon and he tended to talk to people as though they were patients, hanging on his every word for wisdom and guidance.

If he'd ever sought the wisdom and guidance of another psychologist, he might have been told some uncomfortable truths. Yes, the most important part of a man is his mind. The mind controls what he says, what he does and how he behaves. If he uses his mind to be arrogant, smarmy and slightly predatory, if he never thinks that laying off the pies might make him more attractive than the recitation of a couple of third-rate poems, if he really believes that women will be dazzled by his received opinions about the Copernican Revolution or the Categorical Imperative, then he has only himself to blame.

Since Katy now seemed to be the only one remotely interested in his dreary theories about Mike Oldfield's oeuvre and how *Ommadawn* was musically and structurally a far better album than *Tubular Bells*, the conversation was sub-divided back into its original components. Sean found himself talking to Louise, the dark, compactly sexy woman to his left.

'Not Jewish, are you?' was her first enquiry.

It seemed an odd thing to ask. With her caramel complexion, distinctive features, expensive clothes and jewellery, she could hardly have looked more Jewish without donning a hat, beard and ringlets. Sean would have expected her to check that he *was* Jewish rather than check that he wasn't. 'No,' he smiled. 'I'm not Jewish, and if you ask me nicely I'll prove it.'

Louise laughed.

'Irish Catholic,' said Sean. 'All of the guilt, none of the money.' In his case, of course, it wasn't strictly true.

'Didn't think you were,' she said. 'I just wanted to be sure.'

'Why?'

'Because I don't want another Jewish man. They're the luckiest men on earth but they don't realise or appreciate it.'

Sean raised his eyebrows at her and asked, 'What do you mean?'

'A Jewish man,' Louise explained, 'knows that he was born with a sort of marriage voucher that he can redeem thirty years down the line for the sort of girl who, if they weren't both Jewish, wouldn't have looked at him. Once they're married, her life revolves round him. He always comes first.'

'What?' said Sean. 'Literally?'

Again, Louise laughed. 'All that matters for the woman is to be a good, supportive Jewish wife.'

'Well, what's wrong with that?' said Sean, who would have given anything for Nikki to have been a bit more Jewish.

'It means that North London is full of unfulfilled Jewish women with nothing to do but visit beauty salons, have lunch together, then go and pick the kids up from school.'

'Is that what happened to you?'

'Absolutely. I was only twenty-two. What did I know? Don't get me wrong, my husband wasn't a bad man and, materially at least, he treated me very well but, as I say, it was all about him.'

'All about him?'

'Yeah,' said Louise, with a slightly sour smile. 'It's the old Jewish-husbands-on-pedestals problem.'

'Is it such a problem?' asked Sean.

'For a lot of women, no,' said Louise. 'They saw their mothers put their fathers on pedestals and they do the same with their own husbands because it's so culturally ingrained. Finding a nice Jewish husband, even now, is more important than almost anything else, so wives often boast about how handsome and intelligent their husbands are, even though they know deep down that they're not.'

'Well, they might be,' said Sean, feeling the need to show a bit of solidarity for the men of Hampstead Garden Suburb.

'Of course,' said Louise. 'Sometimes it's genuine but quite often it isn't. I sometimes found myself boasting about how wonderful my husband was so that I didn't feel quite so resentful about his plans always taking priority over mine. I mean, I'm not a selfish person but I got fed up with always having to arrange my life round his work, or whether he was playing squash or golf that weekend. Then, a few years ago, he suddenly got into football. Started going to Arsenal every week. He and his friends have got a box at the new stadium.'

'Very nice,' said Sean, who could think of few things worse than watching his beloved team from a corporate box.

'But they're not proper football fans,' said Louise. 'My granddad would walk from Hackney to Highbury to watch the Arsenal. Not this lot. No, no, they get a driver to take them there and pick them up. They have lunch at a posh Italian restaurant in Islington first. Now they've all started going abroad to watch the Champions League games. Portugal last week, Sweden in a few weeks' time. Do you like football?'

'Well, not really,' Sean lied. 'Anyway, most real fans watch it on a big screen down the pub now.'

'Exactly. That's what he and his friends don't seem to understand.'

'So you've split up?' said Sean.

'Yep. He spends a lot of time in Florida. He's in property and they're building a big apartment complex near Key West. The two girls are at university and I'm now in this gorgeous new flat in Belsize Park.'

'Excuse me,' said Sophie, to everyone, as she got up from the table, proving the point that, even now, approximately 110 per cent of Sloaney females smoke, 'I'm desperate for a fag.'

'In which case,' said Jason, with a particularly queeny giggle, 'I'm your man.'

Watching Jason link his arm with Sophie's as they strolled off to share a cigarette in the mews outside, Sean reflected on the genius of Emma Tate.

She knew that homosexuality, or campness at any rate, tends to transcend any class barrier. Jason's immaculate taste and sense of mischief would appeal to Sophie, as would hers to him. Two unlikely people almost certainly paired off already.

However, there was no one here to set Sean's pulse pounding. Louise had come closest and clearly found him attractive, but he suspected it was largely because he ticked the box marked 'Gentile'. Jewishness was still an issue for her, even in reverse. He really didn't want to go out with someone just so that she could rebel against her background. He remembered the North London Jewish girls of his youth, and how he'd enjoyed providing them with a bit of pre-marital slumming. Post-marital slumming, however, was a different matter.

He was just about to make his excuses and leave when the dessert menu arrived and the irresistible promise of dark Valrhona chocolate parfait with home-made vanilla ice-cream persuaded him to hang on for another ten minutes.

Katy, the girl who'd been bored to sobs by Laurence, had seen Sophie vacate the place next to Sean, and seized her chance to claim it. 'Hi,' she said. 'Sean, isn't it? I'm Katy.'

'Hi,' said Sean. 'So we're the only two people who haven't met.'

'Well, we have now,' said Katy, picking up the dessert menu, 'Ooh, dark chocolate parfait. That sounds like heaven. Got to have one of those.'

'Oh, definitely,' said Sean, who immediately warmed to anyone sharing his almost narcotic addiction to chocolate. 'I hate people who think it's somehow sophisticated to prefer savoury things!'

'Me too,' said Katy. 'Anyone who asks for the cheeseboard should be taken out to the kitchens and shot.'

'Could I see the cheeseboard?' asked Laurence.

She and Sean burst out laughing.

'You wait,' said Katy, quietly, 'he'll have some pompous theory about cheese.'

'Have you ever noticed,' said Laurence, in his irritatingly

magisterial tone, 'how cheese has always been a comedy staple? From Monty Python to Wallace and Grommit.'

'Well,' said Sean, 'John Cleese's real name is John Cheese.'

'Don't be silly. Of course it isn't,' said Laurence, who hated the theft of his thunder.

'Suit yourself.' Sean knew it was true: he'd worked with Cleese many times. His attempt to be friendly to Laurence having been repudiated, he turned back to Katy. 'I can only eat cheese,' he said, 'if it has the word "cake" after it.'

'And preferably the words "double" and "chocolate" in front of it,' she agreed.

'Anyway,' asked Sean, 'what do you do?'

'I'm a florist,' said Katy. 'I've got my own little concession in Harrods, just by the food hall.'

'Well, I'm surprised you're here,' said Sean, and he was. Katy seemed relaxed, intelligent and, the more Sean looked at her, very attractive. 'Flower stall in Harrods? You must spend all day meeting rich, handsome men.'

'I do,' she said, 'all buying flowers for their wives or girl-friends. Not the best place to be when you're single and looking for love.'

She seemed to see humour rather than sadness in this irony, which made Sean warm to her even more.

'How about you?' she said.

'Oh, I'm a voiceover artist, recently split up from my wife.'

'Ooh,' said Katy. 'Did you not buy her flowers on her birthday and Valentine's Day?'

'Never,' said Sean. 'I'd buy them on any day *except* her birthday and Valentine's Day. Too obvious. I'd always try to get her some-thing more original than flowers.'

'Like what?'

'Well,' said Sean, 'vouchers, usually.'

'Vouchers?' laughed Katy, dismissively. 'Like John Lewis vouchers? Who said romance was dead?'

'These were home-made vouchers,' explained Sean.

'And what were they for?'

Sean cast his mind back to the most recent 14th February. 'Um . . . the last one said something like, "This voucher guarantees one lie-in on the day of your choice. I will get up, make the kids' breakfast and take them to school. I will then come home and do whatever you tell me."'

Katy, who had always been motivated by gifts and judged a man by the thought he put into them, looked impressed. 'That's brilliant. So what did you have to do?'

'I spent the day mowing the lawn, cleaning out the shed and taking rubbish down to the tip.'

Katy's face fell. 'Oh,' she said. 'That's not quite what I was expecting.'

'Not quite what I was expecting either,' said Sean, 'which is probably why I'm here.'

Jason and Sophie had returned to the table and were knocking back the Chablis. Loosened up and very lively now, Jason had become Clive's self-appointed style guru. 'Shave it all off, dear,' he said. 'Having a shaven head isn't unusual any more. Back in the day, it was just Telly Savalas and Yul Brynner, but now loads of blokes have their heads shaved.'

Sophie added her own stuff-and-nonsense two-penn'orth. 'Come on, old thing,' she said. 'You've lost your hair, not the use of your limbs. Jason's right. Get rid of the rest. You've got a lovely face – show it off a bit.'

Sean expected Clive's cherry-red head to explode with embarrassment but, oddly, it didn't. 'Do you really think so?' he asked, with a shy smile.

There was an assertive chorus of 'Yes' from round the table and a cheer when he promised he would.

Sean and Katy stopped talking for two minutes while they inhaled their Valrhona chocolate parfaits.

Sean's hitherto rather dreary evening seemed to be ending on a high. The dessert was so good that it was almost sexual, and he really liked Katy. However, as they continued their conversation, she did something to shatter his illusions. 'Look, Sean,' she said, 'I can't bear this any more.'

'Can't bear what?'

'The deceit,' she said. 'You seem like a nice guy so I'm going to level with you.'

Sean was perplexed.

'My name's not Katy and I'm not a florist,' she said.

'Oh.'

'My name's Lucy and I'm the Labour MP for Chelmsford South.'

24

Portcullis House, just along from the Palace of Westminster, was opened in 2001 to provide luxurious offices for two hundred MPs. It remains the most expensive, lavishly appointed office block ever built with public money – £235 million of public money, which many people thought could have been better spent elsewhere.

Gone are the days when MPs took pride in their shabby, cramped offices. The bone-hard chairs and rickety old desks reminded them that their personal comfort took second place to the service of their country. Such altruism had long been abandoned as ambitious, grasping newcomers trampled over one another to grab a berth in Portcullis House. Its spectacular glass-topped atrium, home to £150,000 worth of imported fig trees, made the place look and feel like a luxury hotel.

Jack Dodds and Sir Michael Huntley were both offered, and had both declined, beautiful new offices in 'PCH' with jaw-slackening views along the Thames. Neither wished to be part of what Huntley described as an aloof, élite 'political sect'. He'd had a word in the appropriate ear to secure Lucy a pleasingly quaint little broom cupboard in the old building, with just enough room for her desk, chair, laptop and printer. It overlooked the river, but the tiny round window was so high up that she could only see out of it by standing on tiptoe. It made her feel as if she was in steerage class on the *Titanic*. It was quiet, anonymous and, most important of all, private. On the rare occasions that she went there, no one bothered her. She desperately missed the raucous, bitchy conviviality of the open-plan *Cachet* office, particularly Simon's frequent hissy fits. She'd been back a couple of times but it had saddened her to feel like a prisoner on a home visit.

Simon had sensed that she still wanted to be involved with the magazine, which was why he'd called her the previous week and asked her to do an undercover job, posing as a florist called Katy, to write a piece about Top Table.

Now she was staring at the sturdy old-fashioned phone on her desk, knowing that it would soon ring and also who would be at the other end of the line. 'Hello?' she said, when the inevitable happened.

'Hello, Rossy,' said Simon. 'How did it go last night?'

'It was interesting,' she replied.

'Ooh dear,' he teased. 'Already talking like a politician – not committing yourself either way. Come on, dish the dirt. Was it full of freaks and inadequates?'

'Not really,' was the best Lucy could come up with.

'What *is* this? *Newsnight*? Am I Jeremy fucking Paxman? What was it like?'

'The truth?'

'If you're still capable of it.' He laughed.

'It was a disaster.'

'Why? What did you do?'

'I met the man of my dreams.'

'At a fucking dating agency?' shrieked Simon. 'Blimey, that *is* a disaster!'

'I don't know . . . I can't imagine what he was doing there. He was handsome, funny and had this gorgeous deep voice. You'd have loved him. I only met him right at the end.'

'So you didn't blow your cover?'

'I didn't tell him I was a reporter, but I did tell him my real name and that I'm an MP. He looked so shocked and I felt so stupid that I immediately went to the loo.'

'And when you came back?'

'He'd gone. Obviously thought I was psychotic. Either that or he hates politicians. I wouldn't blame him on either count. He disappeared without a word. It's a real shame. There was something special about him. We only chatted for a few minutes but we had a real rapport going and he was so, so sexy.'

Simon's view was unequivocal. 'Forget him, dear. He's a weirdo. If he's so fucking sexy, what's he doing at a dating agency? At least you had an excuse. Move on and find someone a bit less desperate. Anyway, I need you to file by Tuesday. If you invite me for drinks on the terrace, I might give you till Friday. Toodle-pip.'

Lucy went back to her laptop to organise her surgery. She'd thought she'd have them once a week, but Sheila had told her that Brian Marsden only held them every couple of months, and latterly far less frequently than that. 'If they want me,' he'd apparently said, 'they know where to find me.' He was referring to the law that allows people to turn up without an appointment in the Central Lobby and demand to see their MP. If the MP is in the House, he or she is legally obliged to see them.

For London MPs, it is a frequent occupational hazard. As a general rule, the further the MP's constituency is from Westminster, the less chance there is of receiving uninvited guests. Since quite a high proportion of Lucy's constituents got the eighten every morning from Chelmsford to Liverpool Street, she'd already had two such visits. A phone call from Central Lobby informed her that she had a third and, sure enough, a tall bloke with an Essex accent was waiting for her downstairs. 'Hello,' he said. 'Are you Lucy Ross?'

She nodded.

'You're not actually my MP,' he explained, 'but I'm hoping you might be able to help me.'

Lucy wasn't quite sure what to say and waited for him to continue.

'You see, I've got this table booked for dinner tomorrow night and I need someone to share the home-made toffee soufflé with me.'

With a wink and a grin that turned Lucy's knees to water, the man held out his arms and she fell into them.

As he kissed her cheek, Sean looked up at the powerful image of St George and realised that fortune would always favour the brave.

25

It had been years since Sean had taken a girl on a first date, but his policy remained unchanged: always book somewhere fabulous. He did this not because he was out to impress but because he had no idea how, or even if, he and his date would get on. If she turned out to be dull or disagreeable, at least he had the compensation of a wonderful meal.

Within seconds of Lucy's arrival at Bibendum, he could tell that she would be neither. He knew that they could have sat on a park bench with a cheese roll and a bag of crisps and still had a wonderful time. That might be the second date, but for the first, the venue was perfect. Bibendum is housed in the old art-deco Michelin building in South Kensington, which Sean was not alone in thinking was one of the most beautiful buildings in London.

He loved the décor and the unfussy elegance of the cuisine. He loved the crisp white tablecloths and those heavy, pleasingly expensive wine glasses that go 'ting' for a long time after you've tinged them. He loved the huge Edwardian stained-glass windows that depicted the happy, rotund Michelin man, rather than the miserable suffering martyrs that stained the glass of most churches. Most of all, he loved how he felt when he left the restaurant: exactly like the Michelin man.

He was still thrilled by the simple fact that he was going out to dinner. He'd been out to wonderful restaurants hundreds of times yet the novelty had never worn off. Even the most amateur psychologist could have linked this to his childhood. The Irish are noted for many things but *haute cuisine* is not one of them. Since Sean's early life had been soiled by the stench of fatty bacon, overcooked greens and stewed tea, his adoration of fine dining was understandable.

'I like your boots,' was Lucy's first comment, when Sean stood up to welcome her. He was sporting a pair of black buckskin biker boots that he'd bought years ago in Milan.

'Ah, the contraceptive boots,' he replied, with an emerald-eyed twinkle. 'They take at least twenty minutes to heave on and off, so relax, you're quite safe.'

'Delighted to hear it,' she said. 'Now, look, before we go any further – it's been driving me nuts since you arrived at Desperate Diners. What the hell were you doing there? I have a legitimate excuse. I was covering it for *Cachet* magazine. Tell me you weren't there as an ordinary punter.'

'I wasn't.'

'Thank God for that. What was your excuse?'

'I did the voiceover.'

'What voiceover?'

'Top Table did this radio commercial and I was the voiceover. I did it for free because that Emma's a friend of my agent and she invited me along. I thought, Why not?'

'I could give you lots of reasons,' said Lucy.

'I'm sure you could,' said Sean. 'There were ten round the table.'

'Then you just disappeared,' said Lucy. 'I came back from the loo and you'd gone.'

'I had to do a voiceover.'

'At midnight?'

'ISDN link to Australia. I was having such a laugh with you,' he said, 'that I completely lost track of the time and ended up fifteen minutes late. A load of people were sitting in a studio thirteen thousand miles away, wondering what the hell had happened to me. Sorry about that.'

'No,' she said. 'I'm the one who should be apologising. I made you late.'

'Yeah, but I could at least have left you a note.'

'Well, no you were already late. You had to go.'

This exchange told Sean and Lucy almost everything they needed to know about each other. Both had spent the last few years with partners who were cortically incapable of apologising. Petty people who failed to see that contrition was a sign of strength, not weakness, and demonstrated that your feelings were as important as theirs.

Sean found it so refreshing to be with someone who, instead of insisting that she was *right*, kept insisting that she was *wrong*. He said as much.

'I know,' said Lucy. 'The Catholic compulsion to confess. It never leaves you.'

'Fairly unusual in an MP, though,' said Sean. 'I always thought that once you'd taken your oath of allegiance to the Crown, you then had to take another one promising never to apologise or take responsibility for anything.'

'That's one reason why I'm probably not cut out for it.'

'I imagine,' said Sean, with a laugh, 'that there are quite a few more.'

The waiter arrived with a bottle of white burgundy.

'*Nunc est bibendum*,' said Lucy, as they clinked glasses. 'That's the only bit of Latin I know.'

'Now is the time for drinking,' said Sean. He knew it too.

To experience this kind of easy, familiar raillery in the opening couple of minutes of a first date was extraordinary. Sean felt as though he'd stepped on to the relationship equivalent of an airport walkway. Everything was so quick, smooth and effortless. By contrast, his marriage to Nikki had continually given him that horrible feeling of stepping on to the same walkway, only to find it isn't working any more.

The food, though superb, hardly mattered. All Lucy could see on the menu was a tall, dark-haired man, with kindness, mischief and life experience etched into his handsome, clean-shaven face, and all Sean could see was a ravishing Italian-looking girl whose soft brown eyes were ablaze with fun and curiosity.

For starters, they had each other's childhoods. They'd lived about a mile apart and gone to school across the road from each other, though separated by eight years. Lucy had attended the Virgo Fidelis convent, known to one and all as the Virgin Megastore. Her brother Paul had been three years below Sean at St Vincent's, and Lucy wanted verification of all the tales of Catholic brutality with which Paul had come home.

'All true,' said Sean. 'At St Vincent's, they believed very much in the carrot and the stick, only without the carrot.'

It was about now that he suddenly understood why Jewish people married each other. Between Catholics there were also cultural short-cuts and shared understandings. Sean was a staunch atheist, but he was still ethnically a Catholic and always would be. There was a shared hinterland between him and Lucy, a collection of Catholic references, that pulled them together.

For the main course, they moved on to their early working lives. Lucy explained that after college she'd got a job as a secretary on a women's magazine. Since she'd been born and bred in a delicatessen, she began to write the food pages. Then, because she was younger and sassier than anyone else in the office, which, apparently, hadn't been difficult, she'd become the fashion correspondent and her career had flourished from there. Sean told her about working as a sound engineer and about the commercials he'd voiced.

Lucy drove a Volkswagen Polo, had a Barclaycard and shopped in Harvey Nichols. Sean, in a professional sense, had helped persuade her to do all of these things. Neither dwelt too much on their previous relationships, both keen to avoid the almost audible *boi-yoi-yoi-yoing* of a person on the rebound.

Over pudding, their stories reached the present day. That was where they weren't entirely honest with each other. There was mutual relief that neither had been fully paid-up members of a dating agency. 'God, how desperate! How sad! Imagine having to resort to that.'

The truth was that they'd both gone along in the vague hope

of meeting someone. Lucy was still haunted by a lunchtime trip she'd once made to Asprey's, the famous jeweller's on Bond Street, during a pre-Christmas sale. Unable to resist entering any shop with a sign in the window, saying, '70% *off*', she'd wandered in. Even with 70% off, the diamond rings and bracelets were still eye-wateringly expensive but there was a lovely eighteen-carat white gold bangle that was a little more modestly priced. She planned to drop Adam a heavy hint about it when she got home.

Just as she was leaving the shop, she heard a shy, self-conscious voice say, 'Well, that's my Christmas present to myself.'

She almost couldn't bear to look, knowing exactly what the owner of that voice would look like. Her suspicions were confirmed when she turned and saw what appeared to be a Dunkin' Donut in human form buying herself an expensive piece of jewellery. She felt a lump in her throat at the thought of this poor, unloved woman being left for ever on a very sturdy shelf. She hoped she'd never be in that position.

Instead she talked about her new career and Sean admitted that he had the wrong temperament for politics. He regarded himself as a good, decent and truthful person, who was friendly and affable 99 per cent of the time. However, there was still something of the fighting Irish about him, which exploded to the surface when he was faced with lies, cant or hypocrisy.

'In other words,' said Lucy, 'at least ten times a day.'

They didn't notice that the crowded restaurant had gradually emptied and that for the last half-hour they'd been the only people there. For three hours, they'd held each other's undivided attention and neither could remember being so captivated by another human being. Only a polite word from the manager to inform them that the staff were waiting to go home snapped them back into the real world and elicited a cascade of Catholic contrition.

They wandered out on to the street, and as Lucy looked in vain for a cab, Sean realised that they'd lingered so long over dessert and coffee that if he'd been over the limit he certainly wasn't now. He pointed his plipper at the Mini Cooper and held open the passenger door. Twelve minutes later, having turned Albert Bridge and the back-streets of Battersea into an exhilarating blur of tarmac and lights, he pulled up outside Lucy's flat in Clapham.

'Are you coming in?' she asked.

Sean was surprised at the speed of his reply. 'No, thanks,' he said. He'd realised that if this nascent relationship was to blossom, he didn't want it to happen in a flat she'd shared with an ex-lover, even one who was away filming in Argentina. Anyway, he was wearing the contraceptive boots. He kissed her tenderly on the cheek, then sped off into the night thinking that the naughty car hadn't been that naughty, after all.

26

Sean was happily strolling along a quiet street in Notting Hill when he saw it: a London Borough of Kensington and Chelsea clamping van parked illegally on a double yellow line. Furthermore, it was empty, the windows were wide open and the keys were in the ignition. This was temptation beyond endurance. He'd never get another chance like this. Before he'd had time to think, he'd reached through the open window and taken the keys.

Only then did rational thought rear its panic-stricken head. Oh, God, now what? He wanted to hide round the corner and watch the immobilised wheel-clamper's reaction to getting a taste of his own medicine but looking at the bunch of keys, he was suddenly filled with remorse. He knew that if he saw the clamper, he'd probably try to give him back his keys and end up in a police cell, rather than having a picnic in Holland Park with Lucy. Nobody had seen him do it, so it was best to keep walking.

On the corner of Westbourne Park Road, he spotted a dust-cart and hurled the keys in to be buried in half a ton of domestic refuse. Life didn't get much sweeter than this. And even though Lucy was an MP, he knew he could tell her and she'd laugh, just as he knew that Nikki, the born-again prude, would have told him to grow up, play golf and start gardening.

He paused to buy two hot baguettes, only seconds out of the oven, and a bar of Montezuma organic dark chocolate. Tearing open the hot bread and shoving in a few squares of black chocolate created one of the greatest gastronomic experiences known to man. When he demonstrated the limit of his culinary calibre to Lucy ten minutes later, he knew she'd adore it.

'Oh, my God,' she said, her mouth full, of warm bread and melted chocolate, 'this is divine.'

Lying on the grass, with hot chocolate baguettes and cold white wine, they carried on talking. Lucy told Sean that she had been in the area because she and some other novice MPs with nothing better to do had been sent along to a meeting at the Commonwealth Institute. Nobody knew what to do with a famous listed building that people no longer wanted to visit. Every London child had been taken on a school trip there, but pictures of kangaroos, Canadian Mounties and black people harvesting sugarcane seemed a bit patronising now. The world had moved on.

Looking at Lucy as she spoke, Sean felt like a character in an Agatha Christie book who suddenly works out the identity of the murderer. He was nodding slowly to himself as it dawned on him that Lucy Ross of London, SW4, was 'the one' he'd been trying unwittingly to track down since his voice broke. He was romantic enough to believe that there's someone for everyone. Unfortunately, very few people ever find their true other halves. They think they have, Sean thought he had, but, like so many others, he was wrong. Some people accept that the chance of finding their perfect partners is so remote that they settle for whoever they feel comes closest to their ideal before eventually discovering that it was nowhere near close enough.

As Lucy listened to more true tales delivered in the loveliest voice she'd ever heard, she felt the same way about Sean. Like him, she was a lifelong Arsenal fan and, as he did a perfect impression of Arsene Wenger, she felt as though she was listening to her own personal *Jackanory* and wanted to listen to it for ever.

Sean, without realising it, had made it clear to her that Adam had never been the lid to her dustbin. Sean was the real deal – everything that saps like Adam tried to be, knew they never would be, so spent the rest of their lives over-compensating. She couldn't imagine Adam as a small child going into the Arundel

Arms, just behind Pentonville nick, and asking the landlord to let him have the old Jamaican reggae 45s once the jukebox had finished with them. Neither could she imagine him dressing up in second-hand clothes and first-hand lipstick to go out clubbing with Boy George and Marilyn. She certainly couldn't imagine him getting chased through the back-streets of Bermondsey by the CBL, a notoriously vicious mob of Millwall fans, then hiding under a milk float praying that the milkman was of the *Confessions of* variety, who wouldn't emerge from number twenty-six for at least an hour. Most of all, she couldn't imagine Adam stealing a wheel-clamper's keys and tossing them into the bowels of a dustcart. As long as she could hear Sean's deep, protective voice, she was lost in his world and a million miles from the House of Commons.

'So, how's life as an MP?' he asked, bringing the two worlds together in a sudden, unwelcome collision.

'Hideous.' She shuddered. 'I thought fashion writing was trivial and pointless until I discovered politics.'

'I'd have thought fashion and politics were quite similar,' said Sean, 'trying to rehash old ideas into something people might buy.'

'I suppose they are,' she said, 'but at least with fashion it genuinely doesn't matter and you don't have to hold surgeries to sort out people's problems. I haven't held one yet. I know it's unforgivable but I just can't bring myself to do it.'

'Why not?'

'Because I don't know anything.' She sighed. 'There is, famously, no job description for an MP. You have to make it up as you go along. In no other walk of life are you expected to be taken seriously on subjects you know nothing about.'

'Well, don't you have people to help you?'

'Local Party members, and they're the worst of all possible worlds. They're very boring and not terribly bright but they're all politically motivated. All they do is advise me on what the Party expects me to do, regardless of whether or not it's right. I just don't know what to do.'

To Sean, the answer was obvious, so he told her and such was her delight at his suggestion that she leapt up from the picnic blanket and kissed him for the very first time.

The kiss lasted eight and a half minutes.

27

Sean hadn't been frightened of entering rough, unfamiliar pubs since his brother Martin had taught him how to 'time his stare'. 'About four seconds,' was Martin's recommendation. 'Just long enough to show that you're not afraid but you're not looking for trouble. Any less and they'll know you're scared and you may well get a hiding. Any more and they'll think you're cocky and you'll definitely get a hiding. Four seconds. No more, no less.'

This sound advice had ensured that Sean remained inviolate wherever he went, and although it was no longer necessary, old habits die hard.

The four-second stare certainly wasn't necessary at the Rose and Crown on a Sunday lunchtime. 'The Rose' was a huge, rambling pub just outside Chelmsford, popular with locals and visitors alike. A public house is still a house, and what matters most is the person running it. The Rose was, first and foremost, Roy Webb's house and he was very much the guv'nor. Roy was George Webb's brother but unlike George the honest, upright greengrocer, Roy was a bit of a rogue. His grey hair wasn't as closely clipped as his brother's and his Marbella tan, chunky gold jewellery and duty-free cologne betrayed a classic splash of Essex vanity. Despite appearances Roy wasn't a villain, but as he and Sean shook hands Sean saw the tell-tale hardness behind the eyes that suggested he didn't scare easily. Even though he was nearly sixty, Roy Webb looked like a man who could still hold his hands up.

Behind the huge bar a gallery of photos chronicled Roy's thirty-odd years in the pub game. There were pictures of him shaking hands with, among others, Henry Cooper, Vinnie Jones,

Barbara Windsor and Rod Stewart. His personality – big, warm and garrulous – was reflected in the atmosphere at the Rose. He took pride in its place as the centre point for the community, which was why George had thought that the back room would be the ideal venue for Lucy's surgeries.

The place was packed, largely with families sitting down to the Rose and Crown's famous Sunday roast. The huge joints of beef, lamb and pork were served with fresh garden vegetables, and Lucy couldn't understand how Roy could charge so little and still make a profit. 'I know George supplies the veg,' she said to him, 'but all this gorgeous meat?'

'My eldest boy's a porter at Smithfield,' he replied.

No further questions, Your Honour.

Sean, who never did anything if he felt someone else could do it better, had been kissed passionately in the park for suggesting that Lucy enlist the help of people who knew nothing about politics but everything about something.

Roy tapped a big pint glass and called for a bit of hush. 'Ladies and gentlemen,' he announced, 'as you know, we've been happy to host all sorts of events at the Rose and Crown over the years, but it's my pleasure to be hosting the pub's very first constituency surgery. So, please welcome your MP, my MP, our MP, Lucy Ross.'

Lucy stood up to a round of applause and joined Roy at the bar. 'Thank you, Roy,' she said, 'and thank you for letting us use the Rose and Crown for our first surgery. Okay, my name's Lucy and, as an MP, I'm supposed to know everything and help all of you with whatever problems you may have. Of course, I don't, which is why I've enlisted the help of a group of volunteers who do. Sheila here will note the nature of your enquiry and direct you to the relevant adviser.'

The expert advisers were seated behind small tables, like teachers at parents' evening, ready to dispense wisdom on their chosen subjects. Bruno and Ella Ross, (managing a small business and home economics respectively), George Webb (gardening),

Father Sal (spiritual and religious guidance), Darren Crook (building and DIY) and Karen Fisher (relationships) had been first to arrive. They were soon followed by legal, medical and financial specialists, whom Lucy, Karen and Sean had managed to find between them. Sean had persuaded Max, his accountant, to come along since he only lived ten minutes away. 'And, Max,' he'd said, 'don't forget the ruler.'

Max Engelsman always used a plastic ruler to demonstrate his policy on tax avoidance. 'You can bend the rules,' he'd say, bending the ruler almost double, 'but you must never break them.' For Max, accountancy wasn't a job: it was a vocation, A game of financial chess that he played five days a week with the taxman. Max was a grand master and considered it his sworn duty to deny the government every penny he could without breaking the plastic ruler. Given his loathing of taxation, he had been reluctant to help an MP until Sean explained that she was far from typical and disliked the government even more than he did.

'Okay,' said Lucy. 'Any questions?'

A lot of people were filing into the main bar to watch the football live on Sky. It was Arsenal v. West Ham. The overwhelming number of claret and blue shirts made it obvious that the Rose and Crown, like most of Essex, was West Ham territory.

'Who do you support, then?' asked a fan who, instead of hair, had a claret and blue tattoo on his head.

There were three possible answers. The first was the lie: 'West Ham.'

The second was the politician's reply: 'I'm here to support my constituents.'

Lucy heard herself bravely opting for number three: 'I'm from Clerkenwell,' she said, 'a couple of miles from Highbury, so – I've got to be honest – I'm Arsenal through and through.'

This elicited a chorus of boos and hisses, but Lucy could see, from the expressions that accompanied them, that they were good-natured ones.

Sean had told her that, sooner or later, she would be asked this question and it would be best to tell the truth. Real football fans, he said, always prefer other real football fans who are proud to support their own teams to phoneys who pretend to support other people's. When the prime minister had won his seat in the north-east of England, he had suddenly claimed to be a lifelong Newcastle fan. The Toon Army, not quite as gullible as he'd thought, quite rightly despised him for it.

New Labour apparatchiks had never understood football and the fans who follow it. 'Fan', they seemed to forget, is short for 'fanatic', and football fanatics are passionate, tribal and extremely knowledgeable about the beautiful game. Although Geoff Hurst was a hero to the West Ham fanatics in the Rose and Crown, they still hated the way the government had suddenly knighted him thirty-two years after his hat-trick had helped England win the World Cup.

Sir Geoffrey would be the first to admit that, as a player, he was never in the same league as Bobby Charlton or Jimmy Greaves. Since his playing days had ended, he'd worked in insurance and contributed almost nothing to the world of football for twenty years. He must have been delighted, yet slightly embarrassed, when the MBE he'd been awarded shortly after England's triumph was lavishly upgraded to a knighthood.

Having soared in the regulars' estimation for showing herself to be a genuine football fan, Lucy rose even further by explaining that there was a drink on the house for anyone waiting to see either her or her team of experts, courtesy of the credit card that Sean had left behind the bar.

The warm, friendly atmosphere of the Rose and Crown made a welcome change for the people of Chelmsford South from the cold, empty silence of the run-down village hall in which they had waited for Brian Marsden to see them on the rare occasions he had deigned to hold a surgery.

Lucy's unorthodox surgeries took place once a fortnight and quickly became so popular that tickets had to be booked in advance. Originally scheduled to last from three thirty until seven, she never got away before ten thirty. One night, having dealt with yet another complaint about the local council, she turned to Sheila with a slow, weary exhalation. 'Well, that's it for another fortnight,' she said.

'Not quite,' said Sheila.

'Oh, please! Don't tell me we've got any more.'

'Just the one,' said Sheila.

'Who?'

'Me.'

28

Mrs Sheila Webb explained the problem to her MP. 'It's the shops. You know, King's Parade,' she said. 'The council have suddenly put in parking restrictions all along the main road and along most of the side-streets. Completely unnecessary. They say it's to help the flow of the traffic but there's no problem with traffic, never has been. It's just a money-making exercise. Isn't that right, George?'

George, usually so calm, reasonable and articulate, was almost mute with rage. 'My takings are down about forty per cent since it happened,' he muttered, 'but it's not me I'm so worried about. It's Mark.'

Sheila took over: 'Mark had a few problems over the years, you know, drugs and whatnot, but thanks to that record shop, he's really sorted himself out. He's a lovely boy, and I don't know what I'd do if it all went wrong for him again.'

Her eyes brimmed with tears and George stepped in: 'He was really making something of himself. That shop was doing so well. It was great to see him so happy again. He'd found a gap in the market. I mean, you never see proper record shops any more so people were coming from miles away. Well, they won't come if they can't park, will they?'

'Was there a consultation process?' asked Lucy.

Sheila and George looked at each other blankly, and something about their impotence in the face of authority made Lucy realise that she had an important job to do.

For all their toughness, confidence and bravado, working-class people are easily pushed around. Lucy's smart part of Clapham was full of awkward lawyers, journalists and commissioning editors from the BBC. The council there wouldn't have dared try anything like this, and even if they did, the residents would have them for breakfast.

Out here, the residents were a soft target and greedy councils knew it. They would grumble and moan a bit but would still take it on the chin with a 'That's life. What can you do?' sort of fatalism. Ultimately they still doffed their caps to the powers-that-be, which made Lucy wild. Suddenly she could see how dictatorships got started and vowed that her constituents were not going to be bullied like this.

'Trouble is,' said George, 'we can't do nothing about it.'

'You're absolutely right,' said Lucy, also calm, but steely and determined. 'We can't do nothing. And we're not going to do nothing.' She recalled Edmund Burke's famous maxim: 'All that is required for evil to triumph is for good men to do nothing.' At that moment, she realised that 'shopping' was not such a trivial subject. In its own way it was every bit as important as education or the health service. At last she had a subject serious enough for her long overdue maiden speech.

29

One of the advantages of having the letters 'MP' after your name is that it loosens the locks on many doors that would otherwise remain firmly closed, so when Lucy made a request to see Graeme Todd, leader of the council, it was immediately granted.

'Lucy, hi, good to meet you,' said a squidgy, unattractive creature in his forties with a face like runny cheese and the nervous expression of a man who fears he may have left the gas on.

Graeme Todd was in awe of Lucy and, indeed, any Member of Parliament. It was what he'd always wanted to be. Despite a career in local government dating back to the day he'd left school, despite putting himself forward on five separate occasions, he had never been selected to stand for Parliament. Accepting failure, he realised that by staying in local government, he could enjoy a much easier life and end up wielding a lot more power. As leader of the council, he could now park himself behind a big oak desk in a huge corner office on the first floor of the brand new civic centre.

His hand was moist and Lucy found herself looking for a tissue to wipe hers after shaking it.

'So what brings you here?' Graeme was one of those rare people who look worse when they smile. His unappealing beam accentuated the fact that his face didn't seem to have any edges.

'No reason. I just wanted to drop by and see if there's anything I can do to help you.'

Graeme wasn't sure how to take this. On the one hand he

would welcome some extra funding from Westminster, but on the other he was leader of the council and didn't want his authority undermined. Therefore, his answer, 'Well, that's a very good question,' was typically non-committal. Over the next ten minutes, he used an awful lot of words to say absolutely nothing.

It almost wasn't his fault. Like many people in local government, he wouldn't have lasted five minutes in the real world, unprotected by the fully funded feather bed of the public sector. Denying himself an honest opinion and the constant evasion of accountability were now second nature to Graeme Todd. Local government, Lucy had come to realise, was often a good place to train or gain experience at the beginning of your career. Those, like Graeme, who hadn't moved on and had somehow risen to the top of the tree were often the worst of the original intake. Only that morning, she had seen a job with the borough council advertised in the local paper. They were looking for a strategic energy and sustainability co-ordinator to report to the head of Strategic Sourcing to ensure that sustainability was a key priority. The successful applicant would be responsible for procurement in accordance with best-value and take-forward partnership, developing the corporate framework in relation to the agreed sustainability objectives. Knowing that Graeme presided over such nonsense, it was difficult to take him seriously.

Whatever he was saying was translated when it reached Lucy's ears to 'Blah, blah, blah, blah, blah.' 'Graeme,' she wanted to say, 'I've been having trouble sleeping lately. Would you mind coming round tonight, sitting on the end of my bed and talking to me? I'm sure I'll nod off in no time.'

After a further ten minutes, during which she vaguely remembered hearing the words 'outreach co-ordinator', Lucy steered the conversation round to the King's Parade parking restrictions. 'Nothing to do with me,' he said, rather too quickly, spreading those pudgy palms outwards. 'Parking in the borough has been outsourced to a company called Parkfair. You'd need to speak to them about that.'

'Who outsourced it?'

'Well, we did.'

'We?'

'The council made an executive decision,' he said smoothly and fluently, like an actor who'd learned his lines. 'We felt that parking in the borough could be run more efficiently by outside contractors and the money we received for that contract could be put to good use in improving education and social services. Do you have a problem with that?'

'Not personally,' said Lucy, 'but one or two shopkeepers have said that it's destroying their businesses and playing right into the hands of the supermarkets.'

'King's Parade,' he said, 'is an anachronism. People don't want to go to those silly little shops with their stupid names. This isn't London. Neither is it a picturesque village in Suffolk. This is Essex. This is Homebase Heartland. People here are a bit sharp, a bit savvy. They love a hypermarket, the bigger the better. They're not interested in whether a shop is independently run. They just want the best stuff at the best price, all under one roof, if possible.'

'I take your point,' said Lucy. 'It just seems a bit spiteful to put in those parking restrictions and hurt people's businesses.'

'Well, as I say, it's nothing to do with me. Parkfair have the contract, so you'd need to take it up with them.' Apparently sensing that the conversation was taking an awkward turn and he might, God forbid, be held accountable for something, Graeme stood up in that well-it's-been-lovely-talking-to-you-but-I'm-a-very-busy-man sort of way. 'Anyway,' he said, 'no one's interested in King's Parade any more. I mean, look at you – you won't even have your Party HQ there.'

Lucy had disagreed with practically every word Graeme had uttered – those she could remember – but his last remark had been uncomfortably accurate. How could she talk about saving King's Parade when even she had abandoned it?

Without knowing it, the cheese-faced cretin had been more help than he'd ever realise.

30

'Okay,' said Sean. 'That's very good. Bit hesitant at the beginning of the third para. And you can't afford to be hesitant. Once more from the top.'

Lucy was the first, last and only person to have been invited into the voice booth in Sean's flat. Nobody in London, apart from Chelsea Jon, even knew that he had an ISDN link and fully equipped studio. He lived five minutes from all the Soho sound studios, so he had no cause to use it for UK work. It was strictly for overseas jobs. If word got out that his spare room was also home to a fully equipped Dolby-approved mixing desk, he'd be a multi-millionaire but a very unhappy one. He could think of few things worse than having his home and privacy invaded by a constant stream of Matts and Jezes wanting urgent recordings done in the middle of the night.

However, he'd made an exception for Lucy. Since attending her Sunday surgeries at the Rose and Crown, Sean had realised that the skills he possessed were fairly useless to society at large. He'd watched others dispensing vital, practical advice but no constituent's problem would ever be solved by a man whose area of expertise was talking in a really deep voice.

His brilliance as a sound engineer, however, was now being used to help Lucy prepare her maiden speech. He'd advised her to print it off in big, legible type so she'd never have to squint. 'Also,' he'd said, 'leave the bottom halves of the pages blank. That way, you're not glancing down too much, which always looks shifty.' He taught her how to breathe properly and how to ensure that she always had enough puff to reach the end of a paragraph. He showed her the importance of proper punctuation and rhetorical pauses. He told her to underline or italicise words that required more emphasis and shared with her the significance of 'eyebrow'. This was his word for that slightly sardonic delivery he'd learnt from working with wry, intelligent performers like Angus Deayton, Robert Bathurst and Michael Fenton-Stevens.

He told her it was all about rhythm. The reason people laugh, despite themselves, at Bernard Manning or Jim Davidson is because, however vile their material, these comics are experienced professionals who know how to time a gag. It's not so much the gag itself that makes people laugh, but the rhythm with which it's told. All speech has a tune and we know instinctively whether words, like music, are accurately pitched.

Sean, a speaker by trade, had to show Lucy, a writer, the difference between written and spoken English. What looks right when it's written doesn't necessarily sound right when it's spoken. Words have to be added or taken away for reasons of rhythm and cadence.

Above all, he stressed the golden rule: take care of the sense and the sounds will take care of themselves.

After a couple of hours, take twenty-three ended. 'Thank you, Mr Speaker, for allowing me to make my maiden speech.'

Lucy was now pitch perfect and realised that Chelmsford South wasn't the only thing she had grown to love. By inducting her into the tricks of the trade, by showing her that great orators can be taught as well as born, and by convincing her that public speaking was nothing to be afraid of, Sean had made her love him by helping her to love herself.

It was her first visit to his flat and she adored it – the enormous sofas, the even more enormous TV and the immaculate kitchen, which was only immaculate because Sean never used it. To him cooking was just another form of DIY and the process of preparing food somehow diminished the pleasure of eating it.

As if to prove his point, the buzzer sounded and a waiter from the Korean restaurant on Broadwick Street arrived with a sizzling feast for two.

After eating her half of it, Lucy was surprised to discover how tired she was. 'Oh, I can't be bothered to talk any more,' she said, stretching out on the sofa. 'Tell me some more stories.'

With her head cradled in his left arm, Sean used his right to balance the laptop on his knee. Scrolling through to find the right tracks, Sean decided to augment his tales with a sound-track. 'Let me start,' he said, 'by playing you the first record I ever remember hearing,' and clicked on the Dubliners singing 'The Wild Rover'. He moved on to the chunky Jamaican reggae of 'The Whip' by the Ethiopians: 'I loved reggae and I always wanted to be a skinhead. I still do, but I think I might be mistaken for either a neo-Nazi or a homosexual . . .'

'This was the first record I ever bought,' he said, scrolling down to 'Virginia Plain' by Roxy Music, 'down in Ridley Road Market, but I sort of ruined it by asking for "Roxy Music" by Virginia Plain.'

He went through a dewy-eyed journey of seventies and eighties soul, funk and reggae and was rocking accordingly: Trinity's 'Three Piece Suit', Stevie Wonder's 'Higher Ground', then Skipworth and Turner's 'Thinking About Your Love'. Side Effect's rare groove classic 'Always There', however, was a bridge too far. He couldn't sit still any longer. 'What's the matter?' said Lucy. 'I'm loving all this. Where are you going?'

Sean was dancing and, Lucy couldn't help noticing, he danced rather well. Grooving around in his old-skool Adidas trainers he moved with an enviable rhythm that suggested to her that she was watching an inveterate clubber who'd done this sort of thing before.

'Sorry,' said Sean, whose legs had taken on a life of their own. 'I think it might be a class thing.'

'What might be a class thing?'

'Dancing. You see, working-class people,' he explained, 'have to participate. They – I mean we – have no concept of passive appreciation. We weren't entertained by books or visits to art galleries. We have to be involved. That's why football has lost a lot of its old appeal. It's no fun if you're forced to sit down. Same with music – we don't sit down to enjoy it. We don't analyse or discuss it, we take part. Keane can't compare to karaoke. Even slow music demands some sort of participation.'

'Which is?'

'You know the answer to that,' said Sean.

'Play some, then,' said Lucy.

Sean scrolled down to find the slow-dance favourites of his youth and the room filled with the unmistakable intro from the Chi-Lites' 'Have You Seen Her?' followed by Aaron Neville's 'Tell It Like It Is' and Al Green's 'How Do You Mend A Broken Heart?' By this time, just as he always had at Islington youth-club discos, Sean was kissing the most beautiful girl in the place.

This was what he'd wanted. This was what his heart, soul and body had missed. He should have been a bit nervous. Just a bit. This was, after all, the first time in twelve years that he'd become truly intimate with anyone other than his wife. He thought that stage fright might soften his ardour, but it didn't. It just seemed a natural extension, in every sense of the word, of their deep and flourishing friendship. They'd got what they wanted and they wanted what they'd got. After a slow, gentle, almost polite start, Sean and Lucy made love with a passion and prowess that both had almost forgotten they possessed.

Although Sean had only danced for seconds, Lucy had seen enough to get slightly hot. People with good rhythm when they're upright have even better rhythm when they're not.

Lying back afterwards, they fell into the embarrassed reticence of two people who cannot quite believe the things they've just been doing.

Sean glanced at the Adidas trainers he had thrown across the room in frenzied abandon, then broke the silence: 'See what happens,' he said, 'when I don't wear the contraceptive boots.'

31

The rule is the same for all MPs: you're not allowed to speak in the House of Commons until you've delivered your maiden speech. Lucy was the only MP in the country yet to deliver one. She'd been in denial, ashamed and embarrassed by her new career. She'd clung to the ridiculous belief that if she didn't make a speech then she wasn't really an MP. Now, having met Sean and caught some of his contagious confidence, she was finally ready to do her duty.

She arrived for her weekly lunch in the Commons canteen with Huntley and Dodds, the only part of the job she enjoyed.

'So, Wednesday, then?' said Huntley, as he sat down.

'How do you know?' she said, having given up all hope of unmasking his nark.

He just chuckled, winked and tapped the side of his nose.

'Wednesday?' said Dodds. 'What about it?'

'I'm making my maiden speech.'

'About bloody time.'

She'd brought two copies and handed one to each man. 'If you wouldn't mind giving it the once-over,' she said, 'I'd be very grateful.'

Both men took out reading glasses and began to scan the pages.

'Ee, it's good, is this,' said Dodds. 'Just the sort of speech the House needs.'

'Yes, it is,' agreed Huntley. 'It makes a number of interesting points. Have you shown it to the Whips' Office?'

'Not yet,' she replied.

'Thought not,' said Dodds, flatly, 'because they won't let you say any of it.'

'Why not?' she almost wailed. 'There's nothing rude, untrue or defamatory in it.'

'I know, love,' he replied, 'but you've heard all the other maiden speeches, haven't you?'

Lucy nodded.

'They're just polite, insubstantial waffle,' said Huntley, 'paying tribute to your predecessor and prattling on about your constituency, reeling off a few statistics, then thanking the Speaker for allowing you to make your maiden speech.'

'I thought they might want to hear something a bit more interesting.'

Dodds shook his head sagely and cynically. 'Not this lot. It's all changed since our day. All that matters is conformity.'

'So that means I'm going to have to start all over again and that I've wasted all this time?'

'Yes,' said Huntley.

'And no,' said Dodds.

They looked at her enigmatically.

'I don't understand,' she said. 'What do you mean?'

'Well,' said Huntley, 'you'll have to write a new maiden speech. Short, dull, uncontroversial, just like all the others, then get the Whips' Office to approve it.'

'Then?' asked Lucy.

'Tear it up,' laughed Dodds, 'and make your original speech.'

'Can I do that?'

'Well, that depends,' said Huntley, 'on whether you want a career in the Labour Party.'

'I don't.'

'In that case, go ahead. As you say, there's nothing untrue or defamatory in there. You'll simply be in breach of parliamentary procedure. They'll hate it, but ultimately there's nothing they can do. They're not going to lock you up in the Tower.'

'Has anyone else ever done this?'

'I can only remember one chap,' grinned Huntley. 'Must have

been about thirty-five years ago. Can't remember his name now . . .'

Lucy stared at Dodds. 'Was it you?'

'Aye,' he admitted. 'I used my maiden speech to tell Ted Heath that the miners were going to bring down his government. We bloody did an' all.'

'Thing is,' said Huntley, 'it's far easier to pull this sort of stunt if you're in opposition. You can oppose in poetry, but you have to govern in prose. Your party's in government and they'll never forgive you.'

Lucy shrugged like an impudent teenager. 'Am I bovvered?'

From the blank looks on their faces, it was clear that neither Dodds nor Huntley had ever seen *The Catherine Tate Show*. 'That's the spirit,' said Dodds, 'but seriously, one last time, are you sure you don't ever want to rise within the Party?'

'Absolutely sure,' said Lucy. 'I'll serve my time, then I'm off.'

'Okay,' said Huntley, 'as long as you know that, by doing this, you'll be committing political suicide.'

32

'I follow the Honourable Member for Wigan North, who will understand if I do not debate the excellent points that he made in his speech. I congratulate all Honourable Members and Honourable Friends who have made their maiden speeches.'

So far, so good. An ancient parliamentary tradition meant that no one ever heckled or interrupted a maiden speech. Yet the very politeness of that silence can be hugely intimidating. Lucy, thanks to constant practice in a soundproof voice booth, was not fazed. Oddly, she found the echoey resonance of the chamber quite reassuring. Those practice sessions had been invaluable, especially the way Sean had shown her how to take both the treble and the tremble out of her voice, pitch it down and keep it even. Oh, well, she thought, when I get chucked out of Parliament in about ten minutes' time, I can always make a living doing 0898 phone calls.

'Now, Mr Speaker,' she said, 'let's talk shopping.'

The weary old cynics who had been preparing for a snooze suddenly decided to pay attention. Shopping? What on earth was this girl on about?

'Napoleon famously described the British as a nation of shop-keepers. He meant it as an insult but we took it as a compliment, a tribute to our courage, our industry and our spirit of enterprise. The fact is, we like shopping. All human beings do. Show me a woman – in fact, show me a man who says he doesn't and I'll show you a fibber.

'To say you don't like shopping is to say you don't like anything that the world has to offer. To say you don't like shopping is to say that you don't like anyone enough to buy them a gift. To say you don't like shopping, Mr Speaker, is to say you don't like life.

'I can, however, understand why some people *think* they don't like shopping. I can understand how its inherent joys and delights are being slowly destroyed. Town centres in Britain are becoming almost interchangeable, the same shops selling the same things from Exeter to Edinburgh. One huge, soulless supermarket is much like another. The most pleasurable shops to visit are the small independent ones, the ones that this House is allowing to be wiped off the map.

'In my own constituency of Chelmsford South, we're very lucky. We still have a much-loved selection of small shops known as King's Parade. These little shops have served the local community since 1929. They have no trouble competing with the multiples because they offer something priceless: friendliness, diversity and service. We have a butcher and a baker, but sadly no candlestick-maker.

'When I say they have no trouble, I should have said they *had* no trouble because, lately, it's all gone horribly wrong.

'For some reason, Chelmsford Borough Council has introduced draconian parking restrictions and squads of wardens to enforce them. This means that some of those shops may soon have to close, robbing the area of its character, its history and its culture. By doing this, the council are playing straight into the hands of the big supermarkets.

'Mr Speaker, I would be happy to bet that a great many Honourable Members and Honourable Friends have the same problem in their constituencies.

'So what are we going to do about it? The majority of local authorities are Labour-controlled. This is a Labour government. A government that, I'd like to think, takes a dim view of such ruthless profiteering.

'If you regard yourself as a socialist, surely you don't want to see the small community shopkeeper crushed by the might of the multiples. And if you are a capitalist, you don't want to see freedom of enterprise killed off by bullying local authorities.

'In destroying our freedom to shop, they are destroying, in no small way, our freedom to live. That's how important shopping is to each and every one of us. We've all been sent to Westminster to represent our communities, to try to improve the lives of others and to stand up to those who want to take our basic freedoms away. So why aren't we doing that? Isn't it good, once in a while, to forget our political differences and come together for something on which all sides of the House agree?

'Let me return to Napoleon. He tried to destroy this "nation of shopkeepers" but he failed. It's up to us to ensure that greedy local authorities never, ever succeed.

'Thank you, Mr Speaker, for allowing me to make my maiden speech.'

That was when the silence, all three seconds of it, became intimidating. That was when she thought she was going to be sick, and that was when Huntley and Dodds saved her.

'Bravo,' shouted Huntley, and began to clap. On the other side of the House, Dodds went further, rising to his feet to applaud her. More Tories joined in, delighted to discover that not every new Labour MP was a fawning toady. There were a lot of bruised shins among the fawning toadies as they kicked themselves for being so cravenly compliant in their own maiden speeches. They certainly didn't want to applaud but, noticing a number of their more senior colleagues clapping politely, they felt they had no choice but to join in.

The chief whip, seething at having been duped, had been preparing to instigate disciplinary proceedings against the Honourable Member for Chelmsford South until he noticed the prime minister clapping politely. Ever the opportunist, the chief whip now saw the chance to take the credit for allowing an unusually independent maiden speech.

Of course, Lucy's intention had been to bring the plight of local shopkeepers to the attention of Parliament. She was also rather hoping to incur the wrath of the chief whip and be cast into political oblivion. And here she was being applauded by the prime minister, the home secretary and the chancellor of the exchequer.

Another grand plan had spectacularly backfired.

33

In the end, it made no difference. Despite the congratulatory messages, letters of support and ministerial applause, the parking restrictions around King's Parade remained rigorously enforced. The council had sold the responsibility for parking in the borough to a private contractor, whose sole purpose was to make as much money as possible. Although what the company was doing might be viewed as immoral, it wasn't illegal. They had given statutory notice of their plans in the local paper but it had been so deliberately sheathed in legalese that nobody had noticed. Confronted by a page of dense type in which the first line includes the words 'hereby' and 'sub-section' very few people would be tempted to read on.

Though disappointed, Lucy felt she'd had her fifteen minutes of fame and she'd thoroughly enjoyed it. She'd been profiled by the *Independent on Sunday* and realised a lifetime's ambition by sitting on the sofa with Richard and Judy. Now all she wanted to do was sit on the sofa with Sean. She was stretched out, watching TV, while he prepared dinner in the kitchen. This involved unwrapping 'cod and chips twice', then adding salt and vinegar. 'Great British tradition,' he said, bringing it through, served in paper rather than on plates.

'Invented by the Italians,' she said.

'What are you talking about?' said Sean, as he munched into the thick, milky cod and perfectly crisp, dry batter.

'The so-called British national dish was invented by the Italians,' said Lucy. 'Father Sal told me.'

'Didn't he also tell you about a man who was crucified on a Friday and rose from the dead two days later?'

'You can mock,' she laughed, 'but it's true. Some relative of his – it might have been his grandfather's cousin or something – had an ice-cream stall on Farringdon Road and, to whet the customers' appetites, the wife would deep-fry tiny pieces of salty fish and thin strips of potato. The fish and chips quickly became more popular than the ice-cream and that was how it all started.'

'In that case . . .' said Sean, and he disappeared into the kitchen to prepare the second part of the supper. This meant taking a tub of Morelli's authentic Italian *gelato* from the freezer, then leaving it to soften.

'You know, Jack Dodds was right,' said Lucy, screwing up the chip papers, then getting up to put them into the bin. 'Today's front pages are tomorrow's fish-and-chip wrappers.'

'Does that bother you?'

'No,' said Lucy. 'God, I don't want to be famous but I am a bit disappointed. I naïvely thought I could make a difference. I really believed I could save those shops along King's Parade.' She sat down again and snuggled a little closer to Sean so that they could spoon ice-cream into each other's mouths.

'How are the plans for converting Party HQ back into a real shop?'

'In a word,' she said, 'fucked. No one in their right minds is going to open a shop there now they've put in all these parking restrictions.'

'Yeah,' said Sean, 'but you could turn it into a charity shop.'

Lucy grimaced. Charity shops, however noble their aims, were roundly despised by serious retail enthusiasts. Instead of bringing a splash of style and verve to an area, they tended to drag in a dispiriting cloud of desperation. The only ones Lucy had visited were run by worthy old ladies selling belted safari jackets and green polyester skirts to raise money for the local hospice. The shops were invariably hospices themselves for half-read airport novels and chipped china ornaments. 'No,' she said, recalling sad shelves of dead, flattened shoes. 'I couldn't bear it.'

'Not just any old charity shop,' said Sean. 'According to Darren

– and he should know because he lives there – they love a car-
boot sale in Essex. Make it like a car-boot sale in a shop.'

'What do you mean?'

'Well, you just book it out, like a church hall, for a couple of
weeks at a time, to whichever charity wants it. They take it as
it is, with whatever happens to be in there and whatever gets
brought in while it's their turn, and they then get to keep whatever they make. Only thing you'd have to look for, I suppose, is
people unloading hooky gear or hiding drugs in the sleeves of
the Leo Sayer albums. Then, after a couple of weeks, someone
else has a turn.'

The more Lucy thought about it, the more feasible it seemed.
It would appeal to Sheila, whose friends all seem to do some
sort of voluntary work. As a short-term boost for a fundraising
appeal, what could be better than a charity shop that you could
'borrow'? 'You're a genius,' she said to Sean, and fed him another
spoonful of Italian ice-cream. 'That is such a good idea.'

Sean smiled with genuine surprise. It had come to him out of
nowhere, but as he and Lucy ran over it, it became apparent that,
yes, it might work.

As he smiled, a little of the ice-cream ran down his chin.
Putting down her spoon, Lucy removed it with her tongue and
put it back in Sean's mouth where it belonged.

Within seconds, this led to a bout of ferocious carnal activity,
culminating in Lucy panting, 'Yes, yes, yes.'

Sean had a feeling that this may not have been the result of
a glorious orgasm. 'Yes what?' he asked.

'I've thought of a name for the shop.'

'What?'

'Junk and Disorderly.'

Sean laughed. Now it was his turn to say 'Yes, yes, yes'.

34

Lucy had always lived for the moment. She never thought too much about the future and had the credit-card bills to prove it. This was probably why Stuart Brunning, parliamentary secretary to the Foreign and Commonwealth Office, had the uncanny ability to make her flesh creep. With his neat greasy hair, Parker pen clipped into his breast pocket and glasses that wore him rather than the other way round, Brunning embodied everything that Lucy never wanted to be. He could never relax and enjoy the present. Before he was even out of the sixth form this grasping, unappealing little hack had wanted to be a local councillor. As a local councillor, he had wanted to be an MP. Having achieved that, he now wanted to be a junior minister, then he'd want to be a minister, then Prime Minister, then international statesman . . . Like so many of his ilk, Brunning possessed that extra ounce of ambition that isn't quite sane which was why Lucy felt rather sorry for him.

If you can't enjoy the present, how can you ever be happy? Surely there are times when you have to appreciate the moment. If you're relaxing in the sun on an idyllic palm-fringed beach or receiving oral sex from a gorgeous and selfless partner, why would you even be thinking about the future?

Brunning reminded Lucy of Dawn Weller, who was in her class at the Virgo Fidelis. Not physically – Brunning resembled the 'before' in a 'before and after' ad for a bodybuilding course while Dawn had looked like an East German shot-putter. She was a frighteningly good swimmer, who trained unstintingly every morning at Finchley baths and swam for the London Borough of Barnet against the best that Lewisham, Hounslow or Hackney could offer. Yet despite a shelf full of trophies and a neck full of medals, Dawn Weller was never going to make the Olympics, so why had she bothered? Why had she sacrificed so much of her youth just to become Southern Area 200-metres backstroke champion? All she'd gained were an enormous pair of shoulders and the vague but ever-present smell of chlorine.

Brunning, likewise, was never going to become a household name. He lacked the intellect and charisma to go all the way, yet he doggedly persisted in his slow climb up the greasy pole until, before he was even half-way up, he would have to accept that he was sliding back down again.

He saw Lucy as a rising star in the Party and mistakenly believed that her casual insouciance was just a brilliantly contrived façade. He felt that her upward ascent might soon overtake his and that she could therefore be a useful political ally.

He'd left her a message to see him at his office in Portcullis House at two thirty.

'Ah, Lucy,' he said, ushering her towards the small sofa that he had grovelled so hard to acquire. 'Sit down. Now, I'm sure you know about the fact-finding mission the minister has asked me to organise.'

Lucy shook her head. Fact-finding mission? What was he talking about?

'Well, basically,' he explained, 'we occasionally send delegations to various places looking to open up trade opportunities, oiling the wheels of commerce.'

Judging by his hair and complexion, Brunning would be quite good at that.

'Now it's usually something I would attend myself but, as I'm sure you're aware, I have to accompany the minister on his trip to the Middle East.'

Lucy's expression gave nothing away.

She really is brilliant, thought Brunning, unaware that she had no idea what he was talking about. 'Anyway, since you have shown quite a flair for matters retail,' he smiled, as though he was about to give her a CBE, 'I wondered whether you might like to go instead.'

'When is it?' she asked.

'The week after next.'

'Oh, right,' she said, not particularly interested. 'And where?'

'Cape Town.'

Suddenly, for the first time, Brunning had her attention.

'Five-day trip, all expenses paid,' he said. 'To be honest, it's a bit of a junket and it's almost unprecedented for an MP as, well, new as you to be invited. It's quite an honour.'

'Well, thank you, Stuart,' she said. 'I don't know what to say.'

'Well,' he suggested, 'you could try, "Yes."'

'Oh, sorry.' She laughed. 'Um . . . yes.'

'Great,' he said. 'The minister will be delighted. I'll email you all the relevant bumph. Quite a bit of reading, I'm afraid.'

'I've got a ten-hour flight, though, haven't I?'

Cape Town, she thought. Fantastic. Adam had banged on and on and on about how wonderful it was. She was still smarting at having to cancel her holiday there after the election. This trip would exorcise the resentment. She had to go. 'Which hotel are we staying at?' she asked hopefully.

'Let me see,' said Brunning, consulting the document in front of him. 'The Table Bay. Amazing place – right on the Waterfront.'

Damn, she thought, but didn't say. If it had been the Mount Nelson, it would have been perfect.

35

However anonymous she wanted to remain, Lucy was a Member of Parliament and therefore subject to public scrutiny. Anyone at any time could look her up on one of the many parliamentary websites and, in a professional sense at least, find out what she'd been up to. Every detail was there, from how she had voted on key issues to how quickly she responded to constituents' enquiries. Every word she ever said in Parliament was transcribed and recorded. Such intense analysis made her determined to keep her private life extremely private. She loved the thrill of being secretly ensconced in Sean's flat, right in the middle of Soho, looking out over London, all-seeing but unseen.

She loved the fact that, within ten minutes of leaving a theatre in Shaftesbury Avenue or a cinema in Leicester Square, they could be in bed together. Better still, she loved it when they strolled round the corner to any one of a hundred restaurants, asked for the bill after the main course, then had each other for dessert. She had a physical and emotional lust for Sean that was more primal and more powerful than anything she had ever experienced and, from the way he responded, the feeling was mutual.

Sean loved her keenness. He'd never found anything remotely alluring about girls who played it cool. As far as he was concerned, those who played hard to get could stay hard to get. That was what had caused the split in his marriage. Worse, Nikki hadn't even been playing. Had she bothered to make an effort, whatever she'd given him would have been reciprocated with interest in every sense. Lucy was happy to give so she was, in every sense, receiving.

The thought of tearing herself away from Sean, even for a

club-class trip to South Africa, was almost more than she could bear. She declined his offer of a lift to Heathrow because she knew she'd never get on the plane. Instead, she opted to walk down to Piccadilly Circus and get the tube. 'Please don't call me,' she said, as she left, 'until you know I'm too far away to come home. Even now, don't say you're going to miss me, don't tell me that you wish I wasn't going. Simply say that it's only a few days and I'll he home before I know it.'

'It's only a few days and you'll be home before you know it.'

'Kiss me politely on the cheek, as you would a maiden aunt, and wish me a safe journey.'

He kissed her on the cheek, as he would a maiden aunt, and wished her a safe journey.

More than that, he wished he'd met her a long, long time ago.

36

Human beings are usually more attractive when they're happy, and Nikki couldn't help noticing how much happier Sean had become. He'd always had the Londoner's love of a 'run out to the country' as long as it was a return journey, preferably on the same day. Although he'd never wanted to live in Kent, he'd retained an affection for the place ever since Nikki had first taken him there for Sunday lunch with her parents.

He liked the landscape of rolling hills and wooded valleys flecked with apple orchards, vineyards and hop gardens. He liked the little villages, the historic towns, the castles and country houses. He especially liked to gaze up at the huge, open skies on the rare occasions that they were clear and blue. Soho skies were so much smaller, so their frequent murkiness was less noticeable. If Sean happened to experience a grey day in Kent, he felt as though he was trapped inside an enormous Tupperware dish.

Compared with London, Sean regarded Kent as a quaint old-fashioned country called England where the pace of life was slower and the natives nosier, gossiping in the street and chatting at the tills in Tesco.

Kent was a haven for people like Nikki, who'd decided that the capital's frenetic pace and continual challenges were no longer for them. Her parents and many of her oldest friends, who'd never wanted those challenges in the first place, still lived there. Like a lioness once caged in a zoo, Nikki had returned to her natural habitat and seemed blissfully happy. In Sean's eyes, she was all the more attractive for it.

Their separate homes and lives had brought familiarity without contempt and, as they chatted together on a big creamy sofa under the wooden beams by the old inglenook fireplace, the ease and comfort Sean felt was mixed with a simultaneous unease and discomfort. Had he done the right thing in buying his dream home and putting the 'apart' into apartment? Perhaps they'd been too close to appreciate each other. They had lived in domestic discord for years and he had only been able to see her through the distorted prism of a marital magnifying-glass with every imperfection glaringly apparent. Now he was able to stand back and appreciate what a beautiful woman and a wonderful mother she was. And she'd turned a house that had once been a seventies puke-fest of mustard and green into an elegant page from *World of Interiors*.

Sean flicked on the TV and suddenly the prime minister was in the sitting room with them, oozing either sincerity or insincerity, it was impossible to tell.

'Ooh, I can't bear him,' said Nikki. 'Whenever he speaks, it's like he's playing show-and-tell with his little friends.'

Instead of chuckling along, as he normally would have, Sean felt awkward. If the conversation even touched on Labour politicians, he'd have to admit how passionately he'd been touching one of them.

He hadn't mentioned Lucy to Nikki. He'd been careful to avoid falling into 'mentionitis' in case it aroused suspicion. He needn't have worried. Nikki had never been possessive, and although Sean had always liked that about her, he'd sometimes wished she'd shown a tinge of jealousy. It had never seemed to occur to her that he would be attracted to another woman, less still that another woman would be attracted to him, so he'd spent most of his marriage feeling like a rusty old Ford Escort when, now and again, he'd have liked to have felt like a brand new Lamborghini.

'Garden looks nice,' he said, hastily changing the subject. The warmth of her smile made her seem even more attractive. Sean wasn't jealous either, but he was hit now by the realisation that if he could still notice Nikki's physical beauty, it was only a matter of time before another man noticed it too. Later, as he located his favourite part of Kent – the M20 that took him straight back to London – his mind was searing with ambivalence.

Often the greatest revenge you can have on another man for taking your wife is letting him keep her. The same is not true of your children. The thought of his two darling daughters being brought up by another man soon had him doing 120 m.p.h., as if he was trying to escape from this heartbreaking notion.

That afternoon he had been so happy when he arrived in Kent. Then Nikki had made him even happier, but somehow happiness plus more happiness had equalled unhappiness.

He missed Lucy – far more than he had realised he would. Yet here was the irony: missing Lucy had made him miss Nikki. But Lucy would be back from Cape Town in a few days and then everything would be fine, absolutely fine.

37

From the moment she arrived, Lucy had adored Cape Town. As cities go, it's tiny but, as Adam had never tired of telling her, it has 'huge historical significance and cultural diversity'. He'd been there several times. So many films and commercials are shot in Cape Town because parts of it look just like New York, the Bahamas, the South of France or even the Scottish highlands. Busy streets and quaint cobbled ones, glorious beaches, mountains, forests and vineyards: all can be found in or around Cape Town.

The hotel was spectacular, the people were friendly, and the weather was perfect, which was why she hated being there. Adam's other stock phrase about Cape Town was that it 'contains all the things the human heart and soul could desire'.

All the things except one.

Lucy missed Sean more than she had ever imagined she would. She found herself wishing that she'd been sent to a dreary conference centre in Birmingham where it wouldn't seem such a heart-breaking waste to be without him. Her fellow delegates were bland, characterless Labour MPs in their thirties called Andrew, Keith, Deborah and Lesley. They were fairly harmless, but she couldn't think of four people with whom she'd less enjoy spending five days in one of the most beautiful places on earth. Their lives had consisted of little other than Labour Party politics and everything they said or did was skewed by this affliction. Probably without meaning to, they regarded Lucy, who was happy to admit her political inexperience, as a bit of a joke. Just five minutes along the road from the airport she hadn't helped her cause. 'Look,' she said, trying to be friendly. 'Funny place to have a garden centre.' Then she realised that the sheds were shacks and that the 'garden centre' was a roadside squatter camp. Yes, it was a terrible *faux-pas* but an innocent one – had it been necessary for her fellow delegates to look quite so reproving? She knew that Keith, in particular, had wanted to laugh but was so terrified of being seen as politically insensitive that he hadn't dared – even though the driver, who was black, thought it was hilarious.

Despite the brilliant sunshine, the atmosphere inside the people-carrier remained stone cold.

Lucy had travelled all over the world and stayed in some of its finest hotels and had always taken great pleasure in doing so. The others, who clearly hadn't, didn't seem to appreciate that they were staying at the Table Bay, all expenses paid. They behaved as though they were important international dignitaries and this was their divine right. Lucy suspected that they knew, deep down, they were charlatans, were intimidated by the sleek grandeur of their surroundings and thought that the best way to disguise it was to conduct themselves in a pompous, over-polite, almost patronising fashion.

Despite the Table Bay's luxury and impeccable service, Lucy found it too neat, too new and too corporate. It looked more like a shopping mall and lacked the warmth, charm and character that seem woven into the fabric of truly great hotels, even new ones. Still, as a dynamic symbol of the new South Africa, she could see why it had been chosen.

A minibus had taken them all over the region. Like children on a real-life geography project, they were shown orange groves and apple orchards. Bananas, pineapples and mangoes were presented to them as though they'd never been to Sainsbury's. Lucy could remember that, not long ago, it had been considered a heinous ideological crime to buy South African fruit. George Webb had apparently never supported the boycott. He had despised apartheid but continued to sell Cape grapes because he'd believed that 'the people who'll suffer most are the poor buggers whose lives depend on picking them'.

They were taken to film studios to see productions in progress and out into the wine regions of Franschhoek and Stellenbosch to be reminded that South Africa produces some of the finest wines in the world. Here, more than anywhere else, Lucy wished she was sharing the romance of the vineyards and the majesty of the mountains with Sean. He would have loved the silent serenity of Table Mountain, gazing down at the city and the sea, seeing everything but hearing nothing. He would have behaved properly on the trip to Robben Island where Nelson Mandela was incarcerated for twenty-seven years: he would have shown restraint and respect for one man's phenomenal courage, dignity and resilience. He wouldn't have done what Lesley had and burst into crocodile tears over the long imprisonment of that 'poor, poor man'.

Deborah's conduct in the Langa township had been even more embarrassing. Lucy wasn't entirely comfortable with township tourism. She was happy to go there but preferably not with a busload of other tourists as though she were on some sort of human safari. She loved the people with their vibrant street culture and spent every rand she possessed in the little pavement markets, but would gladly have seen Deborah banged up on Robben Island for peering into people's homes and simpering, 'They may not have much, but they have such dignity. They seem so happy and their houses are spotless.'

She had wanted to stay and have lunch at one of the wobbly tin tables outside the butcher's. She watched the locals picking their meat, paying for it, then handing it to the man who did the cooking. Then they sat down, had a drink and waited for their food to arrive. One delicious whiff would have spelled the end for the entire vegan movement, but as Lucy was herded back on to the bus, to return to the sanitised splendour of the Table Bay, she knew that this culinary delight was destined to elude her.

She tried not to ring Sean too often, but they stayed connected by the constant umbilical cord of texts that be-beep, be-beeped their way across the equator.

Back at the hotel, she sat alone at the Terrace Bar gazing out over the Waterfront. Her bag vibrated and she pulled out her phone. *How was the township?* said the message on the screen.

Good and bad.

Chin up. You'll be home in a couple of days.

I know. Can't wait. Wish you were here.

When she read the next message, she almost passed out:

Really? Then look behind you.

38

From the Beatles to Busted, certain groups and performers have always attracted the screams of a million girls. Sheila had told Lucy that in 1963 she'd gone to see the Beatles at the East Ham Granada and all anyone could hear was screaming and the occasional clatter of Ringo's drums. Lucy had never understood how this could be until she saw Sean standing on the Victoria and Albert Waterfront, eight thousand miles from where he was supposed to be. She screamed like a teenybopper. Everyone looked round, convinced that someone was about to be murdered.

After the screams, all motor-neurone skills deserted her. She collapsed into Sean's arms and he half walked, half carried her across to the Cape Grace Hotel for a drink at the Bascule Bar.

Lucy would never know how nervous Sean had been about doing this. Turning up at the House of Commons was one thing – it was within walking distance of his flat. Turning up unannounced on the other side of the world was quite another.

As he placed a triple vodka and tonic in front of her, he said, 'You drink, I'll explain.'

'Yesterday Jon calls me to do an ISDN to Cape Town at eleven o'clock this morning. I said I'd go out and do it in person. He says, "Are you fucking mad? There's no need. There's only an hour's time difference." "Exactly," I said, "no jet lag. I'll get the overnight flight." The job was for a production company called Cape Films – lovely people, I've done stuff for them before. They were delighted. It's much easier for them if I do it in their studio straight to picture, saves them having to mess around with the voice-track afterwards. Anyway, they were always inviting me out to Cape Town. Can't imagine why I picked this occasion to take them up on it.'

Lucy just stared at him, then touched his hand and face to check once more that her parliamentary companions hadn't driven her mad and that she wasn't hallucinating. 'How long are you here for?'

'Till tomorrow night. Same as you.'

'Same flight?' she asked eagerly.

'No. You're going BA, aren't you? I'm going Virgin. My flight leaves about an hour before yours. I'll wait for you at the other end, if you like.'

Lucy nodded, articulacy still not fully restored.

'It was when you said you had a couple of days free at the end of the trip,' said Sean, 'that I got a feeling you wouldn't want to spend them with – is it Lesley? Deborah?'

'Andrew and Keith,' she croaked. 'This is so fantastic. I can just tell them I've got some really good friends in Cape Town.'

'Ones that you strangely hadn't mentioned before.'

'Details, details. They won't care. I'll just say I'm going to stay with them. Are you staying at the Table Bay?'

'Nah,' said Sean. 'It's very nice but a bit corporate for me. I'm at the . . . um . . . Oh, what's it called? The Mount . . . um—'

For the second time, Lucy let out an adolescent scream, and once again lost the ability to speak.

39

For such a grand colonial landmark, Sean found the Mount Nelson remarkably relaxed and informal. He'd grown tired of piss-elegant provincial hotels in Hampshire and Harrogate having ideas above their stations and insisting that 'gentlemen' wear a jacket and tie to dinner. He was delighted to see children running around the 'Nellie', exploring the lovely old building's warren of nooks and crannies.

He led Lucy along a wide corridor to the glorious suite at the end, carried her over the threshold and threw her on to the huge four-poster bed. 'Ten minutes,' he said. 'Ten minutes of looking at the room, the big marble bathroom, that fantastic view across the gardens to the pool, and then we're off.'

Forty-nine per cent of Lucy Ross, MP, wanted never to leave that room. She'd waited years to check in and would have been happy to stay there until she was forcibly escorted to Reception to check out. Fifty-one per cent, however, wanted to go exploring with Sean, and her mind was a strictly democratic arena.

They took a taxi out to Camps Bay and wandered hand in hand for miles along its soft white shoreline, ankle deep in the Atlantic Ocean. Having worked up an appetite, they discovered The Codfather restaurant, overlooking the beach, where the sublime fresh fish was served with a magnificent view of the ocean from which it had just come. The excruciating pun of a name reminded Lucy of the chippie on King's Parade. The Codfather was a world-renowned fish restaurant, from which she and Sean witnessed the most spectacular sunset either of them had ever seen, but when it came to a pun contest, the Essex chippie Oh My Cod was the clear winner.

As the sun disappeared below a purple horizon, the taxi returned to take them on to a little place called the Tiger Tavern, where Sean had promised to meet some people from Cape Films. As they approached the meeting place, Lucy felt as if she'd been there before – and she had: the Tiger Tavern was in Langa the township she'd visited that morning but the whole place looked very different at night.

Without realising it, Sean stared for the statutory four seconds upon entering the bar. They were the only white people there. Unlike certain pubs in North Wales, where the hush of hostility falls when strangers enter, the regulars here were far more welcoming. Something about Sean's relaxed, friendly demeanour told them that these two strangers weren't tourists who'd come to gawp with a condescending mixture of curiosity and pity: they'd come for a drink and a laugh.

The young runners and technicians from Cape Films were surprised and delighted when Sean appeared. Other visitors had made the same promise and broken it, but if Sean had one motto in life it was 'Always do what you say you're going to do'. He drank the home-made beer, dipped the home-made chicken into the fiendishly hot lime pickle, and when the *mbaqanga* band struck up from the corner, he danced like a dervish. Lucy found herself carried along with him and having the time of her life. As the heat and noise got too much even for Sean, Lucy persuaded him to take his bottle of homebrew and drink it up on the little open-air roof bar. As she gazed out over the rickety rooftops of one of the most fascinating, vibrant places on earth, she knew this was one of the best nights of her life especially as she'd be spending the rest of it at one of the most luxurious hotels in the world.

They returned in the early hours, exhausted but with just enough energy to make love in the fairytale four-poster. Afterwards, as Lucy fell in a clear-headed swoon towards sleep, her heart was still racing because Sean had been as desperate to see her as she had to see him – if anything, even more so. He'd travelled eight thousand miles to be with her.

She'd never know that he'd travelled at least a thousand of them because he'd needed to act swiftly and decisively to banish the surprisingly powerful allure of an oast house in Kent.

40

The gang of sinister-looking strangers seemed to know all about Junk and Disorderly. Despite the parking restrictions, the shop had been a runaway success and the men had obviously been tipped off about the surfeit of stock, some items quite valuable, in the dank, smelly, uninhabited flat above it.

Almost as soon as Lucy had left for Cape Town, they had turned up in King's Parade in a white Luton van. At the behest of the swarthy, tattooed gang-master, they went inside and began to remove the contents. Their instructions had been to 'tosh the place out' which meant applying two coats of Dulux Trade Magnolia to the walls, before fitting a cheap and cheerful new kitchen and bathroom from the nearest branch of MFI. Once the paint was dry, another two men arrived and laid plain carpet throughout before the final van arrived from Ikea to deliver a bed, a pair of ex-display sofas plus a couple of tables, lamps and shelves.

Lucy now had a flat in the constituency, courtesy of Darren and paid for by Sean.

When she saw the transformation she gasped like a participant on *Changing Rooms*. In fact, it was better than *Changing Rooms* because the walls weren't orange or purple and nothing had a 'really sort of Moroccan feel'. As soon as she saw the mismatched furnishings and magnolia walls, Lucy knew she wanted to be with Sean for the rest of her life.

His undemanding kindness typified everything she adored about him. Despite his confidence, which sometimes bordered on cockiness, an endearing core of shyness ran right through him. He never wanted to take centre stage. Over the years, cinemagoers had been blown away by a film's crystal-clear digital sound quality yet the man who'd been responsible for it remained anonymous. Countless others had been persuaded to buy things by TV and radio commercials. Their willingness to do so was due in no small part to the deep, warm but nameless voice that had been so devastatingly persuasive.

Sean knew that Lucy would be almost suicidal at the thought of returning to her life as an MP after the idyll of Cape Town, so he had made sure that coming home was the best surprise of all.

She had no intention of staying at the flat but it was good to know that she could if she had to. Its real purpose was as a base for Sheila to do the constituency work. Lucy had been a bit hasty in refusing to use a shop as her constituency office. The Rose and Crown was fine for meetings and surgeries but not for everyday casework, with its armfuls of files and papers. During their first days at their new office, Sheila told Lucy about Brian Marsden's way of dealing with letters from his constituents: he had put them in his 'filing cabinet'. 'It was a wastepaper bin,' said Sheila. 'He may as well have stuck it outside and told the postman to put all the letters straight into it.'

Lucy agreed that it was a disgraceful thing to do, but couldn't help feeling a shred of empathy for Marsden's idle, ruthless approach. It's hard for any MP not to regard constituents' letters as any one else might view the entreaties of beggars. It's impossible to help them all, or even to distinguish those whose needs are genuine from those whose are not. The temptation to transfer all letters from postbag to bin is almost irresistible.

Like all MPs since the invention of the PC, Lucy received far fewer letters than her predecessor. However, this was outweighed by the hundreds of emails that congested her IN box every morning. The vast majority came from people whose demands were either trivial or absurd. This morning's arrivals contained a missive ordering her to intervene in a dispute between two neighbours over who should mend the garden fence. Another

claimed the world was about to be taken over by thousands of
giant stoats and that she should alert the prime minister at once.
At least emails could be either answered or deleted in roughly
the same time as it had taken Marsden to fill his 'filing cabinet'.
She had found that those in serious need of assistance would
usually find their way to the Rose and Crown on a Sunday afternoon, knowing that an adviser would be on hand to help.
However, when she received a polite letter that was not written
in either green ink or human blood, she was inclined to take
notice.

> *Dear Ms Ross,*
>
> *I cannot give you my name but I thought you ought to know
> that the council are about to sell the Jubilee Swimming Pool to
> Fenton Estates, a large property company. It is almost certain
> that Fenton Estates will demolish the pool and build something
> else in its place. No planning permission has yet been given but
> there are strong rumours about them building a huge American-
> style hypermarket. Like many people, I wonder whether this is
> linked to the sudden introduction of parking restrictions around
> King's Parade. Please look into it. If I get any more informa-
> tion, I'll be in touch.*

Lucy wasn't averse to a conspiracy theory – she was happy to
be gulled into believing that Lord Lucan was living with Elvis
in Eastbourne and that Neil Armstrong hadn't really landed on
the moon. She had a quick show of hands in her head: 'All those
brain cells in favour of following this up because it's a bit of a
coincidence, would vindicate everything I said in my maiden
speech and give me the opportunity to use my influence as a
Member of Parliament in a good way and make a real difference to people's lives, please raise their hands . . .

'Okay, all those who believe it's probably not true, and even
if it is, I can't do anything about it, these decisions are taken at
a local level and, as long as no law has been broken, it's none
of my business – and, anyway, I just want to slink back into

political anonymity and spend more time with Sean – (deep breath) please raise yours . . .'

Almost twice as many cerebral hands were raised at the second suggestion so the motion was carried. But something made Lucy fold that letter and place it in a filing cabinet. A real one.

41

As an MP, Lucy could fill her diary several times over with things she didn't want to do. The obligatory visits to local schools, hospitals and old people's homes came with the territory and although invitations to open a fête usually made her want to open a wrist, she didn't like to let people down. Occasionally, she received an invitation that seemed to promise a modicum of enjoyment, like the Sunday-night comedy show at the Prince Edward Theatre in aid of Children in Need.

Sean couldn't go with her because he was seeing his own children. To give Nikki a break, he'd sometimes bring them back to London in the naughty car and take them off to Kensington Gardens to run around the Diana, Princess of Wales, playground. Then they might go on to the Science Museum, and return to Soho for a burger at Ed's Diner. If they'd been good, they might be allowed to watch a DVD on the sixty-inch TV until they dropped off to sleep. It was little wonder that half of the kids at their school wished their daddies lived in Soho, not Kent.

Lucy loved children so much that she couldn't bear to meet Sean's. He was chest-puffingly proud of them and she sensed that he was keen to introduce them to her. However, as she walked along Old Compton Street to meet Karen at the theatre, she saw something that brought her to a sudden, paralysed halt. Sitting at the counter in Ed's Diner, having hot dogs and milkshakes, Lucy saw the man she loved with the kids he adored. Sean had often told her that this kitsch American diner, with its retro décor and jukebox filled with fifties rock 'n' roll, was the children's favourite place in the world. Even from outside, Lucy could hear them. They were singing 'Wake Up Little Suzy' at the top of their tiny voices. Sean kept pretending to fall asleep, but when the children yelled the song into his ear he'd 'wake' with a start, sending them into paroxysms of laughter. It was silly, corny and childish yet to Lucy, peering in from the corner of Moor Street, it was magical.

Watching this little scene had made her mind and body throb with simultaneous sadness and joy. In a way, it was far worse than seeing him with another woman because he was displaying that unique level of love seen only between parent and child.

Standing at the window of Ed's Diner – at the window of Sean's life – she knew that this was one party to which she'd never be invited. Seeing them all together was confirmation that her gorgeous boyfriend had already sired two children with someone else. And as he displayed such love for the children Lucy was reminded uncomfortably of the love he must have felt for the woman who'd produced them. And yet . . . and yet . . . It made him more attractive than ever. She may have been invisible to him but the love and pride in his eyes was clear to her. Also, those beautiful children were living proof of his fecundity: a guarantee that everything was in perfect working order, and that what he had done with Nikki he could do again with her.

She wandered off to the theatre, raw with emotion, hoping that Karen wouldn't pick up on it. Although she was there to help Children in Need, Lucy had never felt so In Need of Children. She and Sean were never together at weekends. Sean was with his children so Lucy used the time to catch up with friends and constituents. The coming weekend would be a rare treat: Nikki was going with two friends for a girls' weekend to Paris. Sean had offered to have the children but so had Nikki's parents, which left him free in London. By happy coincidence, Lucy was similarly unencumbered. Half of her advisers, including Karen, Max and both her parents, were busy that Sunday, so she'd had to cancel her surgery.

Sean felt that weekends were the best time to enjoy London, because those who came in for business were replaced by those who came in for pleasure. Soho, right in the centre, was the best place for him and Lucy to open their arms and embrace the whole metropolis. They started by going north through Regent's Park, all the way to the top of Primrose Hill then headed down to Charing Cross Pier and took a riverboat cruise to Greenwich.

London was originally built to be viewed from the Thames and, meandering along the curves of the river, watching the sights of the city go by on either side, suddenly made sense. Another walk to the top of a hill – this time the one in Greenwich Park because Lucy had always wanted to see the view from the opening credits of *EastEnders*. After a brief stroll round Greenwich market, they walked under the river through the foot tunnel to have a late lunch at the Gun, a riverside gastropub near Canary Wharf that was far more gastro than pub.

'That's where I used to work,' said Lucy, almost wistfully, pointing to a nondescript glass building. 'Whenever I said I worked at Canary Wharf, people would say, 'Oh, it must be great, those amazing views.' Everyone automatically assumes that your office is about thirty floors up, but mine was on the ground floor and nowhere near a window.'

'Do you miss it?'

'Hard to say,' she replied. 'It's my old life, and all the time I was there, I was with Adam. Since I've been an MP, I've been with you so, on balance, no, I don't miss it at all. Oddly enough,' she said, kissing Sean's cheek, 'much as I love having a weekend with you, I quite miss Essex. I've become very fond of the place and, more importantly, the people.'

'Ah, Essex,' said Sean. 'The fifty-first state of America. London's very own New Jersey.'

He had a point. With its low buildings and sprawling flat land, Essex had always embraced US culture wholesale: shopping malls, multiplex cinemas, six-lane highways and its own huge car factory. Dagenham was the Motown of Essex. The original motor town may have produced Stevie Wonder and Marvin Gaye, but its Essex counterpart had given the world Sandie Shaw and Brian Poole and the Tremeloes.

'The people are so honest,' she added.

Sean laughed. 'Well, I wouldn't go that far.'

'I mean honest as in forthright,' said Lucy, 'rather than law-abiding.' Having lived for years with Adam's uptight matt-black minimalism and his terror of being thought vulgar or naff, she welcomed the stone lions and gold-plated bath taps like a Jacuzzi for the soul. In Essex, she'd found a great sense of community. The people tended not to concern themselves with major issues, such as climate change or the war in Iraq, preferring micro to macro politics. They laughed at Essex-girl jokes making fun of themselves in a way that those from other ethnic groups probably wouldn't.

She'd also come to deplore the spiteful brand of nu-snobbery that often made Essex the butt of its invective: it was perfectly all right to call her constituents chavs but somehow wrong to make the same sort of jibes about black people, who shared similar predilections for rap music, sportswear and bling. She loved the fact that Essex people couldn't care less and would hate anyone trying to stick up for them or portray them as an oppressed minority. They were, on the whole, good people, who could teach a lot of others about humour, resilience and having a good time.

It was then she remembered that, for some of them, having a good time meant swimming at the Jubilee Pool and she'd done nothing about her anonymous correspondent's allegations about its imminent closure. Catholic guilt – or conscience – caught up with her. 'So what do you think?' she said, having told Sean about the letter concerning the sale of the pool.

'Hmm. Well, as you say, people in Essex are very honest and this looks like it might have a ring of truth about it.'

42

Sean had always believed that he wasn't political. To him, or to anyone brought up in an Irish household in the seventies, politics meant 'The Troubles', and even as an Irish Catholic he'd detested the Republican sympathisers who could be found in every classroom. 'Smash H Block' and 'Up the Provies' would be carved into desks by ugly boys with big ears who had no real idea what they were talking about.

He'd never understood how any teenager could be interested in politics. Whenever he heard people bemoaning the fact that they weren't, his view was 'And neither should they be.' Surely youth is better spent in constant pursuit of sex, drugs and the contemporary equivalent of rock 'n' roll.

For Sean, the acquisition of age and life experience had brought a greater interest in politics and even greater aversion to the people involved in it. Like George Best at his peak, he could be found on either the right or left wing but was often happy to shoot straight down the middle. He had no pre-set allegiances, and had voted Labour, Tory and Lib Dem, depending on who he thought was best equipped to deal with a given set of circumstances. He couldn't comprehend how some people only ever voted for one party. Voting Labour because 'me dad voted Labour' seemed absurd. Those people's dads might also have worn flat caps, regarded washing-up as 'women's work' and called immigrants 'darkies': did *they* do those things too?

Political parties, like religions and football clubs, rely on the dumb, unswerving support of thousands of people for whom they do absolutely nothing. And yet, individually, not all politicians were bad. Sean had seen how hard Lucy worked, despite her avowed intention to do the opposite. He'd seen her making countless calls to sort out constituents' problems, continually putting herself out and changing her plans to accept dreary invitations from people who failed to appreciate the trouble she'd taken to be there. Although she didn't care about politics, she cared deeply about the people she represented, and while he watched the sixty-inch TV, her eyes were often glued to a much smaller screen, as she sat up late into the night replying personally to hundreds of emails.

She wanted to effect some sort of change but was constantly frustrated by the expediency of other MPs who were often terribly busy doing nothing.

Sean answered the buzzer and Lucy came up to the flat, weighed down with bags from Lina Stores, the famous Italian deli on Brewer Street. 'What's all this?' said Sean. 'I thought we were going out for a bit of dim sum.'

'If it's all the same to you,' she replied, plonking down the bags almost angrily, 'I need to cook. I need to create something. I've spent all day achieving nothing and I want to feel that my life isn't being wasted. This is the bit about politics that I can't bear. The going round and round in circles, the endless buck-passing, arse-covering and evasion of responsibility, the endless meetings but total lack of action.'

It was the first time Sean had seen her upset and it made him realise how lucky he was. He simply walked into a studio, spoke into a microphone, and got paid. All the meetings, the focus groups, the to-ing and fro-ing had been done long before he did his bit. So, although he understood what Lucy meant, he could only imagine how she felt.

'Nothing special,' she said, 'just a bit of pasta and a pudding. Won't take long.'

'Anything I can do to help?' said Sean.

'Not really. Well, I suppose you could open this,' she said, handing him a bottle of Pinot Grigio.

'Tell you what, then,' he drew the cork from the bottle, 'let me find some Italian restaurant music.' He poured the wine into two glasses.

'Perfect,' said Lucy, and took a good long glug. 'Ooh, I needed that. Okay, *la pasta* . . .'

Sean scrolled through the laptop and kicked off with Tony Bennett's 'Rags to Riches', then played 'Volare', preferring Domenico Modugno's original to Dean Martin's cover.

Jerry Vale's 'Inammorata' brought a nostalgic shriek from the kitchen. 'My God, I love this. Where did you get it? My dad used to sing this to my mum.'

In a matter of minutes, Lucy served up two plates of *fazzo-letti di seta al pesto* – silk handkerchiefs with pesto. 'This recipe comes from the north of Italy,' she explained, putting the plates on the table with a big green salad, 'rather than the south. So, for God's sake, don't tell my mum.'

Sean couldn't tell anyone anything because as soon as he tasted the delicate fresh pasta he was speechless. The term 'melt in the mouth' is so over-used that it's almost meaningless, but there was no other way to describe the gastronomic sensation that Sean was experiencing.

It was followed by a home-made tiramisu so delicious that Sean laughed. Unless he'd screamed, like a Beatles fan, no other reaction would have done it justice.

'At least I feel I've achieved something now,' said Lucy, falling back on to the sofa while Sean slid *Roman Holiday* into the DVD player. 'The word *tiramisu* actually means "pick-me-up". I feel much better.'

'God, me too,' said Sean, whose post-prandial delight felt almost post-coital. 'And that, in case you're wondering, is why I've never dared take you to an Italian restaurant. I can't think of one that might serve anything as good as that.'

'You're very kind,' she said, pulling an envelope out of her bag. 'Here, have a look at this.'

Dear Ms Ross,
   Me again. I can now confirm that Fenton Estates have sought

planning permission to build a hypermarket on the Jubilee Pool
site. It hasn't been granted yet. James Fenton, the developer, is
a decent man and it might be worth your while contacting him
to see if he could come to some arrangement with the council
over the parking restrictions in return for a favourable response
to his planning application. You never know, it's always worth
a try.

'Well,' said Sean, 'why not?'

He had flicked the old 'Why not?' switch in Lucy's head, the
one that had made her stand for Parliament in the first place.
'Hmmm,' she said, snuggling up to watch Audrey Hepburn and
Gregory Peck, 'why not indeed?'

43

Sean had always liked actors – good ones, anyway. Just as well, since his job as a sound engineer had involved working with them for eight hours a day, five days a week. Far from being shallow, empty creatures who had spent so long pretending to be other people that they had no idea who they were any more, he found most were splendidly self-aware. Their heightened sensitivities were the tools of their trade, and usually made them great raconteurs and perceptive observers of the world around them. Most were incorrigible gossips, which meant that they had a keen interest in other human beings. This often extended into a desire to know what was going on, socially and culturally, which made them knowledgeable about books, plays, films and television. Being natural performers, they were often wonderfully engaging company. Far from taking themselves too seriously, most understood that what they did wasn't terribly important. Sean remembered a fine Shakespearean actor describing his occupation as 'shouting in the evenings'.

Sean admired their bravery, their willingness to risk a lifetime of penury in pursuing their vocation. This had left him with an intense dislike of am-dram performers, who might have had talent but lacked the courage to turn professional, preferring to keep their steady jobs with software companies in Basingstoke.

He liked actors despite their faults, most of which began with the prefix 'self'. He loved their insecurity, vanity and bitchiness, and saw them as living proof that romantics and cynics are two sides of the same human coin. Like him, most had no interest in anything involving manual labour or fiscal acumen, which he found somehow comforting. He'd come to regard them like human beings, only more so.

There were, of course, exceptions to the rule, and as Sean sat in Reception at Grand Central studios, he was approached by one. 'Hello, mate!'

'Oh, no!' screamed Sean's inner self. 'It's Gary Hardwick.'

Gary was a London actor in his late thirties who'd made his name playing cockney Jack-the-lads. Those meeting him for the first time and expecting him to be anything like his lovable, down-to-earth characters were doomed to disappointment. There has always been a breed of working-class actors best described as 'common luvvies', more pretentious than any grand thespian from the RSC. Gary Hardwick was probably the most loathsome example. Of mediocre talent, not terribly bright and with a repulsive vanity, both professional and physical, Gary could make people want to fake their own deaths rather than spend ten minutes in his company. It had been said that if you ever saw two people talking and one looked really bored, Gary was the other.

'Hello, Gary. How are you?' said Sean, not remotely interested in the answer.

'I'm good, mate, yeah.'

'Just going in for a job?'

'Nah, just finished,' said Gary.

Shit, thought Sean. Please, God, call me down to the studio, I can't bear to get stuck with him.

Just then the receptionist, called over to Sean. Thank you, God. Thank you, thank you, thank you. 'Sean,' she said, 'they're overrunning a bit in Studio Three. They'll be finished in about ten minutes.'

Oh, fuck, fuck, fuck. Never mind, he thought. Look on it as community service. It's either talking to Gary about Gary or painting old people's homes. Best to get it over with. 'So, what are you up to?'

'Oh, mate,' said Gary, 'I'm doing this amazing production.

Polish director, unbelievable. My character is incredibly complex. He sort of hides behind a façade of loyalty. He has to keep his emotions in check while at the same time, right, revealing just a bit to the audience. His motivation is the cruelty inflicted on his boss's daughter by his boss's new wife and her two daughters.'

'Sounds great.'

It was only later that Sean found out that Gary was playing Buttons in panto.

'And when I've finished that, I'm shooting a movie set in London around the time of the Krays.'

Another third-rate Brit gangster movie, thought Sean. Just what the world's crying out for.

'Yeah,' said Gary. 'It's time I moved to the other side of the lens, like. A natural, intuitive actor like me can feel too constrained by the vision of another director. Most of them are fucking crap. You know – when you just know you can do their job so much better than they can.'

Sean understood what he meant. It had been the realisation that he could voice commercials so much better than Gary Hardwick that had persuaded him to become a voiceover artist. 'Yeah.' He nodded. 'I know exactly what you mean, Gal. So, you're going to be directing?'

'Fucking right,' said Gary. 'I think it's my real vocation. I see myself as a sort of cross between Scorsese and Michael Mann.'

'And you've got the money and the backers in place?'

'Yeah,' said Gary, with a conspiratorial wink. 'Between you, me and the gatepost, mate, we've had a bit of a result there.'

'Really?' said Sean, drawing a bit closer.

'Yeah. Pal of my old man put most of the cash up. He's fucking loaded. Bit of a naughty boy back in the day but he's totally legit now. Always looking for good investments.'

'What's his name, then, this heavy mate of your dad's?'

With anyone else Sean wouldn't have bothered asking, but he knew that Gary, who could never resist giving the impression that he was tasty, connected and knew all the right people, would be fantastically indiscreet and tell him.

'His name's Fenton, Jimmy Fenton.'

Sean's jaw must have dropped ever so slightly.

'Do you know him?' asked Gary.

'Me? No,' said Sean. 'How would a bloke like me know a bloke like him?'

'No, s'pose not,' said Gary, with a patronising chuckle. 'Now, listen, mate, don't breathe a word of this to anyone. He's nearly seventy now and he's been straight for years. Only my old man and people from way back would call him Jimmy. He's James Fenton now, hugely respectable. Got a big property company out in Essex but fifty years ago he was Jimmy the Fence, bit of a handful, apparently. My kind of guy.'

Sean was trying to work out which was Fenton's bigger crime: destroying the livelihoods of innocent shopkeepers or inflicting Gary Hardwick the director on the movie-going public.

'They're ready for you now, Sean,' said the receptionist.

'Okay,' said Sean. He turned to Gary. 'Got to shoot, mate, but listen, it was really good to see you.' And for the first time in his life, when referring to Gary Hardwick, Sean was telling the truth.

44

Sean decided not to tell Lucy about James Fenton's criminal past, largely because, if Gary had said it, then it probably wasn't true. Gary Hardwick could never stop acting. As soon as he came off set he began playing the role of 'an actor'. What had started as an affectation had become his personality. He no longer knew when to switch off. The tale he'd told about Fenton might easily be a persona he'd created for someone else, like the one he'd created for himself. As Sean's dad was fond of saying, 'You're better off with a thief than a liar.'

The trouble with liars was that you sometimes caught them telling the truth and, despite Gary's mendacious track record, Sean had a feeling that this was what might have happened.

Lucy's third missive from her anonymous correspondent had directed her to a Companies House website and suggested she click on a number of links to negotiate her way round James Fenton's labyrinthine financial affairs. Having scurried through a maze of money warrens, her mouse had eventually revealed that Fenton had major stakes in several offshore companies, including one called Parkfair Ltd.

Time to make that call.

When Fenton's secretary told him that Lucy Ross, MP, wanted a window in his diary, he wasn't surprised. Ever since his plans to build the hypermarket had become common knowledge, he had been expecting a call from a woman he assumed was a meddling lefty MP, whose hobby-horse this week was a grotty old swimming-pool and an outdated parade of shops. He could have put her off for weeks, even months, but decided not to.

He'd done nothing wrong. He was a successful businessman, perfectly respectable, why should he hide from anyone?

Ultimately, all he wanted was respect. Like every hoodlum from Jack Spot to 50 Cent, James Fenton craved it. Unlike them, however, he'd worked out that the best way to get it was to be respect*able*, and that's what he'd been for the last forty-five years. He'd built up a huge property business and made more money than he could ever dream of spending, but his fatal flaw was greed. Gary Hardwick had been wrong about him: he wasn't quite as legit as he appeared. Still unable to resist the lure of easy money, Fenton occasionally bankrolled the bankrollers who financed criminal activity. Cannily he kept himself so far removed from the sharp end that his involvement would never be suspected, let alone proven.

The head office of Fenton PLC was a huge Jacobean mansion set among acres of perfectly manicured lawns. It gave the chairman such an impressive veneer of respectability that no one, least of all Lucy, could tell it was a veneer.

The Savile Row suit, hand-made shoes and vintage Rolex were all present and correct as he welcomed her into his huge wood-panelled office. She felt as if she was walking into a cigar box. 'Can I get you a drink?' he asked, opening a beautiful cherry-wood drinks cabinet.

'Oh, just a glass of water, please.'

'Coming up,' said the host, taking a bottle of Evian from the fridge and pouring two glasses. Fenton hardly ever drank: it made his face go red and his accent slip. 'Cheers.'

Lucy sat politely on the sofa while Fenton revolved in his captain's club chair, upholstered in deep-buttoned hide.

'The house is beautiful,' she said. 'So much nicer than a boring office block.'

'Glad you like it,' said Fenton. 'It has a great political history – Churchill used it as his campaign HQ when he was MP for Woodford and Wanstead.'

'Late Victorian?' asked Lucy.

'Exactly right – 1898. So, Ms Ross,' he said, 'what can I do for you?'

'Well, I know you're a busy man and I appreciate you taking the time to see me, so I'll cut to the chase. It's about your plans to build this hypermarket on the site of the Jubilee Pool.'

'Yes?' said Fenton, innocently, knowing that legally, at least, he'd done nothing wrong.

'Well, apart from robbing the community of an important leisure centre, the project will destroy the local shops along King's Parade and probably dozens of others within a ten-mile radius.'

'I know what you're saying,' he said smoothly, 'but nothing stays the same for ever. The world has moved on and so have people's shopping habits.'

'And, Mr Fenton, I know what *you*'re saying but does this part of Essex really need another supermarket? There are four within ten minutes' drive of here.'

Not for much longer, thought Fenton. He was going to sell the land to a particularly aggressive American hypermarket chain, who would then introduce a ruthless US business model to Essex. It had been hugely successful in the States. First a giant hypermarket would open, forcing all the little stores to close. Then, instead of being able to walk, local people would have to drive a couple of miles to do their shopping. Having killed a couple of communities, the hypermarket would close down and move to another site twice the size and maybe ten miles further out. Shoppers all over America were having to drive twelve miles to buy a pint of milk. And, of course, whatever happened across the Atlantic transferred quickly to Essex.

'Ms Ross,' said Fenton, 'I know you're passionate about shopping. I was very impressed by the speech you made in the Commons so I don't understand why you'd want to deny your constituents all the benefits of retailing in the twenty-first century. Why shouldn't they be able to buy top-quality jeans for a fiver or a DVD player for twenty quid? When hypermarkets open, no one forces people to go there. They can carry on shopping at their local shops but they never do, do they?'

'No,' said Lucy. 'Not when they can't park.'

If Fenton was in any way rattled by this, he didn't show it. 'Councils have to raise money,' he said. 'They have schools, roads, parks and all sorts of other things to pay for. It's either this or a big increase in council tax.'

Since Lucy had met Sean, and especially since he'd coached her for her maiden speech, she'd taken far more notice of the way people spoke, and there was something distinctly odd about Fenton's speech patterns. She listened as he carried on explaining how hard he'd always worked for the community and how this hypermarket would bring joy and jobs to Essex. She wasn't listening so much to what he was saying, she could have predicted all that, but more to the way he was saying it. Then she realised who he reminded her of. It was Tony Murray.

Murray was the SAS commando turned best-selling author, who now had to live with a false identity. 'Tony Murray' was not his real name and he was never photographed. How much of this was necessary and how much an elaborate marketing ploy was open to debate, but one thing was clear: 'Murray' had had elocution lessons.

Sean had played Lucy a Radio 4 interview with Murray. This was a tearaway who'd grown up on one of the roughest estates in South London and had only joined the army because it was that or prison, yet he spoke in the smooth, modulated tones of a character in *Brideshead Revisited*. All very convincing except that, although elocution can smooth out people's accents it can do nothing about their grammar. Murray's conversation was peppered with expressions like 'them things what I done', which sounded all the more ridiculous in his lovely new accent.

Fenton was a little more practised. He'd been speaking like this for more than half his life, yet the occasional expression betrayed the fact that he'd been born in a two-room slum in Holborn.

This became briefly apparent when Lucy asked him about his shareholding in Parkfair Ltd but, to his credit, he quickly regained his composure. 'The Fenton Group,' he said, a little too calmly, 'has a wide portfolio of interests. To be honest, I'm not sure exactly what's invested where. You'd have to speak to my analysts and advisers. They're far better at that sort of thing than I'll ever be.'

'Good idea,' said Lucy. 'If you'd like to give me their names . . .'

It was probably just as well that Lucy knew nothing about James Fenton's past or, indeed, his present. If she had she might not have been quite so bold. Suddenly, of course, Fenton was a very busy man with a meeting to go to. Lucy could see that she'd annoyed him.

'Look, Ms Ross,' he said, 'I've got nothing against you personally but this is my business. Literally my business. I'm trying to create a fantastic retail opportunity that will bring a lot of investment into the area. It's all legal, all above board.'

'No one's suggesting it isn't, Mr Fenton. I'm just worried about the character of the area.'

'Is that right?' said Fenton, accent slightly ruffled. 'You've only been here five minutes. I've lived here for forty years. I think I know what's best for my own community.'

'I'm sure you do,' said Lucy.

'Look,' he said, clearly not wanting an MP, a member of the establishment, to come away with anything other than a favourable impression of him, 'it'll be great. You wait and see.'

'If you say so, Mr Fenton, but is there nothing you can do about those parking restrictions?'

Fenton gave a nonchalant shrug. He wasn't going to do anything. He'd paid the council a lot of money for that contract and needed to recoup his investment. Greed, as ever, was his fatal flaw.

45

The following morning, Lucy took a trip to the Jubilee Pool and found herself wondering whether her old friend Dawn Weller had ever swum there. Almost certainly, but when Dawn had stepped up on to the podium to be garlanded with yet another medal, the pool would have been fairly new. Opened in 1977, its imaginative name had been inspired by the Queen's Silver Jubilee. After about twenty years as a well-loved and well-maintained leisure facility, the Jubilee had been allowed to fall into dangerous disrepair.

Old pre-war swimming-baths are supposed to be dank and shabby, but Lucy saw something particularly ugly and tragic about public buildings from the seventies and eighties, such recent symbols of civic pride and optimism, that were already falling apart. The reason for the disappearance of public pools like the Jubilee was simple. When councils are strapped for cash or, more usually have badly mismanaged their finances, swimming-pools are the first things to go. Councils have no statutory duty to provide them so they immediately cut their funding. Eventually, sad, disused and in need of a million pounds' worth of maintenance, the pools are sold to developers, swelling both the council's coffers and the nation's obesity problem.

Max, the ruler-bending accountant, was sometimes asked to audit council finances and was always appalled by what he found. 'People assume that all councils are corrupt,' he told Lucy, 'and a lot of them are. But most of them aren't. They're just catastrophically incompetent. Public-sector employees are given huge budgets but have no idea how to run a business, no idea how to run anything. That's why so many places are forced to close down.'

Lucy's mystery correspondent, however, was suggesting that the closure of the Jubilee Pool was not down to incompetence, but corruption.

The pool, Lucy was unsurprised to discover, was 'Closed Until Further Notice' while a leak was allegedly being repaired. As she gazed in at a scene of empty, echoey desolation, she was engulfed by childhood memories of school swimming trips. She was angered that this simple pleasure was now denied to the children in her constituency. If there was corruption at work, she wanted to see James Fenton and his cohorts dropped into the deep end with weights tied to their ankles and left to drown in a sea of urine and verucca plasters.

In the end, however, she knew she'd have to raise the white flag. Unless the law was changed to divest corrupt local councils of their power, the James Fentons of this world would continue to flourish. And what about the councils who weren't corrupt and tried to operate responsibly for the benefit of their communities? It would be unfair for central government to confiscate their authority.

She could carry on the fight but risked being viewed as a one-issue loony, squandering Parliament's time instead of debating matters of global importance.

Sean had decided that what Gary Hardwick had told him, like most things Gary said, didn't matter. Whether or not Fenton was a villain was immaterial. In this case he was a property developer who'd done nothing wrong. Whatever Lucy tried to say would make no difference. As Michael Huntley had told her, and she had told Sean, the average backbench MP has less power than a traffic warden.

Maybe that was a good thing, thought Sean, as he set off for a two-hour wander round London. If politicians had more power, they'd only abuse it.

To cheer Lucy up, he booked a table at Andrew Edmunds, a small romantic and, as he stressed, *independent* restaurant round the corner on Lexington Street. The French onion soup was superb, as was the simple grilled tuna that followed but for Lucy, what came next was even better.

'Just so you always remember,' said Sean, 'that not all shops are hypermarkets. And they never will be.' With that he produced four beautifully wrapped gifts from some of Lucy's favourite shops. There was a plum-coloured cashmere scarf from Sixty-6, a small box of handmade chocolate truffles from Prestat, some Miller Harris tangerine bath oil and a fabulous black suede jewellery box from Pickett. She opened each one with the wide-eyed wonder of a child on Christmas morning.

'There's more to life than politics,' said Sean. 'There's life for a start.'

Lucy flung her arms round him as the waiter approached.

'Would you care for coffee? Dessert?'

'No, thank you,' said Lucy, looking straight into Sean's green eyes. 'Can we just have the bill, please?'

46

Lucy's recent life had been spent either in Soho with Sean, in Essex with Sheila or occasionally with no one in Clapham. The one place she'd neglected was East Finchley with Bruno and Ella.

'Lucia,' said her mother, on the phone, 'we haven't seen you for weeks. Why don't you come home for dinner tomorrow night?'

Lucy loved the way her parents never said, 'come round' or 'come over': it was always 'come home'. Her father, in particular, would have loved it if his entire family all lived together in one big house. 'Okay, great,' said Lucy. 'I will.'

'Why don't you bring this boyfriend of yours? We'd all love to meet him.'

All? Oh, God, that meant at least eight of them. In fact, Sean had met Lucy's parents and Father Sal at the first surgery at the Rose and Crown. She hadn't introduced him as her boyfriend, because it had been very early days; and having set it up, Sean hadn't come to another surgery. He felt a bit useless and, anyway, he was usually down in Kent with his children.

'Um . . . yeah. I'll see what he's doing,' said Lucy.

For some inexplicable reason, she still didn't want to take Sean 'home'. She loved him, he was the best thing that had ever happened to her – so why was she reluctant to let him sit at the huge table and see the biggest bowl of pasta in the world?

She could only link it to her discomfort at being in public life: it had made her desperate to put an electric fence round her privacy. Also, she wasn't sure how her parents would receive him. They were lovely, kind, emotional people but they were still repressed by the Catholic Church. Sean would be ideal because he was handsome, witty, intelligent and the product of a good

Catholic family. But even if they didn't articulate their misgivings, Lucy knew that Bruno and Ella might still regard his separation from his wife in the way that Sir Thomas More had regarded Henry VIII's.

She had another show of hands in her head but this time there was no clear majority – a hung parliament. Oh, God, now what?

Fortunately the decision was made for her when Sean's mobile rang.

'Tomorrow night?' she heard him say. 'Yeah, great. Do you want to come round when you've finished and we'll get a cab from here? . . . Okay, brilliant. See you tomorrow then. 'Bye.'

'Who was that?' she asked.

'Jon,' said Sean. 'He's got a spare ticket for Chelsea–Spurs tomorrow night so for once I'll want Chelsea to win even more than he does.'

Lucy sighed with relief, but wondered whether her inability to make her decision was the result of spending too much time with politicians.

The irony was that Sean would have loved it – the food, the noise, the music, the laughter. Her sister Maria and brother Paul were there with their spouses and children, so were Mr and Mrs Rapacioli from down the road and so, too, inevitably was Father Sal. They weren't particularly interested in Lucy's new career. Compared with the preparations for Maria's daughter's first Holy Communion, it wasn't considered important.

Lucy wondered how the great parliamentary orators would have fared, trying to get a word in edgeways round the dinner table in East Finchley. Eventually, Mr Rapacioli asked her how it was going and she told him about her dealings with Fenton and how, as it turned out, he might be a bit of a crook.

'Of course he is,' said Ella. 'He's a property developer, isn't he? Have you ever met one who isn't?'

'Bit like politicians, eh, Lucy?' said Paul, with a grin, kissing his sister's cheek and rubbing her hair.

There were peals of laughter around the table and, ensconced in the warm bosom of Italian family life, Lucy realised that politics mattered even less to her than it had before she was elected. Unfortunately, what James Fenton was doing was no different from what unscrupulous money-driven people had been doing since time began. She'd tried her best to thwart it but, to quote a cliché, it was the way of the world. All that really mattered to her were the people round this table and the one cheering on Chelsea against Spurs.

She felt, and secretly hoped, that her moment in the spotlight was over. She was happy to be political fish and chip paper for ever.

'So, Lucia,' said Bruno, 'what are you going to do?'

'Not much I can do.'

'I'll pray for you, Lucia,' said Father Sal, less than helpfully. 'We all will. You never know, maybe this Mr Fenton will change his mind. Put your trust in God.'

Lucy remained as sceptical as ever about the tenets of the Catholic Church and the existence of the Almighty, but now was not the time to express her doubts. In fact, there never would be a time to upset Bruno, Ella, and Father Sal by decrying their beliefs. They, and millions like them, were quite content to put their trust in God and it would be easy to ridicule them for it. But, as she wondered constantly, was it any more ridiculous than putting your trust in politicians?

47

The three businessmen turned left when they boarded the American Airlines 747 at JFK. It had been years since any of them had flown economy, yet they took nothing for granted. They appreciated life's little – or, in this case, big – privileges, and were courteous and charming to the airline staff.

They weren't terribly interested in the fripperies of first-class travel – the wonderful food, unlimited champagne and free manicures. The idea of having a flat bed was to sleep on it, and they intended to sleep all the way to Heathrow. For them, this flight wasn't the 'red eye' but the 'bright eye', complete with bushy tail.

Upon arrival a car picked them up – nothing ostentatious, just a plain navy Passat – and whisked them round the M25 to Essex and their meeting with James Fenton to discuss the ruthless US supermarket chain's first big UK venture.

The Passat crunched up the gravel drive and the three men sat and waited. After ten minutes, they saw Fenton park his dark green Bentley. When he got out, so did they.

'Mr Fenton,' said the youngest, a handsome, dark-haired man in his thirties with a polite, Ivy League accent, 'my name's Anthony Rizzo. Is there somewhere we can talk?'

'I'm afraid not,' said Fenton, dismissively. 'If you'd like to make an appointment with my secretary, I'm sure she'll be able to fit you in some time over the next week or two. What's it concerning?'

'I'm here on behalf of Joe Santini.'

Fenton stopped in his tracks. When he turned, the colour had drained from his cheeks. 'Okay, gentlemen,' he said, trying to keep the tremor from his voice, 'If you'd like to come through to my office.'

Rizzo looked nothing like a Mafia hood. Dressed in a blue poplin Brooks Brothers shirt and a pair of Gap chinos, he would have passed unnoticed by anyone. His two colleagues were similarly unremarkable and that was the whole idea. Did anyone really believe that mobsters went around in limos with dark shades and black suits like Ed Harris in *A History of Violence*? Discretion was the order of the day. Organised crime in America was now so beautifully organised that the last thing it looked like was crime. James Fenton was light years behind. For all his practised discretion and *faux*-respectability, he was still just a little too flash.

Fenton sat down in the captain's club chair. Rizzo and his associates preferred to stand.

'Okay, Mr Fenton. As I said, my name is Anthony Rizzo. I'm an attorney and I work for Joe Santini. We're here because we'd like to buy a majority stockholding in Fenton Estates and Parkfair Ltd.'

Fenton was confused. 'Why?'

'Very simple, Mr Fenton. We'd rather you didn't build this huge hypermarket and put all those little mom and pop stores out of business.'

Fenton shook his head in disbelief. 'Why would that be of any interest to you?'

'I'm not at liberty to answer that, Mr Fenton. I've drawn up all the documentation. If you'd like to check that the price we're offering you is fair.'

Fenton looked at the document. It was a reasonable sum but certainly no more than that. 'And what if I don't sign?'

'Well, I thought you might say that, Mr Fenton, so I have our second offer right here.'

Rizzo produced an almost identical document from his attaché case. Fenton looked at it and frowned: it was for half the original amount. 'And if I don't sign that?'

Rizzo smiled. 'Mr Fenton, let's not even go there.'

'The price you're offering – the first price,' he added hastily, 'is still very low.'

'I suppose it is, Mr Fenton,' said Rizzo, 'but we need to hold back a couple of million to restore the Jubilee Pool.'

In a peculiar way, Fenton was pleased. He was egocentric enough to regard it as a huge compliment that Joe Santini, boss of one of the biggest crime families in America, had taken such a keen interest in his business. At sixty-eight, he was getting too old for this sort of caper. Maybe it was time to cash in his chips and retire. Not forgetting, of course, that his bowels were now blancmange and he had never been so scared in his life.

There was something about this Harvard-educated attorney and his smooth, ruthless certainty that frightened him more than any Essex villain ever could. Although he couldn't put his finger on it, what had frightened him was education. If you're educated, articulate and determined, you can take on anyone.

The other two hadn't said a word. They were clearly there just in case education didn't work.

Rizzo handed Fenton a pen. 'If you'd just like to sign here, here and here.'

Sensibly, Fenton did as he was told.

'Thank you, Mr Fenton,' said Rizzo, with a smile. 'Thank you for being so co-operative. You're a smart guy, and for that you should be rewarded. Let me tell you how it is.'

Fenton was ashen. He worshipped money and power and he'd just cravenly signed away several million pounds. He tried to comfort himself by remembering that at least he hadn't signed away his life.

'First thing we're going to do is remove all those parking restrictions. Then we're going to pull out of the deal to build the hypermarket, and restore the swimming-pool. Thing is, Mr Santini's a modest man and he wants you to take the credit for all this. He'd hate to think of you losing face among your associates.'

The face that Fenton hadn't lost had aged about a hundred years in five minutes.

'You're going to make an announcement in the press and on the radio that you've had a change of heart,' said Rizzo, 'and you want to protect these little neighbourhoods and their stores. Think of the respect you'll get for doing that. You'll be remembered for ever. Also, with London holding the Olympics, everyone's going to love you for restoring their sports facilities.'

Fenton was horrified.

'You'll be leaving an everlasting legacy to the people of Great Britain long after you're gone.' Rizzo's tone suddenly turned cold: 'Which, if you don't do exactly as we've told you, will be a lot sooner than you think.'

Fenton knew he was way out of his league. He nodded silently.

'Pleasure doing business with you, Mr Fenton,' said Rizzo, never losing his civility. 'Enjoy your retirement.' He motioned for his two menacing associates to follow him. 'And be grateful that you still have one.'

48

James Fenton's respectable reinvention of himself had been so complete and had taken place so long ago that very few people still remembered his days as Jimmy the Fence. One was Ronnie Hardwick, Gary's dad; another was Father Salvatore de Luca.

Father Sal's success as a priest and as a human being had been helped by his forensic memory. He could remember the names of all his old parishioners and their families, and pretty much every sin they had ever committed. His childhood memories of Clerkenwell before the war were still in sharp focus. He hadn't forgotten life in the shabby tenements of London's Italian quarter, bordered by Farringdon Road, Clerkenwell Road and Rosebery Avenue. He and his family had lived in a tiny tenement in Eyre Street Hill, or 'Aystreet Eel', the core of Little Italy. He remembered the pitiable squalor, redeemed only by the bright clothes and cheery dispositions of the people who lived there. He remembered flat-capped men with black moustaches and bright yellow neckerchiefs, he remembered babies sitting happily on the cobbles in the summer with big, glistering earrings and tiny multicoloured frocks. He remembered the ice-cream vendors singing Neapolitan folk songs as they churned their freshly made *gelati* before loading it on to their barrows. He remembered the barrel-organists with their monkeys and exotic birds. He remembered the warm, comforting smells of washing and cooking coming from the area's countless little alleys and courtyards. He remembered the joy and laughter of a happy, tight-knit community, whose lives revolved around St Peter's Church.

And he remembered the Fentons.

Freddie Fenton was a small-time thug from Holborn who, with

his two brothers, would terrorise the gentle, emotional Italians at every opportunity. Women would be groped and abused, ice-cream carts overturned and their owners pushed to the ground. The whole community was cowed until the arrival from Naples of Louis Santini.

People often wondered why the Mafia had failed to take root in Britain. However, as Father Sal could attest, it did, albeit on a much smaller scale than in America. Louis Santini was a fiery Italian tiler who also lived in a tenement in Eyre Street Hill. Incensed by what he saw, he began by gathering together a little mob in a pub called the Griffin on Clerkenwell Road to protect the community from thugs like Freddie Fenton. Having turned the tables on Fenton, Louis quickly realised that there was more money to be made from crime than tiles, and business boomed.

It was all going well for the Mafia in London until 1940 when Mussolini declared war on Britain. Churchill responded by taking a fairly hardline approach to the many Italians living in London, viewing them all as potential enemies. He issued his famous instruction, 'Collar the lot,' and all men between the ages of eighteen and forty, few of whom had any quarrel with their adopted country, were rounded up and either imprisoned or deported. Overnight, the Italian community in Clerkenwell was decimated.

Father Sal, with his mother and siblings, was put on a boat back to Italy. His father, with thousands of others, was interned in a prisoner-of-war camp on the Isle of Man. Santini was deported to America. Having seen far greater opportunities for organised crime, he decided to stay there. At a stroke, Churchill had wiped out the Mafia in Britain before it had had a chance to get established.

Louis Santini was Father Sal's uncle and Joe, now in his seventies but still very much The Don, was his first cousin. He and Sal had lived together, played together and been deported together. When the war ended, Joe and the other Santinis joined Louis in New York. Father Sal was ordained a priest at Amalfi Cathedral and came back to Clerkenwell in 1960 with his old friend and fellow deportee Bruno Rossi.

Father Sal remained in touch with his cousin. The Santinis loved having a priest in the family. It was as though the vicious and unscrupulous way they made their money and the habitual 'whacking' of rivals was somehow softened by having a man of God as a blood relative. They already had direct access to senators and congressmen, and with Sal on their side, they felt they also had direct access to God and that, come Judgement Day, he would be their celestial attorney and would persuade The Judge to show a little clemency. He was often flown out to the States to officiate at baptisms, weddings and funerals. He never lied to his parishioners: he said he was going to visit family. Omitting to mention, of course, that by 'family' he meant 'Family'.

Never once had he called upon his infamous relatives for help, despite Joe Santini's constant offers. However, when he heard that it was Freddie Fenton's oh-so-respectable son who had ruined Bruno's daughter's laudable crusade to save the little shops in her constituency, he got up from Bruno's table, went to the presbytery and made a call to New Jersey.

Five days later, James Fenton was giving benign interviews to the media about his change of heart and the people of Essex thought he was a hero.

Father Sal had always believed in the power of prayer. However, on this one occasion he had thought it might be more productive to eschew the Pater Noster in favour of the Cosa Nostra.

49

Lucy didn't know whether to laugh or cry. She was delighted, of course that the pool had been saved and that the parking restrictions had been lifted, but she had been thrust back into the limelight, which made her want to weep. She was to be the guest of honour at Roy Webb's bash for two hundred, with a free bar the following evening, at the Rose and Crown. Already King's Parade had held an impromptu party on the pavement, where shopkeepers and residents had been photographed cheering and whooping as the hated pay and display machines were dismantled. The Beer Hunter, the off-licence next door to Junk and Disorderly, had done a roaring trade.

When she arrived at the pub and went in, she realised she'd never noticed the glitterball that hung from the ceiling of the back room. It hadn't played a prominent part in her Sunday-afternoon surgeries but tonight, augmented by the reflection of the mobile disco's multicoloured lights, it was shimmering in all its glory. Lucy developed a when-in-Rome attitude to Malibu and pineapple juice, and when the DJ played Sister Sledge's 'We Are Family' and Beyoncé's 'Crazy in Love' she allowed herself to be corralled with a throng of girls in mini-dresses and stilettos dancing round their handbags, an Essex tradition as noble as morris-dancing.

Although she was feeling a bit tipsy, she wasn't too drunk to notice that Sean was at the bar, having a drink with Roy and a couple of the regulars. Lucy didn't know who they were but, in their too-tight Armani suits, they exuded a combination of stocky menace and garrulous bonhomie. They were the sort of blokes at whom you didn't look twice without very good reason. Sean seemed to know them quite well, and as she watched him laughing and joking, the mist began to clear and she saw him in a new, multicoloured glitterballed light. It might be coincidence. After all, he was one of the friendliest and most clubbable people she'd ever met. Helped in no small measure by his deep voice and strong London accent, he was never fazed or frightened by anyone.

But this was different. He seemed far too familiar with these people, and when they were joined by a third example of Violence in a Suit, and much hand-shaking and back-slapping ensued, Lucy was convinced. Even she'd heard the rumours that Fenton had been leant on by some shadowy gangland figures, and it was now fairly obvious that Sean had had something to do with it. He'd helped her anonymously but immeasurably ever since she'd first met him. She looked at them again, and although she should have been scared and censorious, as her cowardly colleagues would have been, she wasn't. Instead she felt more drawn to Sean than ever. He'd always scoffed at villains and said that 99 per cent were lackeys at the mercy of bosses more ruthless and nasty than any boss from the parallel universe inhabited by 'straight' people. If you added up the money made by the average criminal, he'd said, then factor in the risks and the occasional stretches at Her Majesty's pleasure, most of those mugs would have been better off working at McDonald's.

Well, he was bound to say that, wasn't he? But to help and protect her he'd clearly taken the law into his own hands. Suddenly she saw him as the hero who had made her a heroine. He was, when it came down to it, a very naughty boy. She would never know that her mystery saviour wasn't Sean but was instead the last person on earth she would ever have suspected: a man who'd told her to put her trust in God, conveniently forgetting to suffix the word 'God' with 'father'.

*

Lucy was sitting in the Commons Tea Room with Huntley and Dodds.

'Oh, please,' their *protégée* groaned, 'I don't want to make another speech in the House. Ever.'

'But you must,' insisted Huntley. 'You have to take credit for this. It's a marvellous achievement. Let's hope that other councils follow suit.'

'I can't see that happening,' said Lucy. 'I think this is a one-off. I just got lucky.'

'Are you really not going to make a speech?' asked Dodds. 'Are you not going to lord it over those bastards?'

'No,' she said. 'I'm not interested.'

This was as incomprehensible to Huntley and Dodds as it would have been to any other MP. When you score a rare and magnificent political victory, you seize the chance to rub your rivals' faces in it.

'Well, someone ought to,' said Huntley. 'Leave it to me.'

'No,' said Dodds. 'Leave it to me.'

'I've got an idea,' said Huntley. 'Leave it to both of us.'

'How about all three of us?' suggested Dodds, ever the socialist.

'No, thanks,' said Lucy. 'Count me out.'

'Okay, Mickey,' said Dodds, with a grin. 'Looks like it's thee and me, then.'

Two days later, every seat in the chamber was taken. This was an unprecedented parliamentary spectacle. As far as the public were concerned, Jack Dodds and Sir Michael Huntley were sworn political adversaries, so the idea of them standing up on opposite sides of the House of Commons to make a speech *together* was bound to ignite curiosity.

As soon as Huntley spoke, eloquent, commanding and strong, it was obvious why he was still the star turn at every Conservative Party conference. 'Mr Speaker,' he began, 'let me start by paying tribute to an extraordinary Member of this House. Lucy Ross has only been in Parliament since the last election and already she's had more impact than many people who have sat on these benches for years.'

Dodds was no less impressive. It was easy to see how, when he'd addressed rallies at the South Yorkshire collieries, he could unite and inspire thousands of miners to do whatever he told them. 'By standing up for the little man, the small shopkeeper,' he thundered, 'Lucy Ross has struck a blow against the all-encompassing greed of the supermarkets.'

Over to Huntley: 'Not only that,' he added, 'but she has stood up to the tyranny of local authorities and struck a blow for individualism and freedom of enterprise.'

Back to Dodds: 'Picking up on the Right Honourable Gentleman's point about local authorities. We have a cross-party suggestion. As a nation, we have always had a noble tradition of forming trade unions to protect people against greed and exploitation. I am proud, Mr Speaker, to have been in the vanguard of this movement for more than fifty years.'

This brought applause from the handful of old-style Labour MPs who hadn't yet been pensioned off.

Huntley waited politely for it to abate, then continued: 'Now, I never thought I'd say this but I'm calling for the creation of a new sort of union.'

'A Citizens' Union,' declared Dodds. 'In the same way that we joined together and stood up to the greed and tyranny of employers, we should now be standing together against the greed and tyranny of local authorities.'

Huntley shook his head, like a disappointed schoolmaster. 'They have consistently abused the power that we invested in them,' he said, 'and while it would be undemocratic and wrong to attempt to take that power back, the formation of a Citizens' Union would force local authorities to be more accountable and think more carefully about what they do.'

'It would be like jury service,' explained Dodds, 'but voluntary not compulsory. Each branch of the union would comprise ordinary people from all walks of life.'

'But no one, absolutely no one,' said Huntley, 'who is affiliated to any political party. Local authorities will be required by law to consult representatives from their borough's Citizens' Union before making major decisions. We are proposing a joint private members' bill to get this on to the statute book as soon as possible. We trust that we can count on your support.'

Dodds, unable to resist his famous rallying cry from the early seventies, said slowly and deliberately: 'The people united can never be divided.'

The tumultuous response from both sides of the House indicated that the required cross-party support wouldn't be a problem.

A short stroll away, just across Parliament Square, Lucy and Sean were hiding behind a selection of sorbets at the Inn on the Park right by the lake in the middle of St James's Park. This deceptively smart little restaurant: the building, made of honey-coloured wood, looked like a giant sauna and its picturesque informality provided the perfect antidote to the grandiose splendour of the House of Commons.

'So you didn't want to be there?' said Sean.

'No,' said Lucy. 'In fact, I don't want to go there ever again. I'm quitting while I'm ahead. I've been incredibly lucky.'

'You made your own luck.'

'Not really,' she said. '*You* made my luck. Without you, I still wouldn't have made my maiden speech.'

'Yeah, but—'

'Yeah-but nothing,' said Lucy. 'I'm telling you, and I should know, that most of this is down to you.'

Since the party at the Rose and Crown Lucy had revised her opinion about Sean's villainy. She was still unaffected enough to see the best in people, and was now of the opinion that James Fenton really was a different man, which he was. About £10 million different.

'Who was that goalie you were talking about the other day? Played for Aston Villa?'

'Nigel Spink.'

'Yeah, him. Remind me what he did.'

'He made his first-team début in the European Cup Final. Villa won. How can you ever top that?'

'That's what I mean. I've had a great victory but it will never happen again. Being there today would have been like attending my own memorial service.'

'So you're not even going to watch it on the news?'

'Course I am.' She laughed. 'I may be humble but not quite that humble.'

50

Watching the Huntley and Dodds show on the early-evening news on a sixty-inch TV screen, with Sir Michael booming out of one Bose speaker and Mad Jack booming out of the other, was actually better than being there.

Sean felt his heart swell with pride by proxy as goosebumps popped up all over his body and the hair stood up on the back of his neck. At the end of the joint speech, he leapt off the sofa and jumped around the flat, joining in the parliamentary applause. 'That's fucking brilliant,' he yelled, lifting Lucy up and swinging her round. 'Aren't you proud? Look what you did!'

That was why she loved him so much – for his boundless enthusiasm, generosity of spirit and reluctance to take any credit. 'Look what *you* did,' she insisted. 'How would I have done any of it without you?'

'So, what now?' he asked, still holding her like a hammock, and planted a huge kiss on her lips. 'Have you got the bug yet? Are you happier about staying in politics?'

'Nope. I'm keener than ever to give it all up. I'm Nigel Spink, remember.'

'He went on to play another three hundred games for Villa.'

'Okay,' said Lucy. 'Maybe not.'

And that was what Sean loved so much about Lucy. Her total lack of ego, the absence of vanity. He couldn't imagine other MPs being so honest and modest about their achievements. 'Fair enough,' he said, lowering her back down again. 'When *are* you going to quit?'

'Not sure.' She sighed. She wasn't really sure about anything.

The time was approaching when they would have to take their

relationship up a level, get more 'serious', but she was terrified that the joy of being boyfriend and girlfriend would disappear. They'd ignored the knotty little problem of Sean still being married and, with two children already, whether he really wanted any more. If he didn't, their glorious relationship was on borrowed time, and even if he did, this stupendous flat, which had contributed so much to their happiness, wouldn't lend itself to buggies, cots and changing mats.

Never one to dwell on the future, Lucy snapped back to the present and pulled Sean down on to the sofa. At least, she nearly did. As his lips touched hers, the buzzer sounded and he got up to answer it.

'Hello?'

'Hi, I wondered if Lucy was there. Lucy Ross.'

'Lucy who?'

'Doesn't matter. Wrong buzzer. Sorry to have bothered you.'

Sean turned round. 'Stay here,' he told Lucy. 'Don't answer the door. Won't be a minute.'

He walked down the back stairs and out of the fire escape. He circled the building and, coming back into the mews, saw two men, one with a camera. The one without the camera was still pushing buzzers asking for Lucy.

'Hello, mate,' he said. 'Can I help you?'

'Yeah. Phil Robinson, *Daily Mail*. We're looking for Lucy Ross.'

'Who?'

'That Labour MP. You know the one, bit of a looker. Somebody saw her going in here apparently.'

Sean shrugged his shoulders and let himself back in. He came in, chucked his keys on the table and slumped on to the sofa.

'Who was it?' asked Lucy.

'The *Daily Mail*.'

'Oh, fuck,' said Lucy, real panic in her voice. 'I can't bear it. This has always been my bolt-hole. It's so well hidden that I'd thought no one would find me here.'

'I wouldn't worry about it,' said Sean. 'With all due respect, you're tomorrow's fish-and-chip paper. You know that from last time. It'll all blow over in a couple of days.'

'It's not that I mind talking to journalists,' she explained, 'it's just that I don't want them coming here. This is sacred territory.'

'Well,' said Sean, 'I've got no bookings tomorrow or the next day. Do you fancy buggering off for a couple of days?'

Lucy's panic turned to excitement. 'Yes,' she said, eyes ablaze. 'To somewhere no one will find us. I know just the place.'

51

Sean would have made a very good Italian. He was dark-haired, Catholic, loved good clothes, good food, good wine and good design. Most of all, though, he loved the way the Italians drove and, as he pulled away in a hired Fiat from Naples airport, was delighted to be joining them. 'Look at that,' he said, in admiration rather than admonishment, as a blood-red Alfa Romeo shot through a set of traffic-lights that were exactly the same colour.

'*Benvenuto a Napoli,*' said Lucy. 'This is what it's like.'

'Fine by me,' said Sean, immediately going native and pressing pedal to metal. 'It really pisses me off how pathetically law-abiding British motorists are. They'll sit obediently at traffic-lights at three o'clock in the morning even though there isn't another car on the road.'

'Well,' said Lucy, 'Michael Huntley always maintains that the British, with their servile, mustn't-grumble attitude, are the one race who could live quite happily under Communism.'

'I think he's right,' said Sean. 'Lots of rules and regulations and plenty of opportunities for queuing. The Italians would never put up with all that, and neither would the Irish.'

'That's why I've got to get out of politics,' said Lucy. 'The Labour Party really takes advantage of that aspect of the British people. I don't want any part of it.'

As they approached the Amalfi coastline, Sean wished his parents had been Italian rather than Irish. 'God, this is fabulous. Did you come here every year for your holidays?' he asked enviously, remembering his own dismal, rain-sodden trips to Tipperary.

'Every year,' said Lucy. 'Mum and Dad would shut the deli for two weeks in August and we'd come and stay with Nonna and Nonno.'

Sean wondered if Nonna and Nonno might be cartoon characters like Pinky and Perky, until he remembered that the words meant grandmother and grandfather.

Lucy felt a familiar wave of relaxation wash over her. After the *Daily Mail* incident, she was seized by a sudden yearning to escape to Minori and hide inside her childhood.

Sean gazed out at the sea. He'd never seen a coastline so stunning.

'I know it's tempting,' said Lucy, as the car veered a little too close to the edge, 'but do try to keep your eyes on the road. A lot of people who were gazing at the sea have ended up plummeting into it.'

Sean could see how easily this could happen. To their left, there was a sheer drop into the Mediterranean, to their right an equally vertical ascent to a distant clifftop. Glancing up, Sean saw terraced gardens that tumbled out of the sky and plunged into the pastel-painted houses below. Olive trees and bougainvillaea shrouded the little swimming-pools that clung to the cliff face. The whole effect was spectacular.

This dramatic and unyielding topography had ensured that the Amalfi coast remained relatively unspoilt. Villages balanced precariously near the edge of a cliff can never broaden out into sprawling holiday resorts so they had remained resolutely Italian. This was exactly as Sean had imagined the south of Italy. He was delighted to see that the locals really did wobble along the narrow coastal road on Vespas, without crash helmets, in shorts and flip-flops, balancing boxes of lemons between their knees. Ice-cream was sold on the promenade by men pushing old-fashioned hand-carts, fishermen still took wooden boats out at night to catch the following day's lunch and, yes, washing lines really were strung across tiny cobbled streets.

'Left here,' said Lucy, directing him up a particularly narrow one. Then she announced that they had arrived. They climbed an unfeasibly steep flight of steps and Lucy put her key into a wooden door that Sean wouldn't even have noticed.

'Well,' he said, as they entered the old apartment, 'the *Daily Mail* have got no chance of finding you here.'

'Exactly.' She smiled.

It wasn't because the shutters had been down for the last six weeks and the apartment smelt damp and musty that Sean felt uncomfortable. Neither was it the crucifix above the bed, the holy-water font by the door or the pious, forbidding pictures of St Trofimena, which appeared to be in every room. It was because he felt like a gauche adolescent whose girlfriend had invited him round while her mum and dad were out. It was an awkward sensation and he was about twenty-five years too old to be experiencing it. He'd had a hunch he might feel like this and it was obvious that Lucy did too.

'Very nice,' he said. 'Very quaint, very Italian. But we can't possibly stay here, can we?'

'No,' said Lucy. She knew why, he knew why, so no explanation was necessary.

'Don't worry,' he said. 'I made contingency plans.'

'Where are we going?' she asked.

'It's a surprise.' He winked. 'Come on, take me out and show me Minori.'

It was a few years since Lucy had been there and she was hit by a Proustian rush as soon as she stepped back down to the village. Sweet childhood memories were everywhere: on the beach, along the lemon groves, up the walnut trees and down the little alleyways. Each was waiting to greet her and ask where she'd been. She'd been to a lot of places since she had last come here and that was the trouble. As she strolled around the little streets, she felt as though she was visiting her primary school, giggling at the tiny loos and Lilliputian coat pegs. Like Alice in Wonderland, she'd grown too big and could no longer fit through the door. What had once seemed so exciting and exotic was now just a little village, which took about forty minutes to explore.

Sean loved the hidden, ancient, almost vertical steps, hewn straight out of the cliffs up which you could climb from one village to the next. He also found it incredibly sexy when Lucy spoke fluent Italian to the shopkeepers, waiters and the old man who sold them a bottle of his home-made Limoncello. Sean, had a fairly strong tolerance to alcohol but he knew that if he had more than one shot the car really would end up in the sea.

They drove the few miles up to Amalfi where a large party of middle-aged tourists from Wolverhampton ensured that they saw a distressing collection of sandals worn with socks. Their coaches, Lucy said, would never make it up the mountain to Ravello. It would be challenging enough in the little Fiat – but that was exactly where they took it. It wheezed its way up, able to manage only first and second gear and eventually delivered its passengers to one of planet Earth's top-ten views.

'This,' said Lucy, wrapping her arms round Sean, 'might just be the most romantic place on Earth.'

Ravello was nothing like Minori and it would be hard for anyone to feel that they'd outgrown a place so smart and jaw-droppingly beautiful. Perched right at the top of a cliff, it looked down on the rest of the Amalfi coast both literally and metaphorically. With its serene mix of nature, culture and architecture, combined with breathtaking views across the bay to Capri, Ravello made Sean and Lucy feel as though they'd arrived at the top of the world.

Sean, for once in his loquacious life, was silent.

'Believe it or not,' said Lucy, 'I've only ever been here a couple of times. I always found it quite intimidating. It was so in-accessible, so posh, so grown-up. As a kid, I was never quite ready for Ravello.'

'Are you ready now?' said Sean.

'Yep,' said Lucy. 'I think so.'

'Good,' said Sean, 'because you see that unbelievably gorgeous hotel over there?'

Lucy nodded.

'That's where we're staying.'

Lucy wasn't the only one with a worldwide wish list of hotels. Like Virginia Woolf, Truman Capote and Humphrey Bogart before him, Sean had always wanted to stay at the Hotel Caruso. He'd tried to take Nikki for a romantic weekend there, but she'd ruined it by saying that she'd prefer to go somewhere that was right on the beach rather than 'on top of a bloody cliff'. They'd ended up staying at home

Lucy was, to put it mildly, a little more appreciative. She almost wept at the thought of staying at the Caruso. Since it was so close to her parents' apartment, it had never occurred to her that she ever would. 'Just so you know,' she said, 'this, to me, is even more special than the Mount Nelson. I do not want to leave this hotel until we check out tomorrow. Please don't ask me to.'

Sean had no intention of leaving either. They swam together in a pool deliberately positioned to create a spectacular azure illusion. It was right on the edge of the cliff so, on a sunny day, it was impossible to distinguish between the blue of the pool, the sea and the sky. As night fell, they sat on the terrace and poured a couple more shots of the home-made Limoncello to make them nice and woozy before they went to bed.

Lucy felt they really had raised their relationship several notches, and not just because they were twelve hundred feet above sea level.

As her eyes closed she couldn't help giggling because, considering the Caruso was a former Renaissance monastery, their behaviour between supper and sleep had been far from monastic.

52

It was all a terrible come-down. Sean could only stay in Italy for one night – he had to get home to do an ISDN link to Chicago that evening, followed by a feature-length cartoon the following morning.

Lucy was staying on for two more days. She'd have got on the plane with Sean if her mum and sister hadn't been coming out to join her, and even then she was still tempted to sneak herself into his hand baggage.

The Fiat rolled forlornly back down the big hill to Minori and deposited Lucy at the steps to the apartment, which, compared with the laid-back luxury of the Caruso, seemed depressingly drab and mundane. She tried to take a positive attitude by bearing in mind that life's lows only exist because of the highs with which we compare them. Highs that we're lucky to experience and will, no doubt, experience again.

Sighing heavily, she strolled out towards the promenade and was nearly run over by a white Transit van, which screeched to an unsteady halt a couple of yards from her. Noticing that the van had British number-plates and the driver was sitting on the right, she yelled at him in English: 'What the hell are you doing? You nearly killed me!'

He stuck his head out of the window. 'Oh dear,' he said. 'I'm so sorry . . . I'm a terrible driver.'

There are two things for which the human male cannot bear to be criticised, and driving's the other one, so a man freely acknowledging his ineptitude was both disarming and endearing. Lucy had to smile. As he apologised again, and went to drive off, she thought she recognised him. 'Don't I know you?' she asked.

The man looked at her quizzically. 'Er . . . no, I don't think so.'

'You're a doctor, aren't you?'

'That's right,' he said.

Lucy's hair was scrunched up under a baseball cap and she was wearing sunglasses, so she removed the shades, took off the cap and shook her hair down. 'Now do you recognise me?'

'Yes,' he said. 'Of course. Lucy . . . um . . . Lucy Ross.' He was the trim, handsome, slightly foppish young medic who'd stood in a couple of times when Dr Gerrard, the regular medical adviser, had been unable to attend the Rose and Crown Sunday surgeries.

'I'm sorry,' said Lucy, 'I don't think anyone ever told me your name.'

'Robert,' he smiled, 'Robert Taylor.'

He parked the van at the side of the road, almost up-ending an ice-cream cart and vendor as he did so. 'Whoops,' he said. 'So sorry . . . um . . . *Scusami*.'

'Well,' said Lucy, 'if you're going to be run over, best to be run over by a doctor. At least he might be able to save your life.'

Robert got out of the van. 'I s'pose so. Anyway, Lucy, what are you doing here?'

'I'm Italian,' she said. 'Well, London Italian. This is my parents' home village.'

'Ah, yes, of course,' said Robert, apparently rehearsing for his future life as an absent-minded professor. 'I met them at your surgery thingy. In fact, your father's the reason I'm here.'

'My father?'

'Yes,' said Robert. 'Look, if I can buy you a coffee by way of apology for nearly killing you, I'll explain.'

They stepped into a dark little café that smelt of coffee beans and cigar smoke and ordered two double espressos.

'Thing is,' said Robert, as they sat down, 'I never wanted to be a doctor. I wanted to be . . .'

'A lumberjack?' Lucy smiled.

'Well, anything other than a doctor,' he said. 'My father was a GP and he sort of pushed me into it. Well, actually, that's not strictly true. In fact, it's a complete lie. He never tried to push me at all. I've got two sisters, you see, and I'm the only boy so it was just assumed that I'd follow him into what he regarded as the family profession. It meant so much to him and, well, I just couldn't bear to let him down. He's such a good man, always regarded medicine as a noble calling and devoted his whole life to curing people. He just wanted me to do the same.'

The *barista* brought their espressos and Robert took a sip. 'God, that's strong,' he said.

Lucy tasted hers and, yes, it *was* quite strong, but Robert clearly hadn't experienced the heart-jolting caffeine blast of the espressos served in East Finchley. 'Nothing wrong with following in your father's footsteps,' she said.

'Maybe not,' said Robert. 'Unless you really hate it and don't feel you're cut out for it.'

'I know the feeling,' replied the similarly reluctant MP.

'As a doctor, you have to be able to distance yourself from the unhappiness you see every day,' he explained, 'and, unlike my father, I don't have that clinical detachment.'

Robert had unwittingly identified another disquieting feeling with which Lucy was only too familiar. Her lack of clinical detachment meant that her visits as an MP to paediatric and cancer-care units always had her sobbing as soon as she got home.

'Anyway,' said Robert, taking another apprehensive sip of coffee, 'the profession has changed so much since my dad's day. There were none of these discussions about 'doctor-patient relationships'. For him, it was all very simple. He was the doctor, they were the patients. He sat behind a desk and told them what was wrong with them. At my last group practice, we were told to sit *next to* the patient and empathise. Oh, yes, it was all about empathy and non-judgemental ungendered relativism.'

'Sounds just like being an MP,' laughed Lucy, even though she knew there was nothing funny about the way some politicians manipulated language to confuse people, attached unwarranted importance to simple tasks and distanced themselves from the very people they were supposed to be helping. 'Politics could and should be a noble calling, but I'm not cut out for it.'

Robert seemed surprised. 'But you are,' he insisted. 'Those Sunday surgeries are a brilliant political initiative.'

'But they're not,' said Lucy, always happy to confess. 'They're nothing to do with politics. I just set them up to help my constituents. Or I should say to get other people to help my constituents because I don't know anything about anything.'

'But what about that Citizens' Union thing with Jack Dodds and Michael Huntley?'

'That was their idea,' said Lucy.

'But you started it off and now you're quite famous.'

'Not over here, thank God. And by the time I get back to London on Saturday, people will have found someone else to concentrate on. At least, I hope they will. Anyway, you promised to tell me why you're out here and what it's got to do with my dad.'

'Oh, yes,' said Robert, 'of course. Well, you see, I've always loved food and I really believe that I could do more to improve people's health by encouraging them to eat well rather than wasting any more time in NHS collaborative consensual patient-care programmes.'

'I'm sure you're right.'

'So anyway, the reason I'm in Italy is because I'm about to open a sort of healthy fast-food place.'

'All lentils and lesbians?'

'There may well be a lentil or two,' said Robert, with a smile, 'and lesbians are more than welcome but, no, this place is going to be different.'

'How?' asked Lucy, not wanting to see another hippy joint serving organic wholemeal quiche that was all attitude and no taste.

'Well, it's not going to be vegetarian, for a start. We're going to serve good, simple food. Organic beef, corn-fed chicken, grass-fed lamb, fair-trade coffee, fish from sustainable sources. It's not difficult, just a question of finding the right suppliers.'

'Well, I know a really good greengrocer in Chelmsford,' said Lucy. 'There's even a record shop round the back.'

'That's the sort of thing I need,' he said, 'and I'm out here because your dad very kindly recommended some suppliers to me. Places for the best lemons, olive oil, pecorino, mozzarella and salami. I'm stocking up here, then driving the van back to London.'

'I hope you speak Italian.'

'Well, I can order a pizza.'

'Hmm,' said Lucy, with a frown. 'A lot of my dad's suppliers are farmers right out in the sticks. They don't speak a word of English.'

'Oh, I'm sure I'll be fine,' said Robert, with an expression that suggested otherwise.

Lucy looked at this kind, rather innocent doctor and couldn't bear the thought of any sly salami suppliers taking advantage of him. 'Do you want me to come with you?' she offered. 'I know all his suppliers. They'll give me a much better deal than they'd give you.'

'Well, that would be splendid,' said Robert, almost painfully grateful. 'Are you sure you don't mind?'

'Not at all. My mum and my sister aren't flying in till tonight so I was at a bit of a loose end anyway.' Lucy finished her coffee and knew that a day spent bumping along dusty, unmade roads, tracking down obscure farms and olive groves would make the sharp pain of Sean's departure a little easier to bear. Robert paid for the coffee and they went outside.

'Okay, White Van Man,' Lucy said, jumping into the passenger seat and putting her feet on the dashboard. 'Where do you need to go?'

'Um,' was the best he could manage.

'Shall we start with the lemons?' she suggested. 'The best place is only about ten minutes from here. Oh, and try not to run anyone over.'

Robert started the engine and they began to talk. The more time Lucy spent with him, the more she warmed to him. He was that rare thing, a public-school-educated English Catholic, so he had all the kindness, conscience and cultural parallels topped off with charm, courtesy and beautiful manners. The journalist in her wanted to know more, much more, about him. 'So have you only worked for the NHS?' she asked.

'No,' said Robert. 'And that's the best thing about being a doctor. You can work anywhere at any time, and I did. After a few years at Guy's Hospital, I went to south-west France.'

'Very nice.'

'Not really,' said Robert. 'I was accompanying pilgrims to Lourdes. That's when I saw at first hand how . . . how . . . well, how silly the Catholic Church is.'

'Tell me about it.' Lucy rolled her eyes towards Heaven. If, indeed, there was such a place.

Robert shook his head.

'No,' said Lucy. 'I mean *tell* me about it.'

'Oh, right,' he said. 'Sorry. I just suddenly realised that, you know, coming from an Italian Catholic family, you might find my apostasy rather offensive.'

'I doubt it,' said Lucy.

'Well, when I was in Lourdes, I felt desperately sorry for the pilgrims,' he explained. 'Obviously because they were so sick but also because they really believed they might receive some sort of miracle cure when, as a doctor, I knew they wouldn't. I wondered whether there really had been any miracles so I spoke to Father Kinsella, an Irish priest who was based there.'

'What did he say?'

'He told me that they'd had about eighty thousand sick pilgrims every year for the last hundred years. So that's about eight million people hoping to be cured. How many so-called miracles do you think there have ever been?'

Lucy shrugged.

'Sixty-six,' said Robert.

'What sort of miracles were they?' said Lucy.

'Well, that's just it,' said Robert, 'I asked Father Kinsella if people had, for example, regrown severed limbs, and of course they hadn't. I wasn't trying to catch him out or prove him wrong, I genuinely wanted to know. He had to admit that, in each case, the so-called 'miracle' may well have happened anyway.'

'Fairly harmless, though, isn't it?' said Lucy. 'Like believing in astrology.'

'Yeah, I suppose so, but shortly after that I worked in the Sudan, then moved on to Kenya.'

Lucy was about to mention how she'd always wanted to stay at the luxurious Serena Beach Hotel in Mombasa but realised that that might not be the Kenya Robert was talking about.

'If you saw the orphanages,' he went on, 'the hundreds of babies whose parents have died of Aids as a direct result of the Pope's refusal to allow the use of condoms, if you witnessed the appalling human cost, you'd never set foot inside a Catholic church again.' But it had still been Catholic guilt, he explained, that had made him go out to help the relief efforts in Africa, Pakistan and East Timor. Then he had been truly glad to be a doctor and it was always good to have that vital knowledge and those qualifications to fall back on.

They talked about their pasts and presents. Robert was currently single, having just split up from his girlfriend of three years. Lucy admired the chivalrous way he refused to deride her or blame her for anything. He said that their relationship had simply run its course. His face fell when Lucy told him about Sean.

That said, she had lot in common with Robert. He was only

a year older than her, which made him seven years younger than Sean, so they were at similar stages in their lives, especially when Robert admitted, quite touchingly, that although he'd delivered dozens of babies, he wanted one day to deliver a couple of his own.

'So what are you going to call this restaurant of yours?'

Robert seemed a little embarrassed by this. 'Well, it wasn't my idea,' he said, 'but my two partners are insisting. They want to call it Dr Robert's.'

'After you?'

'Well, more after the Beatles' track on *Revolver*. I suppose the word 'doctor', implies good health even if the Dr Robert in the Beatles' track was a drug-dealer.'

'I think it's a great name,' she said. 'Where is the restaurant?'

'Clerkenwell Road. Do you know it?'

'Know it?' she shrieked. 'I was born there.' Once she found out that his new food emporium would be a few doors from her parents' old one, she felt they'd bonded.

'Thank you again,' he said, as the van, now considerably heavier than it was when it nearly ran Lucy over, rumbled back down the hill to Minori. 'I would never have found those places on my own. I don't know what I'd have done without you.'

'I must admit,' she said, with a grin, 'I don't know what you'd have done either.'

'Promise me you'll drop by when you get back to London.'

'I promise.'

The white van disappeared into the dusk and Lucy thought how interesting and charmingly eccentric Robert was. The depth of his life made her feel, even as an MP who'd achieved so much so quickly, a little shamed by the shallowness of her own.

If she hadn't been with Sean, she'd have fancied Robert, especially as he wasn't burdened with an estranged wife and two small children. She loved his intelligence, his enthusiasm, his quiet determination and his fundamental goodness. His fast-food venture on Clerkenwell Road sounded like a wonderful idea and she was intrigued by 'Dr Robert's'. And, had she not been so in love with Sean, she would have been even more intrigued by Dr Robert.

53

Despite what Robert had said, Lucy did set foot inside a Catholic church. However, St Peter's Italian Church on Clerkenwell Road didn't count. Since 1863 St Peter's had been the focal point of the Italian community in London, and although that community no longer existed within the vicinity of the church and there was no tangible parish, Italians returned every Sunday from as far afield as Watford and Barnet to hear mass in their native tongue. People from little villages reconvened in their hundreds for important occasions such as weddings and baptisms, and it was for her niece's first Holy Communion that Lucy had returned to the fold.

There was something irrefutably sweet and magical about the front pews filled with immaculate dark-haired children – boys in smart little suits, girls in flowing white dresses – all enjoying their special day. The fact that they were being inducted into a weird, rather disturbing ritual that involved pretending to eat the body of a man who died two thousand years ago was conveniently forgotten.

Such was the splendour of St Peter's – its long central nave flanked by towering Ionic columns, its high altar framed by spectacular arches, and the enormous hand-painted frieze, which was Clerkenwell's equivalent of the Sistine Chapel ceiling, the acres of Italian marble, the array of statues, paintings and mosaics – that the place had a grandeur and purpose far greater than the precepts of the Catholic Church.

Although Lucy didn't believe in God she believed in St Peter's, and now that she was no longer made to attend mass there every Sunday, she enjoyed her sporadic visits. With its sense of occasion and warm, emotive embrace, it was far more appealing than the cold, reproving English and Irish parishes that she'd sometimes had the misfortune to visit.

Mass at St Peter's was always in Italian and usually sung, so it was more like going to the opera. The story told was just as nonsensical but there was passion and beauty in the way it was performed. For Lucy, the rhythm and musicality of the language made the perfect accompaniment to daydreaming.

Her mind wandered back to her own first Holy Communion and how proud and pretty she'd felt in her white lace gloves, holding a snow-white missal. She remembered the discos a few years later at St Peter's Italian youth club. She remembered the annual procession in honour of Our Lady of Mount Carmel, and fancying the pants – or in this case the loincloth – off Tony Vitalli, who'd been tied to a cross on one of the many colourful floats that paraded slowly through the streets. She remembered wondering if there was anything wrong or immoral about wanting to snog Jesus.

She remembered kneeling down, mouthing the words of the Lord's Prayer, '*Padre Nostro che sei nei ciell*', while trying to compose a fan letter to the lead singer of Duran Duran. Here she was, doing it again: now she was composing her letter of resignation from the House of Commons, something along the lines of not being cut out for life as an MP, and although it had been her privilege to serve the constituents of Chelmsford South, she felt it better to return to her career in journalism and leave politics to those who would give it the commitment it deserved.

She would receive an insincere reply expressing surprise and regret, but wishing her all the best for the future. No one would try to talk her out of it because they'd be delighted. The Labour Party wanted people who were pliable and obedient, even if they achieved nothing. An MP who did things independently, while remaining resolutely off-message, was their worst nightmare. She was glad to go and they'd be glad to see the back of her. The only losers would be the people of Chelmsford South.

As she watched the children file up to eat their first piece of Jesus, her thoughts turned to Sean. She was in the place where her parents and most of her relatives had been married. She wondered now whether her first Holy Communion all those years ago would be her sole trip to the altar of St Peter's in a flowing white dress. Would she ever stand there with Sean? He was the man of her dreams but he hadn't even hinted at marriage. And, as a divorcee, would he be welcome at this old-fashioned crucible of Roman Catholicism? He knew St Peter's very well and had told Lucy that he, too, thought it the most beautiful church in London. He'd told her how he and his mates had walked down from Islington to go to the Friday-night discos at the Italian youth club next door. The girls were much better-looking, he'd said, than their English and Irish counterparts before adding that, unfortunately, so were the blokes.

When mass ended and she joined the queue to be kissed on both cheeks by Father Roberto, she suddenly remembered the promise she'd made to another Roberto.

54

Lucy decided that no one would miss her if she slipped away for half an hour. All the children had gone downstairs to the crypt for the traditional Holy Communion breakfast. The congregation, meanwhile, would spend at least twenty minutes on the church steps, gossiping, laughing, embracing and gesticulating before settling down in the social club next door. As Lucy wandered off, she could see that, even in the twenty-first century, Clerkenwell Road could still resemble a small village in the south of Italy.

By contrast, Dr Robert's typified what the area had become. The old print works and warehouses had been transformed into loft apartments, and many of their chic, metropolitan inhabitants had converged for Sunday brunch at this wonderful new place they'd found. Its handsome interior, fashioned largely from reclaimed timber, gave people the impression that the restaurant had been there for years but they'd only just discovered it. There was a big industrial-style kitchen at the back, a gigantic communal refectory table in the middle and lots of smaller ones in secluded alcoves round the sides. Best of all, there was a man in a wide-brimmed fedora playing boogie-woogie on an old upright piano in the corner.

The place was rammed and, although she scanned every inch of it, Lucy couldn't see Robert.

'Excuse me,' she said, to a waitress carrying a tray filled with plates of hot wholemeal toast and bowls of Turkish yoghurt, 'I'm looking for Robert – Robert Taylor.'

Since her hands were full, the waitress nodded towards a group of people in the corner. Lucy still couldn't see Robert but, rather than ask again, she went over to the table. She still couldn't see him, then realised that this was because he was the man wearing the wide-brimmed fedora playing the piano. She stood behind him so that he couldn't see her. 'Do you take requests?' she asked.

'Er . . . yes,' said a polite voice from under the hat.

'*Cinque chili dei limoni soddisfano.*'

Robert turned round so quickly that the hat only just stayed on his head. His fingers veered uncontrollably off course, and the whole restaurant glanced up to see what had happened to the pianist. It was the first time he'd been asked for five kilos of lemons.

'Carry on,' said Lucy, with a grin. 'I was enjoying that.'

It was clear from Robert's flustered expression that he couldn't carry on. His mind was elsewhere, his concentration destroyed, and the musical impulses from his brain to his fingertips had gone so haywire that if he'd tried to continue people would have thought he'd been replaced by a chimpanzee.

'No, no,' he said. 'It's okay . . . um . . . Time for a break anyway.' He remembered the fedora and removed it. 'Sorry about the hat. Bit of an affectation, but I always wear it. I can never play in public without a hat and I've had this one for years.'

Lucy smiled.

He called to the barman. 'Andy,' he said, 'can you put on that Oscar Peterson CD? No one will notice.' He turned back to Lucy. 'Probably the world's greatest jazz pianist.' He grinned. 'I flatter myself.'

'I don't know,' she said, 'you play beautifully. Why didn't you mention this before?'

'I suppose I was more interested in buying balsamic vinegar and olive oil.'

'So were you classically trained?'

'My mother was,' said Robert, 'so she had us playing almost before we could walk. Thing is, I never really liked classical music. I much prefer pub stuff. I played quite a lot at Cambridge when I joined Footlights. I always wanted to be up at the front, getting all the laughs, but because I could play the piano, I was always stuck at the back of the stage.'

Lucy had forgotten how much she'd liked Robert's modesty and diffidence. Only he would apologise for, rather than boast about, being a doctor *and* a pianist. She was expecting him to apologise again, for being a successful restaurateur, but he didn't. 'So, what do you think?' he said, gesturing proudly and confidently at the dozens of delighted diners.

'Looks great,' said Lucy, 'but the proof of the pudding . . .'

'Yes, of course,' said Robert. 'Let me get you a menu. What do you fancy?'

At that moment Lucy quite fancied the doctor-pianist-restaurateur. Not in the breathless, heart-in-the-mouth way she fancied Sean, but there was a lovely gentle warmth about Robert and it was hard not to be attracted to a man filled with such talent and goodness.

'Have a bacon sarnie,' he suggested. 'Bacon from a wonderful farm in Dorset, organic mushrooms and tomatoes, with a squidge of homemade ketchup.'

'Sounds great,' she said, 'and of course I have to test your espresso.'

'Marisa,' Robert called, to a beautiful Brazilian-looking waitress. 'Er . . . two bacon sandwiches and two espressos, please. Thank you.'

In less than a minute, the sandwiches and coffee had arrived. 'Real fast food,' said Robert, with a smile.

'Or real food fast,' said Lucy, and took a bite. 'Wow! I never knew a bacon sandwich could taste so good.'

'Congratulations, Ms Ross. That was the right answer,' said Robert. 'Anyway, it's very kind of you to drop in.'

'Well,' said Lucy, between mouthfuls, 'to be honest, I was just across the road at my niece's first Holy Communion.'

'Still,' said Robert, 'it's very good of you.'

'So, is it going well, then?' she said. 'Like I need to ask.'

'We've been packed since we opened,' he said, with the delight of a man who'd found his vocation. 'At long last I'm doing some-thing I really want to do. I became a doctor to please my father, had piano lessons to please my mother and now, ironically, I'm having the time of my life doing both.'

'Both?'

'Ah, well, you see,' explained Robert, 'you were a big influ-ence there. I loved the way you had a constituency surgery at the back of a pub so I've just started a doctor's surgery at the back of the restaurant. Very irregular times, I'm afraid, but usually evenings and weekends when other surgeries are closed. You make an appointment at the bar.'

'That's fantastic!'

'Well, I suffered and slogged to get those qualifications, so it seemed wrong not to use them. Especially as I'm neither a chef nor a businessman. I just like buying all the food. I've always enjoyed shopping.'

'Shopping?' said Lucy, finishing the best bacon sandwich and second-best espresso she'd ever tasted. 'In that case, you're my kind of man,' she said. 'God, that was delicious. So much nicer than the Body of Christ. Right, I'd better get back. I've kept you away from that piano for long enough.'

'Yes,' said Robert. 'And I've kept you away from your rela-tives.'

Lucy stood up. 'Well, best of luck with Dr Robert's, Dr Robert,' she said, 'not that you'll need it. This place is wonderful.'

'Thank you,' said Robert, putting his hat back on. 'Um . . . before you go, I just want to tell you about my car.'

'Your car?'

'Yes,' he replied. 'It's a 1993 Volkswagen Golf convertible. The original shape, you know, the Mark I.'

'Right,' said Lucy, wondering why he was telling her this.

'I'd wanted one since I was about twelve and mine's a special edition, one of the last five hundred ever made.'

'Okay,' said Lucy, nodding slowly.

'Well, a couple of years ago, I was stuck in an awful traffic jam on Battersea Bridge and I noticed this blue Golf convertible in front of me, absolutely immaculate, and I thought, 'that's the car I've always wanted. I've got to have it. I've never seen one in such perfect condition. But in a few minutes we'll be over the bridge, the car will be gone and I'll never get a chance like this again.'

'So what did you do?'

'I jumped out of my car and asked the driver of the Golf whether he'd consider selling it. I'd never done anything quite so impulsive before but I thought, What the hell? No harm in asking. If he doesn't want to sell it, I'll just say, "Sorry to have troubled you," and never see him again.'

'But he said yes, didn't he?'

'He did,' said Robert. 'It turned out that he and his wife had just had a baby and a convertible was no longer practical.'

'So have you still got it?' said Lucy.

'Absolutely,' said Robert. 'I use it every day. It's the best of both worlds – like an old classic car, but not that old.'

'Well, that's great,' said Lucy, still a little confused.

There was a long, awkward pause, and she turned to go.

'You see, the thing is,' said Robert, stammering slightly, 'that taught me a lesson. If you see a chance, you have to take it. I've been following my instincts ever since. This restaurant is the result.'

Looking at him, Lucy realised he wasn't a ditherer but a decision-maker. And a very quick decision-maker at that.

'My dad reckons that that's what's gone wrong with general practice,' he explained. 'Too much analysis, too much discussion. "A good doctor," he says, "relies far more on instinct." That day on Battersea Bridge, I had a hunch that that car should belong to me. What was the worst that could have happened? He could have said no.'

He paused and tugged down the brim of his fedora. 'Or you could say no.'

'Me?' said Lucy.

'Yes,' said Robert. 'You're also about to disappear, and just before you do, I want you to know that I have a hunch we should be together. I've had it since the day I nearly ran you over in Italy. I know we've only ever spent a day together but what happened to me on Battersea Bridge is happening to me again. Times ten. I know you're happy with Sean but, well, if the situation ever changes . . .'

Lucy looked at him, handsome, intelligent, quite wonderful, and found herself swaying, literally. But she didn't know which way to sway. Neither did she know what to say. God, she was tempted. If she hadn't been so besotted with Sean, she would have let herself sway forwards, fall into Robert's arms and stay there for ever.

But she was besotted with Sean and she needed to see him as soon as possible.

55

It was a journey Sean had made many times before. The place he was going had once been Barclays Bank, 160 Piccadilly branch, and he still cringed when he recalled the frequent summonses he had received from Mr D.G. Wilson, the manager. Sean had never discovered what 'D.G.' stood for. Neither, he suspected, had any of the staff, let alone the customers. As far as the world was concerned, D.G. Wilson's Christian name was 'Mister'.

Years before Sean's voice had made him a small fortune, he was often led across the marble-floored, mahogany-countered, high-ceilinged hush of the banking hall. A door was unlocked and he would be ushered along another corridor to Mr Wilson's office.

D.G. would sit solemnly steepling his fingers in grave disappointment at the way Mr Reilly's account had strayed once again into the red. D.G. Wilson took an extremely dim view of this. He regarded going overdrawn and taking money that didn't belong to you as theft, and any customer who did so as a bank robber. It was little wonder that whenever he visited Barclays Bank, 160 Piccadilly, Sean felt not so much a customer as a defendant.

It was a long time since he'd entered the stately Grade-II listed building. D.G. Wilson and his many minions were long gone, and Barclays Bank was now The Wolseley, a superb Viennese-style grand café to which those high, vaulted ceilings and marble floors were beautifully suited. Even at eleven o'clock in the morning, one of the few times you could secure a table without a reservation, the Wolseley was buzzing with a score of crisply attired waiters, who appeared to be on casters, taking and delivering the orders of at least a hundred customers.

The sun was shining through the huge arched windows and Sean could think of no finer place to have brunch with Lucy and yet, as he was shown to a discreet table in the corner, he felt the same sense of doom fall upon him as he had felt when he was shown into Mr Wilson's office.

Lucy's request to meet him at The Wolseley was unusual. She always went to his flat but she'd already decided that she must never go there again. She loved it and its owner so much that she knew if she crossed the threshold she would be seduced immediately by them both.

Resigning from Parliament had been relatively easy. She'd delivered the letter by hand that morning. Resigning from the most perfect relationship she'd ever had would be a lot more difficult. It required courage, willpower and, she kept thinking, insanity. None the less, she knew she had to do it.

Just watching Sean arrive and dispense such easy charm with the rather snooty maître d', then seeing the man's professionally stern features break into a smile at whatever remark Sean had just delivered, made her question her instincts and wonder whether she was doing the right thing.

Sean was perfect. He was the man Lucy was supposed to marry, but she would never get over the hurdle that someone else had married him first. She realised how old-fashioned she was. Although she could easily be with a man who'd left his wife, she wasn't sure she could be with a man who'd left his children.

For Lucy, Mr Reilly was, without question, Mr Right. The core of his being matched and complemented the core of hers, but Robert had made her realise that Sean wasn't the only man in the world who could make her happy. In fact, through no fault of his own but through his circumstances, he might end up making her very unhappy.

A fairytale ending with Sean simply wasn't possible. Like all relationships, it was about timing and, sadly they weren't on the same lines of longitude. Lucy wanted children with a man who didn't have two already. Their lives were at different stages. Robert was a better bet: a cleaner sheet, a hugely attractive proposition. Although he'd never know it, he was very much the silver medallist, but Lucy's instincts told her that, before too long, the silver would turn to gold.

Politics had changed her. She was more courageous and decisive, more able to display, oddly enough, those very characteristics that most politicians lack. With Sean, as with her career in politics, she knew she'd gone as far as she could. This time, she had to quit while they were both ahead, before their relationship had a chance to decline and its passion became forgotten in the corrosive recriminations of custody and divorce.

As she told him that their relationship was over, she found herself trying to remember the tips he'd given her about breathing, pausing and emphasising certain words. It didn't come out quite as she'd intended because this speech meant far more to her than her maiden one in the House of Commons.

He listened in silence and she could see real hurt in his expression and manly misting in his emerald eyes. However, just as he had taken many exasperated lectures and financial penalties from D.G. Wilson, Sean clenched his jaw and took this far more upsetting punishment in exactly the same way . . .

'So what are you going to do?' he asked quietly, that famous deep voice uncharacteristically faint.

'Well, I've finally found a buyer for the flat in Clapham and I've put an offer on a little place in Stoke Newington, just off Church Street.'

Sean nodded. 'What about work?'

'Back to *Cachet*,' she said. 'Simon's so delighted to have an ex-MP on the staff that he's given me a ten grand pay rise. Also, I've had quite a few approaches from the nationals. I've got to do a piece for *The Times* next week. And get this – I'm going to be working as consultant for a deli stroke takeaway that's just opened in Clerkenwell. Full circle, eh?'

Sean managed a watery smile and Lucy started to cry. 'I've

got to do this,' she sobbed, 'and I want you to promise me you won't contact me. Ever. Take that as the biggest compliment you've ever been paid because it is. One look at you and I know I'll want to dump whoever I happen to be with and come running back to you. So promise me – please.'

Reluctantly Sean accepted his fate, and nodded.

'If I see you again,' she sniffed, 'I know I'll have terrible regrets and I don't want to have regrets.'

'Well, I do want to have regrets,' said Sean, slowly finding his voice. 'I want to look back and think wistfully of what might have been. I want to remember being one of the lucky few who knows what it's like to enjoy the perfect relationship, to have loved the girl I should have ended up with, even if I didn't end up with her.'

Yet again, that was why she loved him. Here she was, dumping him when he'd done nothing wrong, and he was trying selflessly to make her feel better.

'Look at James Dean,' he said. 'Would he really have been such an icon if he hadn't died young? If a relationship dies young, it never gets the chance to grow old and stale. It stays perfectly preserved for ever. You know, this has been the happiest time of my life.'

'Mine too.'

'I know you want to have kids, you should have kids, and I'm honestly not sure whether I want any more.'

There, thought Lucy, he's finally admitted it.

'Anyway,' he said, smiling, 'the Mount Nelson, the Caruso, I'm not sure I could keep that up for ever. We might have ended up in the Travel Motel in Chelmsford.'

'I wouldn't have cared,' said Lucy, and she meant it.

There was nothing left to say. Any vague excitement Lucy may have felt about embarking on a new relationship with Robert had been momentarily quelled by having to do this to Sean. They emerged in sad silence on to Piccadilly, and Sean's final walk with Lucy was to the taxi rank outside the Ritz.

Saying nothing, she gave him the tightest, most passionate, rib-crushing embrace he'd ever received. She got in, he clunked the door behind her, the taxi went south and Sean began to walk north.

As he walked away, there were real tears in his eyes. Big, fat salty ones that he could never have allowed Lucy to see.

Despite his misery, he couldn't help thinking how lucky he'd been. Lucky to have met the girl of his dreams and, in such a short time, lucky to have made love with her in three different countries. More than anything else, however, he was so, so lucky not to have been caught.

He'd always been lucky – Napoleon would have loved him. He was lucky to have retained Nikki's love, and luckier still to have kept his relationship with Lucy a secret. He would never have left his children because he'd never really left his wife. They were separated, but the separation had been meant as a cooling-off period to ascertain how they felt. They had never intended it to end with solicitors at dawn. Nikki had insisted on moving to Kent, and it simply wasn't feasible for Sean to live there when so much of his work had to be done at twenty minutes' notice.

One of several strokes of fortune was that Lucy had never pestered to meet the children. Another was that her constituency work had left him free most weekends. Yet another was Nikki's indifference to his life outside the oast house. Like countless couples before them, they had revitalised their relationship by living apart. Absence really had made the heart grow fonder. Lately Nikki had been talking about leaving the kids overnight with her parents and coming up to stay in Soho. She'd even mentioned wanting to be Sean's 'girlfriend' again.

Sean hadn't meant to have an affair. He'd only gone along to Top Table because he was bored. He had never expected to meet someone like Lucy, and the whole thing had got way out of hand.

It was Sean, not Lucy, who'd really panicked when the *Daily Mail* turned up on his doorstep. That was when he knew it couldn't go on for much longer and that somehow he had to get himself out of it. The trouble was, having got himself so ecstatically entangled, he didn't know how to get untangled. Lucky to the last, it was Lucy who had done the untangling for him.

Not for a moment was he trying to excuse himself. He felt horribly guilty about being so spectacularly unfaithful, but if he hadn't, he would have gone mad. Being on the wrong end of Nikki's coldness and indifference had already started to break his heart. Now it was mended, and although he knew that what he'd done was unequivocally wrong, he was sure that he wasn't the only husband whose marriage had been saved, rather than destroyed, by infidelity.

He loved Lucy and he knew he always would. He hoped she would find someone else and would have been relieved, pleased, though slightly wounded, to know that she already had. She was far too special to go to waste but, like him and so many others, she would settle down with her second-best partner because Fate had decreed that neither of them could have their first.

He wiped his eyes, sniffed a bit, then walked back to his magical flat, knowing that a little of its magic was now lost forever. As he crossed Regent Street into Soho, his mobile rang. It was Chelsea Jon with a booking for nine the following morning. 'Another one of those Top Table radio ads,' he said. 'That Emma insists on having you.'

'I don't know, mate,' said Sean, with a heavy sigh. 'I'm really not sure that's a good idea.'

PAUL BURKE

Father Frank

Father Frank Dempsey is a Roman Catholic priest who harbours an almighty secret: he doesn't believe in God.

Despite this, or maybe because of it, he is brilliant and hugely successful as a priest. His unconventional methods, which include driving a taxi to raise funds, bring his flock together and transform what was once a drab North London parish. It's all going beautifully until Sarah Marshall hops into his taxi and into his life, slowly putting his vows under incredible strain.

'A dazzling first novel – funny, thoughtful and original'
Stephen Fry

'A warm, funny, blisteringly good read that has the angels on its side' Tony Parsons

HODDER

PAUL BURKE

Untorn Tickets

Two friends, one scam, heroic possibilities . . .

Notting Hill – 1978. Dave Kelly and Andy Zymanczyk are classmates at a strict Catholic school. Both, desperate to escape their stifling backgrounds, get part-time work in their local cinema.

Here they form a binding friendship and embark on a voyage of discovery. Dave falls in love with Rachel, a Jewish girl who also wants to escape from her strict background, while Andy falls for a girl he knows he can never have.

When the cinema is threatened with closure, the boys realise that more than their new-found freedom is at risk.

'Wonderful. Paul Burke is a natural storyteller and genuinely funny' Dominic Holland

HODDER

PAUL BURKE

The Man Who Fell in Love with his Wife

Meet Frank – the ex-priest who's about to become a father of a very different kind.

Newly-wed Frank Dempsey, a former Catholic priest, can now luxuriate in the sublime joys of his wife's arms.

Yet Frank isn't really off-duty from charitable deeds – when he isn't driving his black cab for a local taxi firm, he is in hot demand to speak at christenings and funerals. Or to inspire people to flock to the dancefloor as a DJ.

Frank soon discovers that the tempting sins of the flesh have consequences; when Frank becomes a real father, he realises he is going to need a miracle to feed the five thousand . . .

'Laughs a-plenty'
Daily Mirror

'A fast and entertaining read . . . It has a Richard Curtis-esque veneer'
Sunday Express

HODDER